UNHINGED

UNHINGED
NECESSARY EVILS

ONLEY JAMES

UNHINGED
NECESSARY EVILS BOOK ONE

Copyright © 2021 Onley James
WWW.ONLEYJAMES.COM

All rights reserved. No part of this publication may be reproduced, stored in a retrieval system, or transmitted, in any form or by any means (electronic, mechanical, photocopying, recording, or otherwise), without the prior written permission of the publisher.

This book is a work of fiction and does not represent any individual living or dead. Names, characters, places, and incidents either are products of the author's imagination or are used fictitiously.

Cover and Interior Design by We Got You Covered Book Design
WWW.WEGOTYOUCOVEREDBOOKDESIGN.COM

ISBN: 979-8-52772448-6

TRIGGER WARNING

This book contains graphic violence, very dark humor, and mentions of past child sexual abuse.

PROLOGUE
DR. THOMAS MULVANEY

This was the hardest part. Finding the boys. But this boy... he would be the last. Then his set would be complete. Dr. Thomas Mulvaney had a small network of like-minded scientists who understood that what he was attempting was worth the risks. The woman beside him, Dr. Arbor, was new to the process. She was a second year resident who worked directly under Thomas's good friend, David.

"Age?" Thomas asked.

The young girl shook her head, hesitant. "Near as we can tell, around six."

He was used to the trepidation. What they were doing was illegal. Some might even say it was unconscionable. Thomas saw it as a necessary evil. "I promise, this is in the boy's best interest," he assured her. "He should be around people like him, people who understand how to meet his specific needs."

They both looked past the glass to the boy who sat at the table. He was calm in a way no child should be. He had a stillness Thomas had only ever seen in predatory animals and military trained snipers.

"Medicated?"

Once more, she shook her head. "No. When he's alone, it's like he simply…powers off. Goes into his own head. It's common in children who've endured the type of trauma he's been through."

Thomas had seen it before. Too often. The child's chart said he was found when police responded to a murder-suicide. He'd been tied to the radiator for such a prolonged amount of time that the rope marks on his ankle were now a permanent ring of scars.

He wasn't the only child found in the home, each filthy, neglected, and in distress. But the other two were young enough that they might still have a chance at a normal life. But this boy? At this age? Attachment disorder had already set in. He knew from experience it was impossible to reverse.

Thomas studied the boy's unnaturally pale skin, husky blue eyes, and inky black hair. If he was put up for adoption, there was a very good chance he'd be picked almost immediately. He was six but could easily pass for younger. Families always wanted the young, white children, especially boys. They'd have no idea what they were taking into their homes. Not until it was too late.

He sighed. "Diagnoses?"

Dr. Arbor folded her arms across her chest. "Officially? Oppositional defiant disorder, conduct disorder, attachment disorder, post traumatic stress disorder."

"Unofficially?"

She cut her gaze to him before quickly returning it to the boy, like she was afraid to take her eyes off him for too long. It was probably a good instinct to have.

"He shows increasing signs of psychopathy. He lies seamlessly, he's charming when he wants something, funny, calculating. His inappropriate touching of adults indicates prolonged abuse. He doesn't actively attempt to harm himself or others, but he shows no compassion for others' suffering. Unsurprising given his living conditions."

"Any bed-wetting, arson, cruelty to animals?"

"It might be too early to tell but, so far, no. In fact, he's quite taken with the smaller children. He treats them almost like…pets. We suspect he was often tasked with trying to keep the younger ones alive. No easy task considering their limited range of motion."

He was perfect. "Interesting. Does he have a name?"

"If he does, he's not saying. We just call him Adam," she said, sounding tired in her bones.

Thomas understood. Working as a pediatric psychiatrist showed a person just how inhuman humans could be, the level of pain and trauma they could inflict on the population's most vulnerable people. It showed that most mental health disorders in children were a direct result of the people who were supposed to love them. It ate away at the soul until, over time, it just became too much for most people to bear.

That was where Thomas came in. There was no fixing these children, no healing their psyche. At best, they would become a burden to whoever agreed to take them in. At worst, they would become a plague on their household, maybe even their neighborhood. Pets would go missing, parents would start putting multiple locks on doors, entire families sleeping together in one room until they just couldn't take it anymore and begged the courts to step in. They wouldn't.

But Thomas would. He'd take them before they became a blight on society. "There's no birth certificate?" he asked.

The doctor flicked her gaze towards him once more. "No. His parents didn't seem like the paperwork type. None of the children in the home had birth certificates. DNA proved they were all biologically related to the mother, so it wasn't a kidnapping situation. The man who killed her was only the father of the youngest, and we have no way of determining who the boy's biological father is. There was no match in the DNA database. Not even familial. As far as the government is concerned, he doesn't exist."

"And his files?"

"It would be easy enough to make them disappear."

These children always fell through the cracks. They were the forgotten, the nobodies. Ghosts in a system that just hadn't killed them yet. Foster families took them in and gave them back, social workers vowed to check on them, but eventually became overwhelmed by their never-ending case loads. It wasn't any one person's fault. The system was a broken wheel, inefficient by design.

That always worked in Thomas's favor. "Excellent. I'd like to meet him now, please."

She swallowed audibly before reaching for her water bottle and taking a few swigs. "What do you do with them?" she finally asked.

It was only fair she'd be curious. A doctor essentially stealing children in the dead of night was the stuff of nightmares. He was a fairy tale villain. Given the type of people these doctors were forced to endure, it was only fair they were suspicious of him. They should be. But he wasn't the problem, he was the solution. "I mold them."

Her brows knitted together, her gaze sharp behind her large glasses. "Into what?"

Into killers. Thomas smiled. "Into exactly what God intended."

She recoiled, her hand flailing at her side. "I can't imagine God had much to do with what happened to Adam."

Thomas shook his head. "Have you ever heard the idiom, 'psychopaths are born, but sociopaths are made'? Research shows it's true, but what if they aren't a design flaw? What if they're here to do what others cannot?"

"What does that even mean?"

"All you need to know is that I run a home for boys just like Adam. He will be well cared for, far better than anything anybody here could offer. He will have access to the best medical care, the finest education, and I will show him exactly what he's capable of."

"Which is what?" Dr. Arbor said, looking at him like *he* was the sociopath.

Thomas made a sweeping gesture. "Using his gifts for good instead of evil."

Dr. Arbor snorted. "Gifts? I'd hardly call this level of disease a gift."

He was already shaking his head. "But that's where you're wrong, Dr. Arbor. You can't fix a psychopath. You can't fix a sociopath. But you can guide them, hone their focus. Teach them how to direct their rage towards those who deserve it."

"Deserve it?" she echoed. "You're teaching them to be monsters?"

"Of course not. They're already monsters. I'm teaching them to kill the ones who made them that way."

She was silent for a long while before finally asking, "Does it work?"

"That's what I aim to find out. These boys are my first test subjects. Over the course of their lives I'll document their progress, teach them how to identify and vet their targets. Teach them to be invisible."

Once more, her gaze dragged to Adam, still blinking at the blank wall. "How many boys do you have?"

"Including Adam? Seven."

It was truly a small sample size, but any more than seven and he wouldn't be able to give them his individual time and attention. It was important that they learned to rely on him and each other. While there was no capacity for love, that didn't mean they couldn't grow to trust each other. They would need that trust. They would need to blend in with society on some level.

"How do you raise a house full of psychopaths, Dr. Mulvaney?" she asked, looking back through the glass at the small boy.

"Very carefully, Dr. Arbor. Very carefully."

After a moment, she walked to the door and opened it,

gesturing for Thomas to enter first. Once inside, Adam's shrewd blue eyes tracked him, though the rest of him remained perfectly still. It was clear he unnerved Dr. Arbor, but Thomas thought he was perfect. A perfect specimen. His final boy.

He crouched down beside the boy and held out his hand. "Hello, Adam, my name is Thomas Mulvaney and I'm here to take you to your new home."

The mask of indifference shattered, replaced by a slow, almost sinister smile. The boy took Thomas's hand and shook it. He could see why he unnerved the other physician. Adam had no baseline for normal. He could only watch and mimic what he saw. He wasn't a six-year-old boy. He was a six-year-old robot currently downloading the software that made a six-year-old boy.

Adam was a gift, Thomas could already tell. "Shall we go?"

ONE
ADAM

Adam tucked his head deeper into his red hoodie, his hand curling around the hilt of the knife buried within the sweatshirt's through and through pocket. It was easy to blend in the middle of the night, swirling from shadow to shadow, avoiding the anemic yellow street lights of the dark, dingy street, but that didn't mean this was a safe neighborhood. Not by any means.

This was the forgotten part of town. Every building had bars on the windows, the roads were pockmarked with potholes, which became oil-slicked pools each time it rained. The prevalence of gun stores, bail bondsmen, and lawyers sat in stark contrast to Adam's neighborhood on the other side of the tracks. But he wasn't trying to 'slum it' with the poor. These were Adam's people. He'd spent the first six years of his life in a dilapidated trailer behind the mini-mart.

Police cars prowled the streets, sometimes shining their flashlights out the window to harass a cluster of people until they dispersed. But they never noticed Adam. Nobody ever noticed him, really. That was why he was still free to roam, to hunt, to kill. But, tonight, the only thing on his to-do list was an early bedtime.

It was strange how seamlessly one could blend if they just pretended they belonged. Even somebody who spent much of his time in the public eye. Somebody famous in certain circles. He supposed it was almost easier to blend in when the alternative seemed preposterous. And the youngest son of billionaire Thomas Mulvaney walking around alone in the worst part of town in the wee hours of the morning seemed pretty preposterous.

But that wasn't who Adam was either. In truth, Adam was nobody. A carefully crafted lie, raised specifically to right the wrongs of others. A lie he had executed so well that, sometimes, even he believed it. But it wasn't real. Any of it. Maybe that was what truly made his walks the best thing about his nights. Nobody gave a shit about him on this side of town. They didn't know the Mulvaney name or who the world thought he was. They didn't care.

He cut through a dark alley to the entrance of the hollowed out shell of a building where he kept his… supplies. He didn't need light to see his way around. He'd been using this particular shelter since he was fifteen. He just needed to drop the knife in his kit and then he'd be on his way. He might even make it home by midnight.

Adam didn't hear the scuffing of sneakers over concrete until it was too late. The sound of a gun's hammer cocking quickly followed, echoing through the empty space. Still, he didn't slow his pace until a wobbly voice shouted, "Stop."

Adam was tempted to ignore the request. The owner of the voice sounded young, uncertain. Terrified, really. It wasn't uncommon for homeless kids to try to find shelter when it grew cold outside. He was probably a junkie. A tweaker looking for quick cash or drugs. But the likelihood of getting shot wasn't zero, and even twitchy junkies sometimes got lucky and hit an artery. His father would resurrect him just to kill him again if he got himself merced in this part of town.

He slowed to a halt with a sigh, turning to face his assailant. He was definitely an amateur. He'd stopped directly in the only pool of light in the darkened space, illuminating his features in great enough detail that Adam could have drawn the boy's sketch from memory.

He was the antithesis of Adam, fair and freckled where he was tan, messy light brown hair where Adam's was jet black, small and delicate boned in direct opposition to Adam's swimmer's body. He most likely wasn't much younger than Adam. He looked to be in his early twenties.

The kid, whoever he was, had never held a gun before. That much was clear by his stance and the way his hand trembled, but his finger hovering directly over the trigger meant Adam gave him the same care he'd give any other predator.

"Okay, you got me. Now what?" Adam asked.

"Put your hood down," the boy demanded, gun twitching in his hand as he spoke.

Adam frowned at the odd request. "Why?"

The kid seemed to hesitate, like he hadn't expected Adam to argue with him. He thought the gun gave him an advantage. It probably did for most. But not to Adam.

He shook the gun. "Don't ask questions. Just do it."

Adam took a single step forward, watching with interest as the boy took a step back. "No."

His eyes bulged. He looked near tears. "No? I'll fucking shoot you in the face."

Lie. "Then do it."

Adam watched as the boy's finger twitched on the trigger. Oh, he wanted to do it. He wanted Adam dead. Interesting. Maybe this was all a misunderstanding. There was no shortage of criminals in this area. Plenty of people to hold a grudge.

"I know who you are," the boy said, confidence edging into his voice.

Adam couldn't help but chuckle. "Oh, yeah? Who do you think I am?"

The boy's eyes narrowed, a pained smile forming on his face. He was sweating despite the cold, but Adam no longer thought he was a drug addict. The boy was terrified, but his eyes were clear, his skin flawless. This boy wasn't a junkie.

"Adam. Mulvaney." He enunciated each syllable, like saying it out loud might invoke some sort of supernatural wrath.

His name on the boy's lips wiped the smirk off his face. If he didn't need to hide his identity, then he might as well show his face. Might as well give the boy the appearance of control. He pushed the hood off his face. "And who are you?"

There was no hesitation. "Noah."

Adam mouthed the boy's name. He hadn't expected him to answer him. People who intended to let their victims live didn't give their names. That didn't bode well for poor

Noah, who looked like life had already run him over more than once.

"Okay. What is it you want, Noah? Cash? Drugs? I have a hundred bucks on me, but if you take my debit card, you can access a lot more. I'll even give you my pin."

The boy's face twisted with a fury that almost looked comical on his innocent freckled little face. Almost. "It's just that easy for you, huh? Just throw money at it. How do you do it?"

"Do what? I'm just trying to make sure we all go home tonight. I have money. You look like you could use some help. Nobody blames you for doing what you have to do to survive."

That only made him more angry, if that was even possible. "People really don't see who you are, do they? You lie so easily."

He wasn't wrong. That probably unsettled Adam more than anything. Whoever Noah was, he'd done his homework. Noah was signing his own fucking death warrant. Adam didn't like the sharp stabbing pain that came thinking this was going to end badly for the boy.

Still, it was best to act as if he had no idea what Noah meant. "I'm not lying about having money. I can show you my bank balance."

"I don't want your fucking money!" Noah shouted, sweat and saliva flying as tears of rage leaked from his eyes.

Adam took two more slow steps in Noah's direction. "Then what is it you want, Noah?"

He scoffed, then sniffled, wiping the back of his hand

across his nose. "To watch you bleed out on the pavement."

Adam's brows made a run for his hairline at the venom in the boy's voice. "I don't even know you, Noah. What could I have done to make you want to kill me?"

Noah's eyes went wide, mouth contorting. "You really don't remember me, do you?"

Nope. "Should I?"

"Have you killed so many people that you really can't remember your victims?"

Yeah. Pretty much. He didn't plan on sharing that with Noah. Besides, if Noah had been one of Adam's victims, he wouldn't still be drawing air into his lungs. "Who is it you think I killed?"

"My father, Wayne Holt."

Adam closed his eyes, letting his brain file through his numerous past victims, plucking the details as he found the name. Wayne Holt, fifty-one years old, serial predator responsible for the assault and murder of at least fifteen children under the age of ten. Had somehow managed to avoid detection for three decades. Police could never find enough evidence to charge him. Luckily, Adam's people had better resources. And a much swifter form of justice.

A shock of awareness hit him as he realized he did know the boy, though years had passed. Wayne Holt had been one of Adam's first kills. Number three, maybe? Roughly a couple of weeks after Adam's sixteenth birthday. The boy was maybe ten at the time. Adam quickly did the math. Yeah, it gelled. It could definitely be the boy who'd stepped out of the shadows that night, calling out timidly for his father, ending Adam's fun almost before it had started.

Thomas had been furious that he hadn't checked for witnesses in the house, but he'd been so excited, so ready to remind Wayne Holt of every single victim and the pain he'd left in his wake. If Noah was truly that boy, there was a very good chance he'd also been a victim.

"Your father was a monster, Noah. Deep down, I think you know that."

Once more, the gun waved wildly. "Fuck you. You don't know shit about my father."

"But I do. I can prove it to you, if that's what you need. But I don't think you want to see what I've seen. Some things can never be erased."

"Shut up! You're full of shit. You're a…serial killer. You have that bored fuckboi act down, but, really, you're the fucking monster."

Adam sighed. What the fuck was he supposed to do about this? About him? He couldn't kill him. Well, he could. But he wouldn't. He knew that, deep down. He couldn't kill him the first night he'd seen him and he certainly couldn't do it now while he was grieving his father. This was clearly something Noah had been thinking about for a really long time. But he also didn't want to die tonight.

"You have three options, Noah. You can just walk away and I pretend this never happened. I can make a phone call and show you who your father really was and ruin every happy memory you ever had of him." Adam closed the distance between them, gripping the gun's barrel and pressing it to his own forehead. "Or you can pull the trigger and kill me. None of those things will change the truth. Your father was a pedophile and a child killer."

This close, Adam could see Noah's deep brown eyes, red rimmed and wet with tears, the freckles dotting his skin, dirt smudging his cheeks and chin. Underneath the anger and the hunger, he was rather unique looking, nothing like the parade of pampered debutantes he was forced to endure every day to maintain his cover.

"What's it going to be, Noah?" he asked softly. "I really hope it's option one."

The boy's eyes darted around the empty warehouse frantically, vibrating with enough energy Adam could feel it in the metal pressed to his skin.

"Make your call," Noah finally said, sounding miserable. "On speaker phone," he added. "So I can hear you."

Adam sighed. "Noah—"

"Do it," he snapped, cutting off Adam's plea.

When Noah lowered the gun, Adam took his hands from his hoodie pocket, leaving the knife where it was so he could slowly reach into his back pocket. He extracted his phone and hit the first name in his frequent contacts.

"What's up, buttercup?"

The female voice on the other end of the line was surprisingly chipper for eleven o'clock at night.

"We're on an open channel," he warned.

Calliope wasn't the kind of girl you put on speakerphone. The sound of long nails furiously typing over keys halted abruptly. "Oh-kay. What's going on? Are you in trouble? If you're in trouble again, Adam—"

"Open. Channel," he reminded, cutting off her rant. "I need you to do me a favor. Can you access some information?"

"Does the tin man have a metal dick?"

Adam frowned. "I don't know what that means."

"Sometimes, I hate this job," she muttered. "What do you need?"

"I need you to send me the evidence file for Wayne Holt."

There was a long pause on the other end of the line. "Why? That case is over a decade old."

"Just do it. Everything."

"Even the—"

"Yeah, even that," Adam snapped before taking a deep breath and letting it out. "Sorry, Cali. It's been a long night. Can you please send it?"

"Yeah. You got it, dollface. Give me five."

With that, she disconnected, leaving Adam and the boy far closer without a gun barrel between them. "You should go," Adam said, his voice pleading. "You don't want to see what we've seen. I promise you, we had more than enough evidence to convict your father."

Noah's face contorted, almost like Adam's words caused physical pain. "Then why didn't you go to the cops?"

"Your father was good at covering his tracks. The police have to worry about warrants and chain of custody. My people don't. We just have to find the truth."

"*We*? Who even are you? You aren't much older than me. You were barely old enough to drive when you killed my dad. I've done my research. What idiot would hire a kid to kill an adult?"

"Nobody hired me. This isn't a job. I don't have benefits and a 401k. Please, Noah. Just go."

Adam's phone chirped. He flicked to his email and the encrypted file blinking at the bottom of it. "Last chance."

Noah snatched the phone from Adam and stabbed a finger against the play button. Adam turned away. He couldn't watch the video again or the boy's reaction to it. Luckily, the video had no sound. Hearing Noah's reaction was bad enough. The way he sucked in a sharp breath, the strangled cry that sounded like a wounded animal, and, finally, vomit splashing onto the concrete as Noah lost the contents of his stomach.

Adam fought the urge to comfort him. What the fuck would he even say? Hallmark didn't make 'sorry your dad was a piece of shit' cards. Though, given the prevalence of shit dads out there, maybe they were really missing out on something. He turned back around and gently took his phone back. It slipped easily from the boy's fingers. "He's not worth your tears or your vengeance. Even if he never touched you. He needed to go. I'm sorry you got hurt in the process."

Noah glowered at him. "Yeah, I'm sure it'll keep you up at night."

Adam just stared as the boy turned and walked away, shoulders slumped, head down. He reminded Adam of a dog who'd been beaten.

Noah's face was a constant companion on Adam's walk home and even hours later as he lay in bed. What had happened to him after his father died? Was he fed? Did he have a roof over his head? Was he somewhere alone, two seconds away from swallowing a bullet?

Adam knew better than anybody that childhood trauma came back to haunt you at the most inopportune moments, in the most incongruous ways. And once somebody turned the key on that part of the brain where those memories lived, it was almost impossible to stuff them back down again.

When the sun came up, Adam hadn't slept a wink. He ground his palms into his eyes until sparks danced behind his lids. He was supposed to meet his father and Atticus at the club for breakfast. He knew he should tell them about Noah. They needed to know that someone out there knew who Adam really was. But he didn't want to tell them. He didn't want to tell anyone. Some weird part of him wanted to keep Noah all to himself.

He stumbled to the shower, letting the molten water blast along his back and shoulders, thinking of big, brown eyes and freckles sprinkled over pale skin. He felt weirdly responsible for the boy. He didn't know why he kept thinking of him as a boy. They couldn't be more than six years apart, but Adam felt like he'd been born an old man—had lived a hundred lives in the twenty-seven years he'd been alive. Noah's life had clearly not been easy, but there'd been a vulnerability, a quiet desperation that had tugged at something buried so deep down inside Adam. Something he didn't know even existed inside him. His conscience.

Would it bring Noah any comfort knowing he had, in fact, kept Adam up all night?

TWO
NOAH

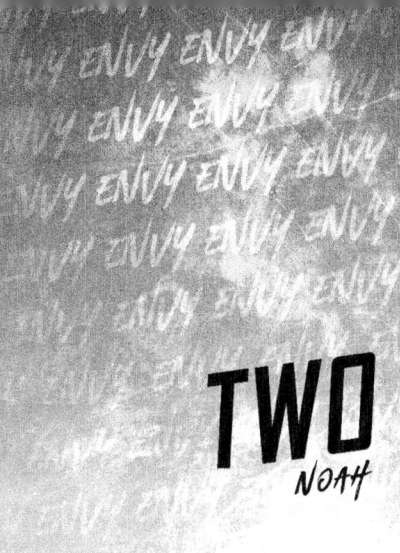

He was watching him again. It was an almost nightly occurrence now. At first, Noah thought he was going crazy, imagining phantoms in the shadows. But no, it was him. Adam Mulvaney. The man who killed his father. His father…the child predator. Noah's stomach lurched at the thought, the images from that video trying to claw their way back into his brain. But he wouldn't let them in and had found a million creative ways to keep them out.

Noah could feel his eyes on him even now. Despite the throbbing bass of the dance music, the dizzying display of neon beams shooting across darkened walls, and the sea of bodies moving in one cohesive wave, Noah could feel Adam's eyes on him. He had no idea what Adam wanted.

At first, he thought maybe he was coming for his revenge or maybe just taking out a witness, but Noah had given him a million chances to end his misery, and the bastard never took them. Instead, he just watched him. Maybe he got some kind of sick thrill seeing Noah suffer. The joke was on him, though, because Noah was too high to feel anything but good.

He fell out the side door of the club into the brisk night air. He didn't bundle up. The synthetic happiness coursing through him made him hot all over. The alley smelled like rotting garbage and piss, but Noah twirled along the alley like a ballet dancer, stumbling when he heard the alley door open and slam shut behind him. He didn't look, didn't acknowledge his stalker in any way. Just stumbled out of the alley and into the parking lot.

It was early enough that others still lingered on corners, in parking lots, outside the bodega. But Noah had never felt so alone. He was always alone, even when people were packed around him. No matter what he tried, nothing filled the hollowness inside him. Not drugs, not alcohol, not meaningless hookups. His lip curled at that last one.

He'd left his friend, Bailey, and her girlfriend at the bar to follow a random stranger into the bathrooms, but the guy was too wasted to get it up. Noah had left him passed out in the stall.

He couldn't help the laugh that escaped, the sound startling in the still of the night. He was destined to be alone. He wished Adam would just do it already. Shoot him in the head, slit his throat, shove him in front of a moving car. Whatever it was, it couldn't be worse than living with what he'd seen.

Maybe he needed to help him along. Maybe Adam didn't want to take him out with a crowd around. The thought of death was a balm that soothed Noah's frayed psyche. It didn't make him sad or scared; it just gave him a sense of peace, a peace he'd never experienced before. He giggled once more, blinking back tears. He retraced his steps, hopscotching over puddles and cracks in the sidewalk. Two blocks over. Three blocks down. The screech of protesting metal as he pushed open the heavy door.

Did he follow? Was he curious? Noah had come to the building a lot after their first encounter, but he never found anything. Whatever Adam had hidden there that kept him coming back again and again had been moved after that night. Not that Noah blamed him. Just because he hadn't killed Adam didn't mean he wouldn't turn him in to the cops. But he hadn't. After the video—after he'd seen what his father had done—it all came back to him in a rush. All of it. A shiver ran through him as he tried to drive the thoughts away. What would he do when the drugs stopped working?

Once inside the abandoned building, he sat on the metal steps that led to the second floor, waiting. Now that he was still, the drugs finally took hold, doing their job. Perspiration gathered at his hairline and beads of sweat slid down his back. Time ticked by, fast then slow, then fast again, like he was in a spaceship, warping through space and time.

He tilted his head back until he was gazing up at the metal rafters. There was a hole in the ceiling framing the night sky above, a singular beam of moonlight spearing through the darkness. How had Noah not noticed it before? He smiled as the stars and moon blurred and sharpened, then danced, chasing each other in and out of the opening on the roof to wind around the supports. He held up his hand and the stars poured through his fingers like sparks, the embers popping against his skin like tiny rubber bands.

"Noah?"

He inhaled sharply at his name on Adam's lips. He jerked upright into a sitting position, hanging onto the rusted metal banister so he didn't tumble forward. Adam glowed. His skin shimmered like he was a vampire in a bad teen movie, like his skin was made of light. His aura throbbed a deep red that made Noah want to touch it. He wished Adam wasn't so beautiful. It would have been better that way.

But he was. Adam was so pretty. His hair was so black it appeared blue in the moonlight, and his eyes were the palest blue. Maybe he was a vampire. No human should look that good. He narrowed his gaze as his eyes fell to the deep vee of his t-shirt. The top of a moth or butterfly wings peeked out from the center of his chest, and his neck was adorned with a large wraparound snake tattoo and a necklace with a bullet hanging from it.

"Are you real?" Noah heard himself ask, then snorted at the wonder in his own voice. What the hell had Bailey given him anyway? It was clearly the good shit.

"Are you high?"

Noah lowered his voice to a stage whisper. "Are you a cop?" His heart caught as Adam grinned, revealing perfect teeth. "Probably veneers," he muttered.

"What?"

Noah could have said nothing, but, instead, he said, "Your teeth. They probably aren't even yours."

Noah knew he wasn't making any sense but he was unable to stop himself from saying whatever popped into his head.

He wanted to touch him, to pet him, to comb his fingers through his hair and taste his skin that still glittered like spun sugar. Did he taste sweet?

"They're mine," Adam assured him. "But if it makes you feel any better, my dad paid a lot of money for them. They were pretty jenky when I was little. My birth mom wasn't real big on dentists. Or hygiene. Or kids for that matter."

Noah processed that bit of information. Adam had a birth mom. Had Noah known that? Maybe. He knew Adam had been adopted. All of Mulvaney's children had been. He was the Gen X Daddy Warbucks.

Noah fell back onto his forearms. "Are you here to kill me?"

Adam moved closer, head cocked like a German Shepherd. "No."

Disappointment settled inside Noah. "Are you following me?"

Another step. "Yes."

"Why?"

That seemed to stop him in his tracks. "I…don't know."

Noah sighed. "You should kill me. I know too much."

"You probably shouldn't say that to somebody you suspect is a murderer."

"If I was going to tell anybody, I would have by now," Noah admitted. "If that's what you're worried about."

"It's not. I'm…not."

"That's good," Noah managed before his eyes unfocused and his head lolled on his shoulders.

Adam's palms suddenly cupped his face. "Hey. What are you on?"

Noah shrugged, his lids going to half-mast. "I don't know."

"You don't know?" Adam echoed, his thumbs pulling at the skin just beneath Noah's eyes, like he'd tattooed the answers under the skin there.

"I told Bailey to surprise me. I have to admit, I'm surprised," Noah confided, his hand reaching out to cup Adam's face the way he was cupping his. "What are we doing?"

Adam snorted. "I'm trying to make sure you don't die of a drug overdose. What are you doing?"

Noah splayed his fingers over Adam's knife-sharp cheekbones. "You're really pretty. Has anybody ever told you that?" Noah asked, examining him for even a single flaw but finding none.

Adam snorted. "Yes."

"Oh," Noah said, letting his hands fall. He hated how defeated he sounded.

Adam didn't drop his arms, though, just continued to cup Noah's face in his large hands.

"You're really…big," Noah said, letting his gaze roam from Adam's booted feet to the top of his head. Well, as much as he could while Adam held his face hostage.

Adam tilted his head once more. "No, I'm average in size. You're just kind of small."

Noah scoffed. "Not where it counts."

That wasn't really the truth either. He was pretty proportionate in every way. He didn't know why he said it, but Adam grinned and Noah's heart tripped in his chest. What was wrong with him?

Noah couldn't help but notice Adam's pointy incisors. He

pressed a finger to the sharpened point. "Are you secretly a Cullen? You have vampire teeth. Is that why you're so pretty?"

The grin slipped from Adam's lips, and he closed his mouth, trapping Noah's finger between his jaws briefly, just enough for Noah to feel the pointed tip press into him. Not hard enough to break the skin but hard enough to leave an indentation. Still, Noah's dick took notice.

When Adam released his finger, Noah ran his thumb over the mark. Adam had marked him. Like an animal. Adam was an animal. A predator. A killer. A killer who was still holding his face. "What are you doing?" he asked again.

"You have stars on your cheeks," Adam mused, a strange look in his eyes, one that made Noah's half-hard cock thicken behind his zipper.

"Bailey's girlfriend turned my freckles into stars," he said, hand raising once more against his will, this time to drag a thumb along Adam's bottom lip, gasping when he felt Adam's tongue against the pad of his finger. "Your lips are so red," he said, voice full of wonder. "Are you wearing lipstick?"

Adam shook his head. "No."

"Why are you following me?" Noah asked again.

"Because I can't stop thinking about you," Adam said, sounding confused, like he hadn't meant to say it.

Noah's eyes widened at the words. "Am I... Are you a hallucination?"

Adam shook his head, leaning into Noah's space. "I'm real."

Noah's head tilted closer, until he could see the pale blue pools of Adam's eyes in the barely-there moonlight. "Nothing about this feels real."

Adam's fingers traced the stars on Noah's cheekbones. "Does that feel real?"

Noah's tongue darted out to lick over his bottom lip. "Yes. Your hands are so warm."

"I run hot. Always have," Adam said, kneeling on the riser just below the one where Noah sat, forcing his legs wider.

"Are you going to hurt me?" Noah asked, voice almost hopeful.

Adam scanned his face for a long moment. "Probably, yeah. But you might like it."

Noah surged forward, crashing their mouths together. For a second, Adam's lips were unyielding, but then they softened, and the hand on Noah's cheek slid to his chin, tugging it down so he could slide his tongue inside.

Noah didn't know what he'd been thinking but he wasn't sorry. None of this seemed real, not the metal risers digging into his back or Adam's thighs parting his or the heat of his body trapping Noah in place against the staircase.

Adam controlled the kiss, tilting Noah's head however he wanted, lazily exploring his mouth like he had all the time in the world, like he had a right to take what he wanted. Maybe that should have made Noah mad, but it just turned him on. He finally let himself bury his hands in Adam's silky tresses, whimpering when Adam shifted and their hips met. Adam was just as hard as Noah, maybe harder. Definitely bigger.

Noah didn't think anybody had ever kissed him like this before. Kissing—when there even was kissing—was always just a precursor to the main event, it wasn't ever the goal.

The more they kissed, the more Noah thought this was just a vivid fever dream. There was no way he was kissing the man who killed his father in a dirty, deserted warehouse. He was probably passed out in that disgusting club bathroom.

"You smell good," Adam growled against his lips.

"That can't possibly be true. I smell like sweat."

"Yeah, but beneath that…you smell different. Something that's just you."

"I don't know what that means," Noah whispered before kissing him again.

Noah startled as his body vibrated. In his haze, he thought he'd been tazed. Then he realized it was Adam's phone buzzing in his pocket. He ignored it, his hands threading in Noah's hair, holding him in place so he could bite at his lips, his chin, his earlobe.

Once more, the phone began to vibrate. Adam dropped his forehead to Noah's, breathing hard, before sitting up and retrieving his phone. "Yeah?" Noah couldn't hear what the voice on the other end was saying, but they seemed just as irritated as Adam sounded. "Busy. Yeah, busy. None of your business?" Adam snorted. "I'll be there. I said I'll be there, Atticus. Damn."

Atticus Mulvaney. Adam's brother. A doctor. Both MD and PhD. Left practicing medicine to research rare diseases. Another golden child.

When Adam hung up, he examined Noah's face. "Give me your cell phone."

Noah frowned. "What?"

"Your cell phone. Give it to me."

Noah fumbled in his pocket until he pulled out the ugly flip phone. Adam frowned at it like he'd never seen one before. "What? It's all I can afford."

Adam didn't say anything after that, just punched something into the keypad. When Adam's phone rang, he disconnected the call and saved it, then handed the phone back. "I have to go. I'm calling you an Uber. Text me when you get home."

"What—"

"Don't argue with me. Just do it." Noah opened his mouth to tell him to fuck off but then snapped it shut. Adam pushed off from the bottom riser and walked three steps before turning back around and coming at Noah with enough momentum it triggered an instinct to run. Before he could get his addled brain to comply, Adam's lips were on his again, kissing him in a way that had his toes curling in his sneakers.

Then he was gone and Noah was alone, wondering if he really had just hallucinated all of that. What the fuck was happening?

THREE
ADAM

Adam's lip curled as he heaved the bloody corpse towards the drain in the middle of the floor. He'd thought he was in really good shape before he'd had to haul his brother's latest victim—a six foot four, three hundred pound rapist—from said victim's car to the center of the abandoned slaughterhouse. While Adam was fit, his brother…wasn't.

Atticus was tall and fair with a gym body and ginger hair. He looked like a Mormon and a tax attorney had a baby with shitty eyesight. Even now, while they were attempting to dispose of his brother's fuckup, he was wearing a pair of seersucker pants and a white button down shirt, though both were covered in blood.

"Seriously, dude? Wet work is not my thing. How could shit go this completely sideways? And what the fuck are you wearing?" Adam finally asked after they got the man where they wanted him.

Atticus gave him a pissy look, using the back of his hand to push his glasses up his nose. "I had a work thing."

"A work thing?"

"Yeah, you know work? That shit you do and they pay you for it? Oh, wait. No, you still live on Dad's dime."

Adam snickered. "You need to let that go. You might have a medical degree, but you work in the sciences. Dad pays your bills, too. You can't afford that luxury mom car you drive playing mad scientist at the research center."

"Fuck you," Atticus said, voice testy.

After a minute, Adam sighed. "What was your work thing?"

Atticus brightened a bit. "The research center threw me a party because I scored a grant that will fund our program for the next five years."

"Congrats. But don't forget our real job."

Atticus bristled. "This isn't our job."

"What would you consider it then? A passion project? Community service?" Adam placed his foot on the dead man's chest, grabbing the handle of the blade, which was embedded in the man's head, pulling with all his might. "What the fuck is this thing? Excalibur?" Adam grunted, starting to sweat through his now ruined Armani t-shirt. He gave his brother a disgusted look. "Seriously, man. How did you fuck up this bad?"

Atticus's eyes bulged behind his glasses, his face contorting. "My fucking gun jammed. I had to improvise."

Adam gaped at him. "And your first thought was a hatchet?"

Atticus snorted, his voice full of derision when he said, "It's a meat cleaver, you miscreant. We were in his kitchen. It was that or a butcher knife, and when you have three hundred pounds barreling towards you, you make a decision and you let it play out."

"Well, now, it's two in the morning and we're stuck here, in Satan's tiled asshole, trying to pry a cleaver out of this fucker's skull."

"I'm sorry to pull you away from the coke you were probably snorting off some rent boy's ass."

Adam scoffed. "Coke? What are you, eighty? Who the fuck does coke anymore?"

"Haven't you heard, it's making a comeback. It's all about nineties fashion and eighties drugs. Kids today," August said, pushing through the clear thick plastic sheets that separated one room from the other. They reminded Adam of the things you saw in an automatic car wash.

Adam's head snapped around to glare at Atticus. Why was Adam there if Atticus had already called August? This was August's *raison d'être*. He loved the blood and guts. He was the cleaner, the enforcer, the stone cold killer with an iron stomach. Ironic given he looked like a taller, more terrifying version of Harry Potter, minus the glasses. He was the second oldest, going by their adoption order, and had the least magnetic personality of them all as far as Adam was concerned. The family nerd with a dark side who would terrify the most hardened criminal.

August held up an electric saw, giving a smile even Adam found unsettling. "Found this," he said, unnaturally cheery given their surroundings. He pulled the trigger and the blade roared to life until he let it go. "It's cordless." His mouth turned down in an *imagine that* expression that probably would have sent most people screaming.

But that was August. He had taken to killing as easily as he'd taken to quantum mechanics. He had a way of compartmentalizing that was almost supernatural. Adam had once watched his brother torture a man for five hours, then strip off his gloves, change his clothes, and go give a three hour talk on particle acceleration in magnetic fields.

"What are we supposed to do with that?" Adam asked.

August looked at him like he was stupid. "We have no idea how much of Atticus ended up on our friend here. So we're going to dismember him, bleach him, package him up in nice little pieces, and chuck him into the river with some cement blocks. By the time he floats to the surface, any and all trace evidence should be gone. And then we won't have to tell Dad that his pride and joy fucked up."

Atticus plopped his gloved hands on his apron-covered hips. "You know, it's not my fault I excelled at everything growing up. Maybe if you had all tried a little harder, Dad could have doted on one of you instead."

Adam rolled his eyes, crouching beside the body to start undressing their recently deceased serial rapist. "Oh, yes. Please tell us again how being Dad's favorite is so hard." Adam got some perverse pleasure out of knowing that the man who'd forced himself on others without their consent was now being stripped and dismembered against his will. Too bad he was already dead.

"It was!" Atticus cried, indignant. "He always expected me to be perfect and to make sure you guys were perfect, too, and we all see how well that turned out."

Atticus and August looked down at Adam with their

patented older sibling superiority. "Oh, fuck you both. I'm sorry I'm not a doctor or an egghead professor. Has it ever occurred to you that I did you all a favor by never applying myself?"

Atticus snorted. "How so?"

Adam grinned. "I half-ass everything and still rise to the top. Imagine if I was using my full potential. I'd leave both of you in the dust. I'm the black sheep by choice."

August snorted, but Atticus looked like a fish out of water, mouth opening and closing before he sputtered, "You're a fucking supermodel. What exactly did you intend to ace, Tyra? Smizing 101?" August gave Atticus a smug look. "What? Kendra liked *America's Next Top Model*. I know some things."

Adam wrinkled his nose at the mention of Atticus's ex-girlfriend. She was a fucking nightmare. A total gold digger who'd descended on the Mulvaney household like a plague, her army of skanks doing their best to land the Mulvaney brothers one at a time, like they thought they could clear the board in one shot.

They were definitely barking up the wrong family tree. Half of his brothers liked dick, two of them didn't care about gender at all, and August…well, Adam was pretty sure he was a fucking android. He couldn't imagine his brother sticking his dick in anything that didn't require batteries.

"Look, I'm not saying modeling required the same amount of skill as brain surgery or gene splicing or whatever the fuck you do when you're in mad scientist mode, but at least I didn't get a hatchet stuck in the head of a three hundred pound rapist."

"It's a meat cleaver," Atticus and August said in unison.

"Whatever. Can we please get this done? It's hot as fuck in here and it smells like rotting meat and shit."

"You're such a baby," Atticus muttered.

"You're such a baby," Adam mimicked. "Fine. Next time, call Archer. Or Asa and Avi. The murder twins are always down for a little slice and dice," Adam reminded him with a grunt, straining as he tried to get the man's shirt off. "A little help here?"

Atticus sighed and August dropped his new toy. Together, the three of them wrestled the man's clothes off and into a burn bag. August pulled the hose with the spray nozzle from its home on the wall. At least they still had the deserted factory to use in a pinch. As August hosed down the man's mottled body, Atticus left and went to the van, returning with two bottles of industrial strength bleach, handing them masks and goggles before they uncorked the chemicals.

He was a stickler for the rules.

It was likely overkill, but they couldn't take any chances. If they got caught, the whole family went down. Mutually assured destruction was the glue that held their fucked up little family together.

"Next time, can we just acid bath a bitch?" Adam asked, dumping the bleach over the corpse, nose and eyes burning despite the proper personal protection equipment.

"Those chemicals leave a paper trail. Besides, remember when Archer tried that and the barrel spilled?"

Adam shuddered. "Yeah, enough said."

The rest of the job took about three hours to complete. By the time they were done, they were all covered in blood and bone shards. They loaded the now clean pieces into the cooler in August's car before loading a layer of fish over top. They stripped out of their bloody clothes and took turns blasting each other with the icy hose water. Once they were changed into fresh clothes, they gave the place one more scrub with the bleach and the hose and August dumped the electric saw in a bucket of bleach before closing the place back up.

"You know what to do?" Atticus asked Adam.

Adam rolled his eyes. "Yeah, I've only done this about a thousand times." He pulled his phone out, threw an arm around his brother, and sent the picture to Calliope.

Adam: Photoshop that into some nondescript bar and post it on our socials.

Her response came back lightning fast. **Is that how you ask for something?**

Adam: Sorry. Long night. Can you please do it for me, beautiful?

She sent two kissy face emojis and one suspicious one followed by: **Yeah, done.**

Adam was about to put his phone away when he saw he had another text. It was just one word. **Home.**

Noah. A jolt of awareness shot through Adam. He'd told him to text when he'd gotten home and he'd listened. The sound that escaped his throat was almost a growl. There was something about Noah following his orders that went straight to his dick and ignited a primal instinct that had his mind delving into the gutter thinking about all the other things he'd like to make Noah do for him…and to him.

Adam fell into the front seat of his father's Land Rover but made no move to start the car, too busy thinking about what had happened between them just a couple of hours ago. Noah had been so easy, had melted into Adam, had let him do as he pleased.

But Noah had also been high. Maybe that was why he'd given in so easily, had made those sounds each time their mouths met. What other noises could he bring out of Noah if he had the time? He turned over the car's engine, tempted to throw it in drive and go find him.

He hadn't been invited. But his cock was hard just thinking about Noah's sweet face and his slight body. There was so much fire packed in such a little frame. He'd been so fierce the day they met and so willing just a few hours ago. He'd wanted Adam, there was no denying that. And he didn't think it was the drugs. At least, not just the drugs.

That kind of power was dangerous for someone like Adam. He lacked the gauge needed to temper his wants with Noah's needs. If Noah gave him permission, Adam didn't know if he could stop himself from pushing him to the limits. Adam liked being in control, taking charge, forcing others to bend to his wants. It was something he'd accepted about himself long ago. And there was always somebody willing to play with him, but since that very first night with Noah, there'd been nobody *but* Noah.

Adam hadn't been able to stop thinking about him. No matter what he did, Noah was never far from his mind. At first, Adam thought it was the guilt. Adam had broken

Noah's heart to save himself. He'd shown him who his father was, the disgusting things he'd done, probably triggering repressed memories Noah hadn't been ready to face.

But it wasn't guilt, or rather, it wasn't *only* guilt. He just wanted to be near him. Adam spent his life dwelling in darkness and Noah felt like the light. He felt like the sun on Adam's face. Whenever he saw him, something unknotted deep inside him and he could breathe…even if Noah didn't know he was there.

And that was the problem.

Adam didn't understand boundaries. As a child, he'd broken a lot of toys trying to make them do things they weren't meant for. He didn't want Noah to be another broken toy. He was already popping mystery pills and making out with murderous strangers in abandoned buildings. When he'd found out Adam wasn't there to kill him, he'd sounded disappointed.

Maybe Noah needed Adam? Maybe he needed somebody to take care of him, watch over him, show him what he was capable of. Adam snorted. He couldn't be Noah's guardian angel—not when every time he closed his eyes, he pictured him on his knees, begging Adam to do increasingly dirty things to him.

He threw the car into drive, leaving the parking lot and pulling out onto the road with no real destination in mind. He should go out somewhere, make himself known, give himself an alibi. Adam crawled to a stop at the red light. He itched to make a left and head to The Landing Strip, the strip club by the airport. That was where Noah called home—a rusted out Airstream trailer parked in the lot. Noah worked there as a dishwasher.

An angel and devil were squabbling on Adam's shoulder. Left brought him to Noah who he knew for a fact was home. Right took him to his studio apartment in the heart of the city. He needed to go home. He needed to leave Noah alone. He was vulnerable; small and sweet and so fucking malleable. Adam wanted to be the one who made him cry, who made him whimper and moan and sigh. Maybe even the one who made him scream.

When he'd asked Adam if he was going to hurt him, Adam hadn't lied. If given the chance, he would hurt Noah. That was what he did. It was who he was. But Noah had smashed their mouths together only after Adam had said yes. Did he want Adam to hurt him? Or had he somehow convinced Noah he wasn't the bad guy? Fuck, he hoped Noah didn't somehow think he was a good person.

Adam was the worst, a bad guy who did bad things to bad people for good reasons. The scales of good and evil would never tip back in the right direction for him. He didn't just kill people, he enjoyed it, and that wasn't ever going to change. The world needed people like him and his brothers. His father called them a necessary evil.

Necessary or not, Noah deserved something good in his life, and that would never be Adam. The least he could do was stay away from him. But when the light turned green, Adam made a left.

Fuck.

FOUR
NOAH

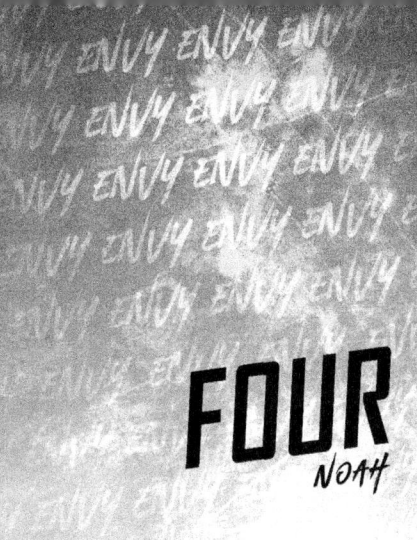

Noah had almost made it to his trailer when a beer bottle crashed against its side, inches from his head, beer and glass hitting his skin. Noah might have startled if not for Bailey's little pink pills. It wasn't the first time a bottle had been chucked at his head, wasn't even the first time that month. People in cheap strip clubs often made poor decisions.

"Hey, you little shit. Don't you run from me."

Gary whirled him around and slammed him up against the trailer, his head thudding hard enough to make him see little cartoon stars. "Hey, Gary. What's up?" Noah asked, a giggle falling from his lips.

They must have looked comical to outside observers. Gary was a foot taller and a hundred pounds heavier, and his meaty hand around Noah's throat might have been able to encircle his whole neck if he wasn't pressed against the metal siding of his Airstream.

Noah's stomach soured at the stench of sweat and beer and bad breath coming from Gary, who was an inch from his face. "Did you take it?"

Noah frowned, then blinked, forcing himself to concentrate. *What was in those pills?* "Take what?"

His head jerked to the side as Gary slapped him in the face hard enough to send the world spinning. "My backpack. Did you take it from my office?"

Noah could feel himself grinning, then laughing, but he couldn't stop. "I didn't even work tonight. I've been out with friends. Why would I steal a backpack?" He schooled his face into a serious expression. "What was in it? Was it your sense of humor?"

Once more, Gary slapped him.

"If you keep doing that, I'm going to make you buy me dinner," Noah taunted, licking his top teeth mockingly, stumbling as Gary released him abruptly.

"Your dad was a friend, but you're pushing your luck. If I find out it was you, I'm gonna bury you in this tin can you call a home. You hear me, fucker?"

Before Noah could formulate a response, Gary turned, trudging back towards the entrance of the club.

Noah managed to get into the Airstream, shoving the flimsy lock in place. He gave another cursory look through the window to make sure Gary was gone before heading to the ugly floral couch in the tiny living area and popping the bench seat off, pulling the ugly camo backpack from its hiding spot.

Gary was a fucking moron. Noah had swiped it last night, and he spent so much time fucking his dancers he hadn't even noticed it was missing until almost twenty-four hours later. He knew exactly what was in the backpack. A fuck ton of cash, all fake, a Ruger snub nose revolver, some scraps of paper, and his keys.

The keys were what he was after. He'd already made molds and taken them to Kevin at the key shop to have copies made. He'd also made a copy of Gary's license, hoping his address was current. Somewhere in Gary's house was the key to solving Noah's mystery. A shudder wracked his body, like somebody had walked over his grave.

He'd planned to put the backpack back where he'd found it, but then Bailey and her girlfriend had conned him into hitting the club. Drinking, dancing, and partying seemed like a much better prospect than sitting in his beat up trailer, obsessing over his current project. He didn't regret his decision either. If he hadn't gone out, he never would have kissed Adam, felt his hands on his face, had him look at him with that same overwhelming intensity he had the first night they'd spoken.

The night he'd tried to kill him. That night had changed everything. In some ways, everything was now so much worse, but some things were better, too. He no longer felt guilty for not saving his father. He now knew the truth about what happened to him as a child, for better or worse. Mostly worse. Definitely worse. Maybe not all of it. But enough.

What he couldn't remember was probably best left buried, but that didn't mean he was going to let it go. Because the things he did remember...well, they were fucking awful. Nightmarish shit that no child should have to endure, and Noah didn't know much, but he knew he wasn't alone. His father hadn't been alone either.

Noah shook the thoughts away. He didn't want to think about that tonight. He wanted to think about Adam's lips on his and the way he'd sounded when he said he couldn't stop thinking about him. It didn't seem real. Noah was nothing special, small in stature, slender build, definitely no six-pack. He had blah brown eyes and freckles.

Adam was a fucking runway model. He used to be anyway. He looked more like a rock star with his inky black hair and painted fingernails and lashes so black it looked like he was wearing eyeliner. And those blue eyes, so pale they were almost white. He didn't seem real. It was like somebody had ripped him from a teen drama. The bad boy. The supermodel. The killer.

Noah made his way back to the bed that took up the back half of his trailer, stripping down to his underwear before falling face first into the mattress, Adam still on his mind.

He supposed wanting to fuck his father's killer was a level of fucked up that would probably require years of therapy that Noah couldn't afford. But Noah had felt something between them that very first night. He'd known the instant Adam had taken control of the situation, had felt the balance in power shift even with Noah holding the gun. Adam could have killed him at any time. In the moment, that thought was as exhilarating as heroin. Sometimes, he wished he had killed him. Death seemed peaceful where Noah's life was chaos. Death seemed preferable to loneliness. And Noah couldn't remember the last time he wasn't lonely. Had he ever felt like somebody cared?

He rubbed his face on his pillow like he could wipe away his depression. He'd rather think of Adam. Adam with his big warm hands cupping his face and just moving him where he wanted him, like Noah had been made just for Adam's pleasure. What did pleasuring Adam look like? His dick hardened. It definitely wanted to know the answer, too.

Even tonight, Adam had taken charge immediately, not because he wanted to throw his weight around or because he had some kind of alpha male complex. Adam just naturally dominated a space. And, God help him, Noah liked it.

Or maybe it was the drugs talking. Maybe sober Noah would find Adam saying he was probably going to hurt him not sexy, but, for tonight, Noah chose to fall asleep with a smile on his lips, replaying the memory of Adam's kisses until he finally dozed off.

Noah woke to the hinges of his trailer door protesting. He jerked upright, his heart hammering in his chest as he watched a large figure stalk closer. Gary. He scrambled into the corner of his mattress but then ran out of space. It was too late to hide, there was only one way in or out. He slammed his hand down on the light, the forty watt bulb not taking away the horror of the situation but giving it a much more cinematic feel, like a Stanley Kubrick film.

Noah wasn't sure which of them looked more shocked. Him or Adam. When Adam's face came into view, a shock of awareness ran through Noah, part of him excited but the other half furious he'd just scared the shit out of him. "Did you just break into my house?"

Adam frowned, turning back to look at the door like Noah might be talking to somebody else. When he looked back, he shrugged. "Technically, I just pulled really hard and it opened."

Noah's mouth fell open at the matter-of-fact tone in Adam's voice. "Have you ever heard of knocking?"

Adam crawled onto Noah's bed, like it was a given he'd end up there. "I did knock. You didn't answer."

Noah pulled his pillow into his lap, hugging it, wondering if he was dreaming or hallucinating for the second time that night. "Maybe I didn't want to see you. Did that even occur to you?" he asked, sounding unconvincing even to his own ears.

Adam's brows furrowed together as he leaned into Noah's space. "No, it didn't. Why wouldn't you want to see me?"

"Um, it's, like, four in the morning? I was sleeping? I don't actually know you?" Noah countered.

"You knew me earlier. That was you underneath me, right?"

Noah gripped his pillow tighter. "And you took that to mean you have an engraved invitation to my house?"

Adam actually seemed to be pondering the question, like he wasn't certain of his own motives. Finally, he said, "You said you were home. I knocked. You didn't answer. I thought maybe you'd overdosed. I needed to see for myself you were alive."

Noah screwed the heels of his palms into his eyes. "I'm alive."

Adam didn't leave, just moved closer. "Why would you do a drug when you didn't even know what it was?"

Noah shrugged. "What are you, the morality police? You kill people, like, as a hobby."

"It's more like community service," Adam said, his expression blank.

Noah blinked at him before shaking his head. "I can't figure out what your deal is. I can never tell if you're making fun of me or if you just have zero idea of what's considered appropriate behavior."

Adam reached out and took Noah's hand, looking at him with a potency that made him swallow audibly. "I'm well versed in how to behave in polite society. My father made very sure of that. But…that's for other people, not you."

Noah tried to pull his hand away. "I don't deserve politeness?"

Adam's brow furrowed, seemingly growing frustrated. "No, you don't deserve the fake version of me. You know who I am… What I am. I don't have to be fake around you."

Noah should have been terrified of the intensity of Adam's words, the way he stared at Noah like he saw something… magical. Maybe Adam was high? "I know you murdered my father. I know you've killed people. I don't know who you are. I just know what you've done. That can't be who you are."

Adam seemed almost hurt by Noah's words. He definitely seemed confused. "But it is. I was raised for this. We all were."

Noah pondered Adam's words. "You were raised to kill?"

"We were raised to level the playing field. To right the wrongs of the justice system. There are a lot of bad people in this world and the law rarely makes the right call. We do our homework. We save lives. We keep people safe."

Noah should tell Adam to go. He'd seen enough murder documentaries to know a sociopath when he saw one, knew anybody who looked at him the way Adam did was probably batshit crazy. But he wasn't wrong. Killing Noah's father, no matter how painful it had seemed at the time, had most definitely saved lives. It had saved Noah. He just hadn't remembered that until he'd forced Adam's hand and those memories had started floating to the surface.

His skin crawled just thinking of him. He had no idea how or why he'd turned his father into a saint after his death. He'd definitely been a monster. Now, his memories were the monster, lurking in the most unlikely of corners, popping up when Noah least expected and tearing him apart.

Sometimes, it was like it had happened to somebody else, but other days, it was like it was still going on. Sometimes, the only way to quiet the voices was to swallow some pills, drink some alcohol. Sometimes, the drugs were his only safe space.

"Why are you here?"

"I wanted to see you," Adam said with such sincerity that Noah couldn't help but smile.

"You just saw me a few hours ago."

Adam flopped on his back, making himself at home on Noah's bed, looking way better than he should there. "It wasn't enough. I needed to see you more."

"You know I'm not going to have sex with you, right?"

Adam's gaze darted away from Noah and back again, his

heavy black brows furrowing once more. "Okay."

"So, if that's why you're here, you should go," Noah prompted.

Adam's brows raised. "But…that's not why I'm here. So, I'm gonna stay. Okay?"

Noah could only stare at Adam, who was pulling his shoes off and then his jeans, tossing them over the edge of the mattress. "Why are you taking your clothes off?"

"Did you want me to sleep with my boots on?"

Noah's hands gesticulated wildly. "Why did you take your pants off?"

"Chafing," Adam said, deadpan.

"You're certifiable. Like chasing butterflies, bats in the belfry, not all there."

"That's rude. I am a psychopath. Words hurt, you know." Noah opened his mouth to apologize when Adam grinned. "I'm kidding. Do you have more questions or can we go to sleep now?"

Noah's brain was turning a mile a minute. "Don't you live in a mansion on the other side of town?"

Adam shook his head with a smile. "No, my dad does. I live in a studio apartment on the other side of town."

"And why can't you go sleep there?"

Adam shrugged. "Because you're not there and I want to be with you."

Noah blinked at him stupidly. "I—" He broke off. Why was he fighting this? He'd been thinking of nothing but Adam since they parted ways hours ago. "Yeah, okay. You win. Let's go to sleep. Don't get handsy," Noah ordered, secretly hoping he would.

Adam grinned, slipping his way under the covers and holding the comforter up for Noah to do the same. Before he could do anything more, Adam slipped his arm behind Noah's neck, drawing him against him. Noah let himself rest his head on Adam's chest, noting absently that it was a different shirt than earlier. Beneath his ear, Adam's heartbeat thudded steadily, luring Noah into a light doze.

"What's that?" Adam asked.

Noah's eyes flew open, looking to Adam, who was staring at Noah's ceiling. He tried wriggling out of Adam's grip, but he held him in place. "It's nothing. Just a project."

Adam's gaze cut to his. "I know a murder board when I see one."

Noah glanced up at the ceiling where he'd tacked up numerous pictures, paperwork, articles, and pictures of possible suspects, connecting them all with red string. "I'm not lying. It's a project."

"One involving your father?"

Noah looked up at his father's picture in the center of his ceiling. "Yeah, something like that."

"You do know I'm not going to stop asking until you tell me, right?" Adam asked.

Noah sighed. "I'll make you a deal. If we can sleep now, I'll explain everything tomorrow. I've had a long night."

Noah startled as Adam lifted his hand and stroked Noah's cheek. "Okay. We talk in the morning. I'll take you to get breakfast."

It wasn't a question, so Noah didn't take it as such. Adam's weight shifted and he lifted Noah's chin, giving him a soft kiss. "Good night."

"Good night," Noah echoed, voice raw.

FIVE
ADAM

Adam woke with his arms around Noah, his body tucked snuggly against him. He was small compared to Adam's six foot two, but he fit perfectly, allowing Adam to all but envelop him when they spooned. He liked the idea of people having to go through him to get to Noah. It was a foreign concept. He didn't know how to describe it. From the moment he'd seen him standing there, holding that gun on him, Adam had just known he wasn't going to let him go.

Ever.

He nuzzled his nose against Noah's neck, inhaling deeply. Noah had said he smelled like sweat, which would have been fine with Adam, but it wasn't true. Noah had his own peculiar scent, something that evoked a sense memory deep in Adam's lizard brain. Something that made him think *home*.

"Are you sniffing me?" Noah asked sleepily.

Adam liked Noah's voice, not too high, not too deep. Everything about Noah was just right. "Yes."

He felt Noah's body shake with laughter. "You're so weird."

Adam grinned, even though Noah couldn't see it. "Other people think I'm charming."

Noah stretched deeply, craning his head around to look at Adam but making no attempt to leave his arms. "But you also said last night that other people don't know the real you, so..."

Adam let that tumble around in his head for a minute before saying, "So, you think people only find me charming because they don't know me, but you don't find me charming because you do?" He didn't like the idea of Noah not liking him, but he wanted whatever Noah wanted. "Do you want me to be fake charming me or real me?"

Noah sighed, rolling to face Adam, wiggling up until they were all but nose to nose on his pillow. "No. I guess I like how weird you are."

"I like your face," Adam said, sweeping his hand over Noah's freckles. "Your stars are gone."

"Sorry."

"Don't be. I like your freckles. They were the first thing I noticed about you."

Noah smiled ruefully. "And here I thought it would be the gun in my hand."

"Nah, I'm used to people pulling guns on me. I'm not used to wanting to kiss those people."

"You wanted to kiss me?" Noah asked.

Adam stuck his tongue out and licked the tip of Noah's nose. "I wanted you to walk out of that warehouse alive so that I could eventually kiss you."

Noah searched his face, like he was trying to figure out if Adam might be lying, then leaned in and brushed his lips across Adam's in a barely-there kiss. Something caught fire in his blood. He rolled Noah so he was beneath him, catching his hands over his head as he separated his thighs with his hips. When Noah made a whimpering sound beneath him, Adam pulled back. "Too much?"

Adam started to move away when Noah threaded their fingers together, hooking his legs around Adam's thighs so he couldn't go anywhere. "I didn't say stop."

This time, it was Adam studying Noah's face for any sign he wasn't serious, but he got lost staring into Noah's eyes. He'd never understood that phrase before, but now, he did. Noah's eyes weren't just brown; there were flecks of green and gold in them, visible even in the dim light of the trailer.

When he captured Noah's mouth again, his kiss was greedy and consuming, like he couldn't get enough. Because he couldn't. He liked having Noah underneath him, held hostage beneath his weight, leaving Adam free to do whatever he wanted.

Noah liked it, too. He whined when Adam nipped at his lip, his hips bucking up against him like he couldn't help himself. Adam could feel how hard he was just from their kiss. Just like last night. Had it only been last night? Time seemed to blur around Noah, like it was Adam who was high. Maybe he was high and Noah was his drug. If so, he was already hooked.

He gripped his fingers tighter, rocked his lower body against Noah's, their erections slotting together with only two thin layers of cotton between them. Adam dragged his mouth away, biting at Noah's earlobe. "If I don't stop, this is going to get messy."

"I don't care. Don't stop. Make me come," Noah gasped.

Adam couldn't help the near feral sound that fell from his lips. He released Noah only so he could shove their underwear out of the way. Once they were skin to skin, Adam caught both of Noah's wrists in his hand, the other wrapping around his shoulder, holding him steady so he could drive against him.

Adam had never done this before, had never wanted anything but a quick fuck and a quicker exit, but this, the slick slide of their bodies working against each other, Noah panting and whining beneath him, had him ready to blow faster than sex ever had. Especially when Noah started talking—babbling, really—a stream of consciousness ramble that was a road map for Adam to follow. "Oh, fuck. Oh, God. Don't stop, right there. You feel so fucking good. Harder. Oh…fuck. Yes. Yes. Please. Please. Please."

Every word that fell from Noah's lips drove Adam closer. He tried to keep from falling over the edge until Noah got there first, but he wasn't going to last much longer.

"Adam," Noah gasped, lifting his head to capture his lips, but it wasn't a kiss so much as him moaning into Adam's mouth as he came. That was more than enough to push Adam over the edge. He surged against Noah a few more times, his hand clamping around his wrists even harder as he spilled between them, his hips spasming as pleasure dragged him under.

When he finally released Noah's wrists, they were both still breathing hard. Adam pressed his forehead to Noah's. "You talk a lot."

Noah flushed. "Sorry, I guess I just get caught u—"

Adam kissed him. "It's the hottest fucking thing ever. Never stop."

"Okay," Noah said, breathless.

Adam rolled off of him to stare up at the murder board overhead. He'd almost forgotten. "So, what conspiracy are you trying to *Beautiful Mind* your way through?"

Noah sat up and grabbed a towel, cleaning himself off and throwing it to Adam, who did the same. Once their clothing was righted, Adam tugged Noah back down so they were both staring at the ceiling.

"You might as well tell me because I'm not going to stop asking, and when I don't get what I want one way, I get it another. I'd rather just hear it from you."

"You sound fucking crazy, you know."

Adam's face contorted into a look of disbelief. "I am crazy. I kill people. Remember?"

"Community service, remember?" Noah countered with a shake of his head.

Adam grinned. "Spill. What are you doing? Stop distracting me. What are you involved in?"

Noah took a big breath, blowing it out and chewing his bottom lip. Adam threaded their fingers together, squeezing in what he hoped was a reassuring gesture. Noah looked away. "After you showed me the video…of my dad and that boy…" Noah swallowed audibly. "Things started to come rushing back. Memories from when I was younger, a lot fucking younger…"

Once more, Adam squeezed his hand. "He hurt you."

It wasn't a question. "Yeah. I don't remember all of it. I can't… If I do, I'll lose my fucking mind. You know?"

"That's why you took those pills. To keep the memories at bay?"

Noah did look at him then. He nodded. "Sometimes, being fucked up is the only way to keep him from crawling back inside me. I don't like being high, I just hate remembering. Things were easier when I didn't remember."

Adam could only nod. He knew what it was like to have the horrors of your past seep through the cracks in your foundation like some kind of toxic gas, poisoning your thoughts. "I'm sorry," he said, surprised to find it wasn't just a meaningless platitude given because society dictated it as the proper response. He meant it. He didn't want to be the cause of Noah's misery.

"I forced your hand. You could have just killed me. You gave me the chance to go. I refused. It's nobody's fault but mine."

"I'm still sorry. But why is your father in the center of the board? I promise you, he's definitely dead. It wasn't as bloody as I'd hoped, but he's dead."

Noah shook his head. "I know. I'm the one who found him. Remember?"

Pain spiked through Adam's chest. He'd done that. He'd traumatized Noah when he was barely ten years old. "Yeah."

"He wasn't the only one."

Adam cut his gaze to Noah. "What?"

Noah set his mouth in a grim line. "My father wasn't the only one to…do things to me. There were others. Friends. Strangers. Five whose faces I can remember. Others who just watched in the shadows."

Adam's rage was instantaneous, a match to gasoline. His vision was a deep throbbing red. He released Noah's hand to slam his fist into the pillow. "I should have killed that piece of shit slowly. I should have looked deeper." He could feel his body trembling, his blood pulsing in his veins. He needed to hit something. Kill it. Rip it apart. He was a bomb ticking down, and if he didn't get out of there, he was going to explode all over Noah, and he didn't need Noah seeing him like that.

Before he could think to stop him, Noah threw a leg over his hips, settling in his lap and taking his face in his hands. "Stop."

It was said with such gentleness that Adam's brain ground to a halt, the dog throwing itself against its cage inside him as confused by Noah's serene expression as Adam.

"Stop," he said again. "You couldn't have saved me. By the time you came along, I'd aged out of my father's preferential victim pool. I'd already locked all those memories up."

"I want to dig him up just so I can kill him again. I hate that he hurt you."

Noah gave him a humorless smile. "I know. But, as a result, I now crave being hurt. The brain sure is a fucked up thing, huh?"

Adam blinked at him. "What?"

"Bite me, spank me, pull my hair? Tell me I'm bad, tell me all the things you're gonna do to me. Make me take it. Pin me down by my wrists and trap me against a mattress. Dry hump me until I come?" Adam swallowed audibly, his cock desperately trying to rally at the words falling from Noah's lips. He leaned forward and nipped his bottom lip, drawing blood, before sucking on it. "Lucky for you, Daddy issues aren't just for girls." He held up his wrists, where the blood was starting to pool in the shape of Adam's hands.

"Sorry," Adam said, not really sorry at all but wishing he was for Noah's sake. He liked marking Noah, wanted everybody to know he was his to protect.

"I just told you, I'm fucked up. I like the pain. The rougher the better. A shrink would have a field day with me."

"You're not fucked up," Adam said fiercely. "You're perfect."

"Said the killer," Noah said with a smirk. His smile faded as he examined Adam. "You good?"

Shock reverberated through Adam as he realized he was. Noah had somehow disarmed him with just one word. "Yeah. Please, finish telling me your story. I'll try not to lose my shit again."

Noah slid off him and back onto his back, gazing up at the ceiling and his father's face. "He looks so evil now. I never thought that before my memories came flooding back. That's weird, right?"

"Our brains are tricky. They employ all kinds of tactics to keep us functioning. My parents abused me until I simply shut off my emotions. Your brain took all the bad things that happened to you and it locked them away so you could function. Once you started to remember, your perceptions of your father changed."

Adam watched as Noah swallowed hard, nodding. "I'm sure I could remember more details if I tried. But I don't want to dig any deeper. What I remember is bad enough. But I need to know their names. I need to make sure they get put down the way my father was."

"Let me do that for you."

Noah was already shaking his head. "No."

Adam's heart rate shot up at Noah's refusal. "It's what I do."

"Not for me it isn't. I need to do this myself. Maybe not the killing, but at least the naming. I'm the only one who remembers enough to feel my way to the light switch. I've already gotten one name. My father's best friend, Gary, the owner of the club. He was definitely there. I feel like cracking him might be the key to cracking all the others."

Adam would happily crack this Gary like a fucking glow stick if that was what Noah needed. "At least let me help. I'm excellent at extracting information from unwilling targets."

"Fine. But I call the shots."

This time, it was Adam who smirked. "I thought you liked being told what to do." He rolled on top of Noah again, pinning him beneath him. "'Bite me, spank me, pull my hair'? That's what you said, right?" There was no heat to his words, just a teasing tone that had Noah smiling up at him. Fuck, he liked making him smile.

"Only in the bedroom. You can do whatever you want to me in here. But out there"—he jabbed his thumb towards the window—"I'm in charge. That's my offer. Take it or leave it."

Adam pushed Noah's hair off his face, grinning. "Whatever I want, huh?"

"Within reason," Noah qualified.

"What's within reason?" Adam asked, sliding his tongue between Noah's lips in a kiss that lingered long enough to distract.

"No circus animals. No permanent damage. You can't pee on me."

Adam barked out a laugh. "What?"

"It's a thing. Oh, and no spitting in my mouth. That's a hard limit."

Adam was starting to think he and Noah watched entirely different porn. "Noted. But the others weren't?"

Noah hit him in the shoulder, face flushing. "Shut up."

"Hey, you're the one setting the rules. I'm just clarifying."

"Deal or no deal?" Noah asked.

Adam kissed him once more. "Deal."

SIX
NOAH

The restaurant was nothing fancy, but it was one of Noah's favorite places. An old school diner with black and white checkered floors and where everything was red and chrome. He'd been frequenting Moe's since the year after his father died. The wait staff used to give him free food after school because they knew it would likely be his only meal. In all the time he'd been going there, he'd never once set eyes on the man whose name glowed in the window in red neon. He suspected there was no Moe.

The scent of maple bacon and buttermilk pancakes hit Noah the moment they walked in the door, making his stomach growl comically loud. Noah was sure everyone could probably hear it over the clanking of forks on plates and the animated conversations of the patrons.

Adam was glued to Noah's back, his hands on Noah's hips and his chin resting on his head, like they'd been dating for a decade when, in reality, they were little more than strangers. If what they were could be reduced to such a simple word. Still, Noah felt himself leaning into the reassuring heat of Adam's torso but hated how comfortable he already was with him. Hated how much he liked the feel of his hands on his body.

He flushed as he thought about their kiss that had turned into orgasms just ninety minutes ago. Noah had had a dozen meaningless hookups in his time, each with the understanding that it had meant nothing; they were just scratching an itch. But kissing Adam in that warehouse had sparked something deep in Noah's core, something that seemed to smolder within until Adam had pinned him to the mattress and kissed him like he was dying and Noah's lips were the only thing that could save him.

Noah had never experienced that kind of combustible chemistry. Adam was a match and Noah was gasoline-soaked paper, and that was a volatile combination that could easily blow up in his face. Still, he would have let Adam do anything to him, had *wanted* to let Adam do dirty things to him.

But Adam—despite his weird intensity—had seemed so comfortable letting Noah set the pace. He seemed to be this strange mixture of brute force and childlike possessiveness, like Noah was his new favorite toy and he'd smash it before he'd let anybody else play with it. That shouldn't have been hot…but it was. Noah had never been anybody's favorite anything.

Before Noah could fall any further down the rabbit hole of existential crisis, Cindi 'with an i' swayed her ample figure towards them, loudly chomping her gum. Moe's really leaned into their retro aesthetic.

Cindi had on a red polyester uniform the same color as the red vinyl booths. She wore horn-rimmed glasses and her hair in a sky high rat's nest. Noah knew she was in her sixties and had eight grandkids, but she honestly didn't look a day over fifty. She had good genes.

She smiled warmly when she saw Noah, smacking a kiss on his cheek. "Hey, doll. Haven't seen you here in forever. I was starting to think you'd abandoned us for that new age place with their wheat grass shots down the block."

Noah grinned. "Like I could ever give up the cinnamon roll pancakes here."

She flicked her gaze to Adam, smirking when she noted the way he clung to Noah. "Who's your friend?"

Noah craned his head up and back to glance behind him. "Cindi, this is Adam. Adam, Cindi."

"Hi," Adam said, not releasing Noah's waist.

"Hey there, yourself. You look really familiar," she said. "Are you an actor?"

"No. Definitely not," Adam said with a laugh.

That wasn't entirely true but hardly anything Noah could voice out loud.

Cindi grabbed two menus and led them to a back booth. Adam slid in across from Noah, but his long legs quickly entangled with his beneath the table. "What can I get ya to drink, cuties?"

Coffees ordered, Adam snagged Noah's hand. "You have freckles on your fingers, too," he mused.

"You're obsessed with freckles," Noah teased.

Adam flicked pale blue eyes upwards, snagging Noah's gaze. "No. Just yours."

If he didn't stop saying things like that, Noah was going to do something stupid like fall in love with a murderer.

Cindi returned with two mugs, and Noah watched as Adam dumped enough sugar into his coffee to stand a spoon in. "That can't be healthy," Noah said, smiling when Adam took a sip and sighed deeply.

Noah drank his black. Mostly because he usually couldn't afford anything but powdered creamers, which gave him the creeps. All those lumps just floating around, waiting to be dissolved in boiling liquid. No, thank you.

Once they had their food—cinnamon roll pancakes for Noah and a Belgian waffle buried in syrup and powdered sugar for Adam—the real conversation began. The one they'd put on hold in the trailer until they could get some sustenance.

They could talk freely. The restaurant provided the perfect amount of white noise to keep their conversation private. Still, he kept his voice low, leaning in just a bit to talk in-between mouthfuls.

"Okay, what's step one?" Adam asked.

Noah was tempted to play dumb just to put off the inevitable for a while. But this was why they were there. To solve a mystery. "I stole Gary's backpack and made copies of all his keys. He gets to the club at seven each night and doesn't leave until ten or eleven in the morning. I swapped shifts with another dishwasher so we have the whole night to look through all of his shit."

"You want to break into his house and look for…" Adam prompted.

"If he's got the same…tastes…in porn as my father, then there's a chance, maybe, he kept souvenirs of his time with my dad and these other men. If I can find those tapes, I can possibly find them."

Adam nodded. "Makes sense. I can have my people deep dive into his internet history, bank statements, background?"

Noah gave him a flat stare. "You have people?"

"Yeah. Doesn't everybody?" he asked, tone teasing.

Noah still didn't quite understand who Adam worked for. It had taken years just to identify Adam in the first place. If his father hadn't been so paranoid, he might not have even had a place to start. He hadn't known about Adam working for a group of people until the night he confronted him and he'd made the phone call that had shattered Noah's fragile existence. Would Adam tell him the truth?

"What is this group you work for?" He dropped his voice. "Who hires a—what?—sixteen-year-old to kill people? That's how old you were when you did my dad, right?"

Adam nodded, looking impressed, Noah wasn't sure why. "I wasn't hired. I don't get paid. Community service, remember? I'm a mandatory volunteer."

Noah scoffed. "You can't make it mandatory for somebody to volunteer their time."

"Tell that to my father," Adam muttered.

The pieces began falling into place for Noah. In the trailer, Adam had said, 'we were raised for this.' It had sounded like some Batman level vigilante bullshit last night when he was half asleep and fully high. But maybe Adam was serious.

"Wait…your dad? Thomas Mulvaney is a…murderer?" Noah whispered.

Adam snorted a laugh; then took a long drink of his coffee before saying, "Please, my father would never get his hands dirty like that. No, my father trained *us* to be murderers."

Noah sat on that sentence for a minute. "Us? Like…your brothers?"

Adam shrugged, seemingly unbothered by the conversation, like they were discussing traffic. "I mean, you can't fault his logic. My brothers and I are uniquely qualified to do what we do. And honestly, we turned out better than the doctors could have hoped, given our initial diagnoses."

A finger of unease ran along his spine. "Which was what?"

Adam smiled softly, shaking his head. "I told you, I'm a psychopath."

Noah choked on the bite of pancake he'd just forked into his mouth, sparking a coughing fit that drew far more attention than he wanted.

When it was over and the others went back to their eggs and toast, Noah managed, "Yeah, but when people say that, it's a joke or exaggeration."

Adam raised his hand to get Cindi's attention before pointing to his cup with a sweet smile Noah found laughable considering the conversation.

When he looked at Noah again, he shrugged. "When I say it, I mean I had a team of board certified psychiatrists who determined I lacked the emotional capacity to feel love, regret, guilt, remorse. Psychopath or sociopath is relative, I suppose. They don't know if I was born this way or if my trauma created my eternally broken psyche. The outcome is similar either way."

Noah's brain snagged on the unable to love part, trying to ignore the stabbing pain that shot through him. It figured Noah would be attracted to a man who couldn't love him by design. He really was hopeless. He tried to push the thought away. "So, are all your brothers like you?"

"Psychopaths, you mean?" Adam asked. "Yeah, that's why he chose us."

A thought suddenly occurred to Noah. "Am I going to get merced for knowing this information?"

Adam's face grew serious. "I would *never* let anybody hurt you." The rawness in his declaration almost made Noah teary despite its absurdity. Nobody had ever protected him. Ever. He'd always told himself he didn't need it. But now, here was this dangerous stranger swearing to protect him from his family. Adam threaded their fingers together on the table. "Besides, are you planning on telling anybody?"

Noah gave a humorless laugh. "And proclaim that a group of billionaire vigilantes killed my pedophile father? They'd either think I was certifiable or they'd throw you a fucking parade and build a statue in your father's honor."

Adam nodded. "You're probably right. But you don't have to worry about my family. Like I said, I'll keep you safe."

Noah's heart did a little dance behind his ribcage. Adam was so fucking intense. He was like one of those characters in a teen romance novel where the naive girl ignores every instinct with catastrophic consequences. Except, in this scenario, Noah was the naive girl. He liked the attention. For better or worse. The catastrophic consequences were likely to follow but it was so hard to care. Was it wrong that he wanted somebody to love him and look at him with movie level *fuck me* eyes?

Except, Adam didn't have the capacity to love anybody. He'd said so himself.

So, what the fuck were they doing?

Before he could formulate a response, a shadow descended over the table and a teen girl stood gazing at Adam like he was Beyoncé. "I'm sorry," she said, face bright red. "But are you Adam Mulvaney?"

Adam grinned, and the girl looked like she might faint. "Yeah. Hi."

Noah tried to untangle their fingers, but Adam tightened his grip, his gaze never leaving the girl in her white shorts and crop top.

She glanced back over her shoulder at a group of girls gawking at them before telling Adam, "I'm such a huge fan. Can I get a picture with you?"

Adam glanced at Noah. Was he asking his permission? Only after Noah shrugged did Adam say, "Sure."

The girl slid into the booth, pressing her cheek to Adam's, snapping a selfie before extricating herself quickly. Adam never once let go of Noah's hand. When she spotted this, she giggled. "Oh, my God. Is this your boyfriend?"

Adam looked at him. "Yeah. This is Noah."

Was Adam his boyfriend? After only a day? Why wasn't Noah more alarmed by that? Instead, his whole body flushed hot until he was sure he was redder than Adam's biggest fan. She looked between the two of them, then said to Adam, "He's so cute," as if Noah wasn't actually sitting there.

Adam gave Noah a knowing smirk. "The cutest."

"Anyway, thank you so much."

With that, she was gone, racing back over to the table where her friends were now all babbling excitedly, crowding together to look at the girl's coveted selfie with *the* Adam Mulvaney.

With the girl now gone, it was like somebody had flipped a switch and Adam's superficial charm disappeared, replaced by that piercing look he seemed to save just for Noah.

"Does that happen a lot?" Noah asked.

Adam seemed to ponder the question. "Nah. Most of the people uptown don't give a fuck about a hack model with a trust fund."

"Why did you tell her I'm your boyfriend?"

Adam frowned. "Because telling her that you're the son of one of my murder victims and we're together because I happened to get off with you this morning sounded like a mouthful."

Noah shook his head. "You could have just said friend?"

Adam's brows furrowed. "But then she might think you're available."

Noah's brain stumbled. "But I'm not? Available?"

"No."

"Do I get a say in this?" Noah asked, not even mad, just feeling like he'd definitely slipped into an alternate universe.

Adam tilted his head. "Yeah. Did you not want to be my

boyfriend?"

Noah laughed at the genuine confusion in Adam's tone, like the notion was preposterous. Maybe it was.

"I hate to keep harping on this one point because it's starting to feel a little mean to keep bringing it up, but we don't know each other."

"You know me," Adam insisted.

"But you don't know me," Noah countered, voice a harsh whisper.

"I don't need to know everything about you to know that you're what I want."

"That makes no sense."

"It will eventually," Adam promised. "But if this is too much for you…if I'm too much for you, I get it. I'm…a lot."

"Why would you want to be in a relationship if you can't love somebody?"

Once more, Adam pondered the question. "What does that word even mean? Lots of people throw the word love around without actually treating the people they supposedly love like they are loved. I don't have the same signals firing in my brain that you do. I have to rely on instinct. My instincts tell me you're the one. What do yours tell you?"

That you're going to rip my heart out some day, maybe literally. "My instincts have really never done anything for me. If you give me two choices, I make the wrong one every time."

Adam leaned in. "Instinctively, what do you think you should do?"

"Run fast and far away from you," Noah said without thought.

Adam grinned like he'd just somehow put Noah in check mate. "Then, by your own logic, you should do the opposite. And stay. With me."

"This is crazy."

"All the best things are."

SEVEN
ADAM

Adam was well versed in being where he didn't belong. He'd been breaking into people's houses almost since he was old enough to cross the street unassisted. Noah clearly had not. He sat beside Adam in the car, staring at Gary's front door like he expected a SWAT team waited on the other side.

Noah's worried face made Adam want to forget all about the plan. He was sure he could think of something else for the two of them to do, something that didn't involve triggering Noah's worst memories. But he knew that wasn't going to happen.

Adam sighed, looking out across the well-manicured lawn of Gary's ranch style home. The guy was paranoid, but he wasn't very bright. He had surveillance at every corner of his house. Hell, even his doorbell had a camera, but they were all on his wi-fi. His easily hackable wi-fi. It had only taken Calliope minutes to take control of his feeds and loop them so he'd never know they were there. She'd also run a background check, looked at his bank accounts, and attempted to access his laptop.

That was where they'd run into an issue. Gary had NSA-level encryption software, making his system unhackable from the outside. So, not that stupid, Adam supposed. Still, he had more than one computer, so all they could do was clone whichever computer Gary had left behind and hope there was something incriminating behind that encryption software.

"You ready?" Adam asked.

Noah worried his bottom lip between his teeth. "What if we get caught?"

"We won't get caught. The cameras are looped, the alarm is deactivated. We have the key to his front door. Just look like we belong here and nobody is going to bat an eye. We're just friends watering his plants."

"So, we just go in and ransack his house? Won't he know we've been there?"

"No, we go in and you carefully look through his stuff for anything related to his…extracurricular activities. I'm going to clone his hard drive and give it to Calliope so she can take her time cracking it. Chances are Gary has been doing this so long he thinks he's untouchable. That's what happens with all these guys. Eventually, they get lazy, and that's how they get caught."

Noah swallowed audibly, giving a nervous nod. "Yeah, okay."

"Hey, you good?" Adam asked, gripping Noah's chin and tipping it upwards, examining his face. Most people were easy to read, but Noah's face either said nothing or everything, just like Noah himself. Adam merely wanted to give him what he needed.

"Yeah. Part of me is just afraid of what I'll find in there."

Adam leaned into Noah's space, wrapping a hand around the back of his neck and tugging him in close. "Listen, there's a good chance that while we're in there, we'll find something you can't unsee. So, look but don't absorb. Got it? Turn your brain off. Take pictures of whatever you think is important, but don't look at any one thing for too long. Don't let anything in."

"Yeah. Yeah, okay. Let's do this." Noah pulled the handle, swinging the passenger door wide.

Adam snagged his arm before he could leave. "I can go alone if you want me to?"

Noah's eyes widened, then went kind of soft. "No. I need to do this."

Adam got that. He did. But he also didn't want to see Noah break under the weight of what he learned. There was already a strange hollow look in his eyes, a kind of misery that came from years of struggle and disappointment, like an animal that had been beaten enough to never trust another human. Adam didn't want one more thing to disappoint Noah, but he also knew this crusade was going to be a burden he carried for life.

Noah was already learning that he'd endured the worst kind of abuse at a young age. No matter how much he thought he could shut down any memories from surfacing in the future, it just wasn't possible. The more he poked at his past, the more likely he was going to remember the minute details. And that was going to hurt more than he knew.

They'd dressed in civilian clothes, jeans and t-shirts, making sure to look like two regular guys with every right to be in this surprisingly upper class suburban neighborhood. The only precautions they'd taken in advance were the thin medical grade gloves they'd donned in the car, but they'd be undetected at a distance.

They used the keys to enter the house, closing the door and locking it behind them. There were two open rooms off the foyer, one which held a pool table, the other office equipment.

Adam pointed to the desktop computer and then his backpack. "I'm going to get this started. I'll come find you in a few minutes. I know you said we have all night, but the faster we're in and out, the better."

Noah nodded, moving deeper into the darkened recesses of the house.

Once Adam began cloning the hard drive of Gary's desktop computer, a window popped up telling him it would take approximately fifteen minutes, standard for an average home computer. He spent those fifteen minutes rifling through Gary's desk drawers, finding little of interest in the top two. The bottom drawer was locked. Interesting. Adam opened the top drawer, searching for something to pick the lock, rolling his eyes when he saw the key under a desk organizer tray. The man really was stupid. Adam unlocked the drawer, heart rate accelerating as he saw the laptop inside.

He pulled it free just as the other hard drive finished. He then repeated the process with the newly found laptop, but, this time, when the window popped up, the wait time for cloning was three hours. Three hours? Adam's jaw set in a hard line as he did the math. That kind of time meant there was about one terabyte of data on that encrypted server. He shook his head. He wasn't surprised. These men were all the same, slaves to their impulses.

While Adam lacked the empathy necessary to feel the pain and horror for what these children endured—a blessing given what he'd seen—he did have a disgust for people who preyed on the population's most vulnerable. It was weakness. Pure and simple. Wolves feasting off the sick and the lame.

But when these predators were cornered, Adam was the wolf and he was indifferent to their cries, their screams, their hollow apologies. He had no problem putting them down with extreme prejudice. For the greater good.

Adam left the laptop to do its thing and wandered the house, opening drawers and cabinets, looking for anything unusual, anything that might give them some idea of who Gary's friends were.

In the kitchen, under some random mail, Adam found a strangely shaped key. It looked like it belonged to a storage unit or a bus locker. He pocketed the key, certain it wasn't something Gary used frequently enough to notice it was missing.

He found Noah crouched in a spare room closet, rifling through a file box filled to the brim with papers. When he dropped beside him, he saw it was bank statements and other important documents. "Find anything good?"

Noah shook his head. "No, it's all just the same boring paperwork everybody else seems to have," he muttered, shoving the lid back on the box with a grunt of frustration.

Adam nodded. "Yeah, it's not like in the movies. Sometimes, there's not going to be a magical paper trail. I did find a hidden laptop that seems promising. I don't know what's on it, but chances are, it's nothing good. We just have to hope Calliope can crack the encryption."

With the encryption software blowing their quick in and out timeline, they took their time, searching Gary's house room by room. While he wasn't a hoarder by any means, he kept boxes of meaningless papers, each more disappointing than the last. Adam was certain there would be something there. A picture, a video, something. All these creeps kept souvenirs. The laptop had to be the key.

They ended their search in the office, scouring the credenza behind the desk, again finding nothing of interest. Adam checked the hard drive. They still had ninety minutes. Shit. Adam opened his mouth to give Noah a time update when he saw him staring at a picture on the wall.

He was visibly shaking, his hand reaching up to touch the photo and pull it from the wall. Adam came to stand beside him. It was a picture of Gary and Noah's father standing outside a cabin in the woods, arms around each other's shoulders and big smiles on their faces.

"I know that cabin," he said, voice dull.

"Know it how?" Adam gently prompted.

"My dad and Gary used to take me there." He closed his eyes and swayed on his feet. "I can smell the pine needles."

He shuddered. "They built a campfire. I can still smell it and the oil in the lamps from when the power went out. And sweat." A sharp gasp ripped from him, head turning like he could somehow look away from whatever memory was playing out in his head, the photo slipping from his fingers. They both watched as the frame hit the floor, the sound of the cracking glass loud in the silence.

Noah looked to Adam with wild eyes. "Shit. Shit."

When Noah went to retrieve it, Adam snagged his arm. "No. Leave it. Shit falls off walls all the time."

There were too many chances for something to go wrong if Noah tried to clean up the glass. A picture falling off the wall wasn't nearly as noticeable as a picture disappearing or returning to the wall with no glass protecting it. Besides, if he cut himself on the glass, those gloves wouldn't protect him from DNA transfer.

Noah gave a stilted nod.

Adam's gaze darted to the window as he heard the sound of a car door slamming and then a car alarm activating. He looked out the window to see a man walking up the drive in their direction. "Shit. We got company."

He snagged the hard drive, dumping the laptop back in the drawer, quickly locking the cabinet and tossing the key back in the drawer, snagging Noah's arm and dragging him deeper into the house, into the back bedroom, quietly closing the door just as the front one opened.

He slipped the window open and helped Noah out first, sliding it closed behind them. They crept through two neighbors' unfenced yards, staying low to avoid windows.

Only when they were a safe distance from the house did they head back to the sidewalk.

Adam took Noah's hand as a woman walking her dog passed. He gave her a wave and she gave them a reserved smile after she saw Adam click the lock on his BMW. These suburbanites were all the same. Fancy car equaled they belonged in that neighborhood. She wouldn't give them a second thought.

Once in the car, Noah dropped his head back against the seat, looking worn out and shell-shocked. He didn't protest when Adam clicked him into his seatbelt before fastening his own. He then snapped a few pictures of the man's Ford sedan and the license plate, shooting it to Calliope before pulling out of the neighborhood.

Noah didn't speak the whole drive back, just stared out the window, though he didn't pull away when Adam rested his hand on his knee. He didn't take them back to Noah's, instead hopping on the freeway towards Adam's loft uptown. There was less chance of anything further triggering Noah at Adam's place.

It was only when they pulled into the garage that Noah seemed to snap out of his trance, looking around like he'd been teleported to another place and time. "Where are we?"

"My apartment."

Noah gave a hollow, "Oh."

Adam exited the car and came around to the other side, opening Noah's door for him. He took Adam's offered hand, not releasing it once he was on his feet. That was fine with Adam. He liked Noah touching him and Adam didn't really like touching anybody unless they were fighting or fucking. And he wasn't fucking Noah tonight. He was too raw.

Once they were outside Adam's fifth floor apartment, he pulled the keys from his pocket, watching as the loose key from Gary's tumbled to the carpeted floor. He retrieved it, opening the door and swinging it wide for Noah to enter. "What was that?" he asked.

"Not sure. Found it at Gary's. Maybe something. Maybe nothing."

Noah just nodded, not asking any more questions. Once inside, Adam unzipped his hoodie and tossed it over the chair, watching as Noah wandered around his small loft. Adam could have chosen a bigger space like his brothers, a sprawling house or some sleek luxury penthouse apartment, but he liked the small space with its exposed brick and minimalist design.

Noah looked at the narrow staircase, following it upward with his gaze. "What's up there?"

"My bed."

Noah didn't look at him, didn't say a word, just started climbing the stairs. Adam stood frozen. If he followed Noah up those stairs, he knew what would happen. Noah wasn't okay, clearly. That photo had triggered something inside him. But who was Adam to tell Noah how best to cope with his trauma?

Adam followed him up the stairs. When he reached the top, he found Noah sitting on the edge of his bed.

"Whatcha doing?" Adam asked.

Noah's gaze flicked to his. "I said you could be in charge

in the bedroom, right?"

Adam's cock hardened so fast he started to sweat. "Yeah," he managed.

Noah leaned back, putting his weight on his palms. "We're in your bedroom. What are you waiting for?"

Adam watched Noah carefully. "I don't know if that's a good idea."

"You don't want me?" Noah challenged.

Adam arched a brow. "You know that's not true. I just don't want to do anything you're not ready for."

Noah's eyes drifted away from Adam's face and then back again. "I'm hardly a blushing virgin. Besides, I don't want to think about him…them…what they did to me. I don't want to think at all. Just stop me from thinking about anything but you. Us."

Adam didn't know how Noah intended the words to come out, but they sounded a lot like a plea instead of a demand. Why was he fighting the inevitable? Noah was sitting on his bed, demanding Adam touch him. What was the point of being the villain if he let the right thing get in the way of what he wanted? And he wanted Noah.

He peeled his shirt over his head, dropping it on the floor, before wandering closer. Noah let his legs fall open as he approached. Adam stepped between them. Noah sat forward, eyes locked on Adam's as he licked over the deep groove of his hip.

"Christ." He tipped Noah's chin upwards, running a thumb over his bottom lip before pushing it into his mouth.

Noah sucked eagerly, his thighs squeezing Adam like this

was a test and he was determined to ace it. Adam's cock throbbed as he imagined Noah giving it the same attention as his finger, but he still wasn't certain if this was the right thing to do.

He hissed as Noah's teeth clamped down on his skin hard enough to leave a mark. He snatched his finger free.

"Is that how this is going to go?" he asked, voice low, the threat more than implied.

Noah's pupils blew wide at Adam's change in demeanor. "I guess that depends on you. I thought you'd be a lot… rougher."

Gauntlet thrown.

Adam had no problem being the aggressor; it was his default setting. If Noah wanted it rough, he'd give him what he wanted.

He slapped his face, just hard enough to get his attention, carding his hands through his hair and yanking it back to look him in the eye. "Careful what you wish for."

EIGHT
NOAH

Noah's cheek stung but his cock throbbed from Adam's slap, and when Adam reached down and wrapped his hands around Noah's throat, tugging him to his feet, a shiver of awareness shot through his whole body, thoughts of everything but the two of them slipping away.

Adam's mouth took his in a greedy kiss that brought Noah up onto his toes, a tiny whimper escaping. His hand slid from Noah's throat to grip his chin tightly between thumb and forefinger, holding him in place so he could lick over his bottom lip, nipping it with his teeth before darting his tongue inside once more.

Noah's whole body flushed, pleasure rolling over him. It was hardly Noah's first kiss. It wasn't even his first kiss with Adam, but the possessive way he explored Noah's mouth had him grasping at Adam's waistband, desperate for something to hold onto.

"I want your mouth on me," Adam murmured into his open mouth. "You can do that for me. Can't you, baby?"

Noah swallowed hard, tongue sliding out to wet his lower lip. He gave a stilted nod, brain hazy as he sank to his knees. He felt like a virgin, hands shaking as he fumbled to undo Adam's belt and open his zipper, tugging the denim down. When the jeans pooled at Adam's feet, he stepped out of them and kicked them free, fingers knotting in Noah's hair, forcing his mouth against the rigid outline of his cock.

Noah inhaled deeply, eyes rolling at Adam's scent, mouthing over the fabric of his underwear, noting it was already damp. Was Adam just as hot for him? Seemed hard to believe. He hooked his fingers into Adam's waistband, dragging the underwear to mid-thigh before going back to nosing along the length of his now freed erection. His cock was perfect, heavy, and flushed, leaking at the tip. And Noah ached to taste it.

Sitting back on his heels, he gripped Adam's length, tonguing at his slit and relishing the bitter pre-cum. Moaning, he leaned forward to suck him, head bobbing awkwardly with Adam's fingers still tangled in his hair.

Adam yanked his head back, the sharp tug pulling another harsh sound from him. He looked down at Noah, his voice a warm rasp. "Oh, you can do better than that. Open your fucking mouth and show me how bad you want it."

Adam's words shot lightning through Noah's core, stoking a fire within him. He did as he was told, lips parting, but unable to do more with Adam controlling his movements. He didn't have to wait long. Adam fed him his cock an inch at a time, the weight heavy on his tongue, the tang of his skin making Noah's already hard dick leak behind his zipper. His hands settled on Adam's thighs, the hair tickling his palms, as he lost himself in making Adam feel good, sucking greedily.

Adam wasn't done playing with him, though. He would pull free from Noah's lips, only to slide back in deeper each time until he was fucking into Noah's mouth in a brutal rhythm, stopping only to pull out and slap his cock on Noah's tongue, like he was getting too close, too fast. The thought made Noah shiver.

"Fuck, baby. Your mouth feels so good. You're doing so fucking good for me," Adam muttered, his voice a harsh whisper. "Open up a little more. That's it," he crooned. "Fuck, yeah. That's it, baby. That's it." He blew out a harsh breath, teeth clenched as he said, "That's my good boy."

Noah moaned around Adam's cock, half afraid he might embarrass himself by coming in his pants just from his words and how much he seemed to love Noah's mouth on him.

He grunted in pain as Adam's other hand joined the first, twisting in his hair, holding him in place so he could drive into Noah's throat, cutting off his air and triggering his gag reflex, his muscles convulsing around Adam's cock until the world grew hazy. It was painful…terrifying…and also the single hottest moment of Noah's life to date.

Adam held him hostage, hips moving in tiny aborted thrusts, his pubic hair tickling Noah's nose as his air supply ran out.

Adam's next words dragged over Noah's ragged nerves like silk, his voice panting and raw. "That's it. There you go. You're doing so good. Just a little more. Oh, fuck. A little more. You're so tight. So fucking tight for me."

Noah's blunt nails scratched at Adam's thighs, eyes watering and saliva filling his mouth as a sense of euphoria kicked in. Just when he thought he might lose consciousness, Adam pulled free, jerking Noah's head back. Tears streamed down his face as he took in big, gulping breaths, lungs burning like he'd just been pulled from the water.

"You're so fucking perfect," Adam murmured as he smeared his cock over Noah's spit-slick lips.

Noah's heart hammered in his ears, his whole body trembling. Fuck. There was definitely something wrong with him because he just wanted more. He wanted Adam to use him up, take what he wanted, uttering those filthy words while he did it. Even if it fucking killed him.

Adam's gaze softened a little as he looked at him. "You're so pretty, baby. You like being on your knees for me?"

Noah's cock throbbed at his words. "Yeah," he said, breathless.

Adam smiled, his hand running along Noah's cheek. "Yeah? You like being good for me?"

"Yes," Noah managed, blood on fire.

Adam slapped his face once again, a little harder this time. "I bet you'd like being bad for me even more."

Noah's brain fell briefly offline, wondering what being bad for Adam might look like. Adam dragged him to his feet before pulling him in for another dirty kiss. "I want you naked. Now," he snarled, pushing him away.

Noah struggled to lose his clothes under Adam's careful scrutiny. It was easier when they'd just been hot and heavy in Noah's trailer, but now, in Adam's room with its vast lighting, the differences in their appearances were glaring. Not that Noah thought he was ugly, but he was shorter than Adam, his body soft where his was hard, pale where his was golden brown.

But when he looked up, Adam was studying him with a wolfish look. "On the bed." Noah sat heavily, mouth dry as Adam lost his underwear. Noah reached for him, but he shook his head. "Uh-uh, not like that. I want you on all fours."

Shock reverberated through Noah. Was Adam going to fuck him? Something shivered deep inside at the thought of him working Noah open, sliding his cock home, driving into him. He needed to shut down his brain before he came untouched just thinking about all the things Adam might do. He was already so close.

Noah did as he was told, feeling weirdly vulnerable, naked with his back to Adam. Not afraid exactly, just aware, every one of his senses on high alert.

The bed dipped behind him and then Adam's blunt nails gently scraped along the backs of Noah's thighs, causing goosebumps to erupt along his skin, before disappearing. "I like you like this," Adam mused. He trailed his finger between Noah's cheeks, teasing over his hole. "Completely open to me."

Noah sucked in a sharp breath as Adam's hand cracked across his ass, fire trailing in its wake. He whimpered when Adam's lips ghosted over the abused flesh before his hand came down hard on the other side. Noah bit down on his bottom lip, stifling another helpless noise as Adam's mouth soothed that wound, too.

He braced himself for the next slap, but it never came.

Noah cried out as Adam's tongue suddenly laved over his entrance. "Fuck," he whined, falling to his forearms, back arching, hands fisting in Adam's pillowcase. "Oh, God."

"Oh, yeah. That's it. Arch your back for me. Fuck, you taste amazing," Adam growled against him, gripping Noah's hips, holding him still so he could bury his face in the heart of him, mouthing over his hole.

Noah couldn't think of a response. He couldn't think at all. He dragged the pillow closer, burying his face, moaning like a whore when Adam's hand closed around his aching cock, working just the head, thumbing over his slit as he stroked in time with the tongue probing Noah's hole. He wasn't going to last.

When Adam's mouth slid lower, to suck Noah's balls, he ripped his face from the pillow. "Oh, fuck. I'm so close. Please, don't stop. Please." He knew he was babbling, fucking Adam's tightened fist, eyes rolling as he picked up the pace. "Please, Adam. I need to come." Another desperate noise fell from his lips as he picked up the pace. "Oh, fuck. Yes. Please. Please. I'm so close. I'm so close. Just a little more. Please, Adam…"

The sound Adam made was animalistic, teeth sinking into Noah's ass cheek before going back to spearing his tongue against his hole. "You gonna come for me, baby?" he asked.

Noah was nodding, even though Adam couldn't see him, his hands mangling his fancy pillowcase as pleas continued to spill from his lips. "Yes. Oh, fuck. Right there. Oh, yes. Please, Adam," Noah begged. "Please, can I come?"

Adam chuckled. "You can come, baby. Let me hear you."

One more twisting pull of Adam's hand over Noah's cock and he was gone, crying out as he spilled onto the comforter, Adam's hand working him until he batted it away with a hiss of pain.

Noah's stomach fluttered when Adam rumbled, "My turn," flipping Noah onto his back and dragging him down the bed before crawling over him.

He gripped the headboard with one hand, feeding Noah his cock with the other. His hands flailed before finally coming to rest on Adam's ass, muscles flexing beneath his fingertips with each shallow thrust. His panting grunts and the increasingly protesting headboard told Noah that Adam was close, but that was his only warning. Then he was pulling free of Noah, jerking himself a few more times before cum painted over his lips, his tongue, his cheeks. Once more, Adam rocked forward, smearing his cock over the mess on Noah's face before slipping back in for Noah to suck him clean.

When he had nothing left, Adam sat back on Noah's chest, panting, a smile spreading across his face as he used his thumbs to attempt to clean Noah off. He finally rolled off Noah and the mattress, grabbing his t-shirt, carefully wiping Noah's face before cleaning himself off and tossing it away.

"You okay?" he asked, smiling soft enough to make Noah's heart ache.

Noah nodded. "Yeah, better than okay. You?"

"I'm good. Yeah," Adam said. Noah's smile faded as Adam leaned down and kissed him softly. "That was really hot."

Noah shook his head in wonderment. "You're definitely too good to be true." His eyes widened. He hadn't meant to say that out loud.

Adam's responding grin was teasing. "I'm a murderer. And you"—he dipped his head once more to trail kisses over Noah's chest—"are sexy as hell. I love how you just babble whenever you're about to come. It drives me crazy."

Noah snickered. "Thanks?"

When Adam laid down beside him, Noah snuggled up against him, letting his fingers trace the outlines of his tattoos. The snake he'd seen that first night wrapped around Adam's neck. But there was also a butterfly in the center of his chest with angel wings on either side, a rose on either arm and a dagger piercing his side. All seemingly unrelated but, somehow, all Adam.

Noah wasn't sure what they were supposed to do now. He'd already slept with Adam—just slept—but most of his sexual encounters ended with him rolling out of bed and shoving his clothes on before the cum had even dried on the sheets. He didn't know if he was supposed to stay and cuddle, sleep in Adam's arms. Should he leave? Or at least offer to go?

Before he could think on it too much, Adam's phone began to vibrate from somewhere over the edge of the bed. It had to be after midnight. "Who's that?"

Adam groaned, not even bothering to look. "One of my idiot brothers, I'm sure."

Noah frowned. "You're not going to answer it?"

Adam's fingers began to trail along Noah's arm. "If they're calling this late, they want something. If I don't answer, I can pretend I was sleeping."

Noah mulled that over while Adam's phone vibrated three more times, then stopped, before starting once more.

On the third attempt, Noah said, "I don't think they're going away."

Adam blew out a breath through his nose like an angry bull, crawling to the foot of the bed to fish his phone from his jeans pocket. "What?" he growled into the phone. "I'm busy, can't this wait?" Noah could hear a tinny sounding voice speaking rapid-fire but not what was said. "In the morning. No, in the morning. August, I'm fucking naked in bed. I was almost asleep. Yes, I was. None of your business?" Adam's mouth formed a hard line as the voice once again spoke angrily. "Oh, my God. Fine. Fine. Fuck you."

When he disconnected, he looked at Noah. "I gotta go to my dad's for an hour or so." Noah's heart sank, but he sat up, prepared to find his clothes. Adam's hand pushed him back onto the mattress as he crawled over him. "What do you think you're doing?"

"Getting my clothes?" Noah said, frowning.

"Did I say you could go?" Adam asked, his voice sexy enough to make Noah's dick try to rally.

"You don't want me to leave?"

"No, stay here and wait for me. Naked. I love having you naked in my bed."

Noah hated the smile he could feel forming on his face.

"You sure?"

Adam gazed at him with that same feral tenacity that sent a knife of pleasure through his belly. "I'm positive." He kissed him deeply. "Besides, who says I'm done with you yet?"

NINE
ADAM

Adam slouched in one of his father's Brabbu dining chairs, knife in hand, casually twisting the point into his fingertip as he eyed his brothers warily. There were only three of them for the time being. At least Atticus hadn't assembled all the Avengers for his little intervention. His father was also absent, which meant this was a non-sanctioned scolding. That was good to know. Well, maybe.

Might as well rip off the Band-Aid. "So, what is it that was important enough for you to call me to Dad's house in the dead of night?"

Atticus ran a hand through his hair, shooting a look at August, like he expected him to be the one to handle Adam. Adam didn't know why they always thought he needed handling.

August arched a brow, shrugging one shoulder. "Don't look at me. This is your party."

Atticus gave a low grunt of frustration, snagging his phone from in front of him and tapping a few keys before sliding it across the large table to Adam. He picked up the phone and saw several pictures of him and Noah at the diner eating breakfast. "Are you having me followed?"

"No, dumbass. Those are screenshots. They're all over the internet," Atticus snapped.

"Okay. So, what?" Adam asked. "You called me here at one in the morning because I had breakfast?"

"You're being obtuse," August chided. "It's not the meal we object to, it's the company you're keeping."

Adam's nostrils flared. "Noah?"

Atticus removed his glasses, pinching the bridge of his nose. "Yes, Noah."

"Why? What the fuck do you care who I date?"

"Date!" Atticus shouted. "You can't be this stupid."

"I think you underestimate him," August said, amused by his brother's fury.

Archer ran his hands over his face. He clearly was just coming off yet another bender. He had three days of stubble on his chin and his dark brown hair stood on end. The buttons of his white shirt were mismatched. "We care because you're dating the son of one of your victims. You have to see that's a bad idea."

"Why?" Adam asked, flouncing back in his chair.

"It's a six degrees of separation thing," Archer explained. "People are going to wonder why a spoiled rich kid is dating trailer trash."

Adam flicked his gaze to Archer. "Don't call him that," he warned.

"Christ. He likes this kid," Archer muttered.

"Yeah. I don't have to hide who I am from him. He knows I'm a killer. It's just…easy with him."

Atticus looked like he was choking on a golf ball. "Has it not occurred to you that he's setting you up?"

Adam scoffed. "What? No, he's not. You're fucking paranoid."

"The foundation of this family was forged from a thousand corpses. Of course, we're paranoid. That's how we're able to do what we do," August reminded him.

Adam could feel his pulse bounding in his veins. His fury bubbled just below the surface, tempered only by the knowledge that, if they really had a leg to stand on, Atticus would have called their father.

"Noah had his chance to get his revenge. He stuck a gun in my face. He wanted to kill me. When I showed him who his father really was, he instantly backed down. He doesn't want to ruin us. He just likes being with me. Why is that so hard to believe?"

Atticus sighed. "How is he going to feel when he realizes your whole life is a fraud? That you're not this charming playboy supermodel?"

"He knows. I don't have to pretend around him. He knows exactly who and what I am and he accepts me."

Atticus darted his gaze to August, aggressively gesturing to Adam in a *do something with him* gesture.

August shook his head. "Adam, you're putting us all in danger by associating with this boy."

"Atticus almost married that psycho Kendra, and none of you batted an eye at that train wreck," Adam snapped.

"She didn't know about our secrets," Archer said, sounding bored.

Adam could feel his anger rising. "Exactly. If she had, she would have used it to drain our family dry. She was an absolute fucking nightmare. Noah doesn't want anything from us. Besides, if you're so concerned he's going to go run and tell the world, wouldn't the more prudent move be to keep him close, not alienate him further?"

"Adam, you're being childish," Atticus said.

Adam shot a glare in Atticus's direction. "Why are you even here? Shouldn't you be synthesizing a protein or growing ears on the back of rats or something? Why do you care who or what I'm doing all of a sudden?"

"I care for the same reason we all do. There are a million guys you can stick your dick into—what is your deal with this one? Is this just another cry for attention? Haven't you gotten enough?"

Adam sent the knife in his hand sailing towards Atticus, feeling some satisfaction at the way his brother flinched when it embedded into the wall just behind his head.

Atticus blew a breath out of his nose. "There. That right there is what I'm talking about. You're almost thirty years old. Stop acting like a spoiled brat."

Adam leaned forward. "I'm twenty-seven and, yes, I am an adult. As an adult, I can stick my dick in whoever I want."

"So, you *are* fucking him? The child of the man you murdered?" Archer asked.

"Don't say it like that. He's twenty-one." *I think.*

"He's setting you up," August said again, voice almost

completely devoid of emotion.

"No. He's not. I've been following him for weeks. He had the chance to kill me and he never took it."

"Because you decided to show him evidence that his father was a child molester," Atticus said, fuming.

"What should I have done, Atticus? Let him kill me? Kill him? That goes against our code. It's not Noah's fault he was raised by a sick fuck like Wayne Holt. He was one of his victims, too, you know."

"So, what?" August asked.

Adam froze. "So, what?"

"Yeah, so, what? What do you care if he had a shitty childhood? I know we've all been taught to act as if we have emotions, but you aren't pretending. So, what's happening here?"

"What do you care? I like him. I like being with him."

"Calliope says she sent you that information two weeks ago. Why are you fighting this hard for a guy you don't know?"

"Because I do know him. And he knows me. In all the ways that matter."

"Oh, Christ," August muttered. "I might have expected this *Romeo and Juliet* bullshit from Avi or Asa, but not you."

Adam gripped tightly to the one nerve he had left, spitting, "Oh, fuck you, August."

"Lower your voice," August cautioned, leaning back in his seat. "The closer you get to him, the worse it's going to be when you have to let him go. End it. Now. Because if you don't, we'll have to tell Dad, and I don't think you'll like how he chooses to end it."

Adam shoved his chair away from the table, the feet scraping loudly over the marble floor. "Go ahead. Tell Dad. And while you're at it, tell him this. I'm keeping Noah. He's mine."

"He's not a toy. He's a human being," Archer muttered.

His rage took hold, and his hands fisted at his sides. "He's mine. I won't give him up. Don't push me on this or I swear to fucking God, I'll burn it all down. Do you hear me? If you make me choose, I'll choose him."

"You don't even know him, Adam. And you don't get to make these decisions for all of us."

Adam stalked towards Atticus, snatching his knife from the wall before storming out of the room. He walked through the kitchen to the garage, pulling a set of keys from the array on the board, choosing his father's Audi R8 before jamming his finger on the button to retract the garage door. As soon as he dropped into the leather seat, he turned the engine over. It purred like a kitten.

He threw the car in reverse and slammed his foot on the gas, only seeing the older man behind him at the last possible moment. The breaks screeched as the car's bumper stopped a hair's breadth away from his kneecaps. Adam's heart jackhammered behind his ribcage as he watched his father approach the driver's side, using a single finger to indicate he needed to roll down the window.

As always, his father's voice was deceptively calm. "Adam."

"Dad."

He sighed. "Why are you trying to run me down at

midnight with my own car?"

"I-I wasn't. I just needed to clear my head, and I didn't want to walk."

"I'm quite certain I paid for a rather expensive BMW not six months ago. Please, don't tell me you totaled it already."

"No. I just wanted the R8. I need to break the law."

His father chuckled. "Who pissed you off this time? Archer? Atticus? It couldn't have been August. Avi and Asa aren't even in town. Aiden doesn't talk enough to piss you off. So, who was it?"

"Nobody. I just need to think."

"You can't lie to me, you know. I'm the one who taught you how. I know all your tells."

Adam blew a breath out through his nose. "They were staging an intervention."

"And why is that?"

"Because they don't like my new boyfriend."

His father gave a sage nod. "The Holt boy."

Adam's gaze went wide. "You know?"

"I know everything my boys get up to. It's my job," his father said. "How much have you told him?"

"He already knew a lot of it. But I filled in some blanks for him," Adam admitted. He'd never been able to lie to his father, not even when he was little. It was hard to lie to somebody who seemed to love you unconditionally. No matter how unlovable you were.

"Do you think that was the wisest course of action?"

Adam nodded. "You tell us to trust our instincts. That's what I did. Instinctively, I know Noah would never betray me," he said. "Or you."

"This could complicate things for the whole family if it goes sideways," his father cautioned.

"I'm not giving him up," Adam said defiantly. "I told them and I'm telling you. Noah's mine. I choose him."

His father chuckled. "Relax, Adam. I'm not going to tell you to stop seeing him. But he is your responsibility. The more he knows, the more of a liability he becomes. If he betrays us, the consequences will be…dire."

The tone in his father's voice sent an icy chill along his spine. "He wouldn't do that. Not to me. Not to anybody. He's…a good person."

His father studied him for a long moment. "Alright. I'll talk to your brothers."

"They're going to be pissed," Adam warned.

"Why's that?"

"Because as much as Atticus likes to say he's your favorite, they really think I am."

Once more, his father gave a low chuckle. "They think? But you're not?"

"No."

His father crossed his arms over his chest, tilting his head. "You think I prefer any of my children over the others?"

Adam knew for a fact that his father had a favorite, but nobody talked about it. Aiden was his father's favorite. He was the sixth adopted, after the murder twins, and his father had just always had a weird soft spot for him. Maybe it was because Aiden rarely talked while the rest of them never shut up. It was hard to say, but none of them dared state the obvious.

"No, Dad. I think you find us all equally annoying," Adam lied smoothly.

His father gave a smile as fake as the one Adam returned. "Okay, go back to your boy. But remember what I said. He's your responsibility now. I hope your instincts are good."

Adam nodded before throwing the car back in reverse and slowly pulling out of the driveway. There was a lightness to him now that he had his father's blessing. His brothers liked to huff and puff, but they'd never go against their dad. Ever.

Still, his father's words wormed their way deeper into his head. Noah was his responsibility. Adam didn't think Noah would ever betray him or his family, but the deeper they dove into Noah's past, the more dangerous it became for him and, by extension, all of them. They needed to get to the bottom of Wayne Holt's suspected pedophile ring and get Noah the justice he'd been denied.

But not tonight. Tonight, Noah was waiting for him. Adam's cock twitched at the thought of Noah warm and willing in his bed. He'd been so fucking good for him earlier. So responsive. Could he push him further? Harder? How dark did Noah's fantasies get? Adam was eager to find out.

TEN
NOAH

Noah didn't sleep well in strange beds. Years of foster care, hopping from house to house without ever having a home, had left him with an ever present sense of anxiety about sleeping in any bed but his own. Even when those beds felt like clouds and had pillows with just the right support and sheets with a thread count higher than his credit score. It was why he'd scraped every penny to buy his ugly ass trailer outright, so nobody could take his bed away ever again.

But sleeping in anybody's bed but his own had really never been an issue. Noah didn't date, didn't have boyfriends or friends with benefits. That would've required having friends, and Noah didn't have those either. It was easier that way. If you didn't get close to someone, they couldn't leave. That was what he told himself.

Or, at least, he had before Adam.

Noah hadn't anticipated the sleepover, even when they'd pulled into Adam's garage. Maybe it had been implied, but Noah hadn't been in the best headspace after their deep dive at Gary's house. It was his own fault. He let his guard down after Adam had specifically told him not to, but they'd been so close to getting out of there. He'd thought it was safe.

But then there was the picture. That stupid fucking picture of Gary and his dad, smiling and laughing. He knew why they were so fucking happy, knew that he'd been inside that cabin. Knew what would happen to him once they returned.

His stomach churned, bile rising in his throat, as his memories tried to fight their way to the surface. He shoved them back down with a frustrated growl, flopping on his stomach and burying his face in Adam's pillow. His stomach swooped as the scent of spicy soap and expensive cologne filled his nose, triggering heat low in his belly.

What was he going to do about Adam? Adam, who had claimed Noah as his after just forty-eight hours, like some prehistoric caveman. Adam, who swore he'd never let anybody hurt Noah, like he was taking a blood oath. Adam, who had given him the most intense orgasm of his entire life before tucking him into bed and kissing his forehead.

Fuck. Noah wanted to believe Adam's instincts. He wanted to think that the part of Adam that could feel had somehow recognized the parts of Noah that couldn't and tried to close the gap. But the realist in him screamed that he was just ignoring a million red flags and, at best, he'd get his heart broken and, at worst, he'd end up in a ditch. He honestly wasn't sure which was worse.

But as uncertain as he was of Adam's intentions, he was very certain he wasn't leaving. He wasn't going to run.

Noah had spent so much of his life feeling sad and lonely or feeling nothing at all. Adam made him feel good, made him feel excited. When he woke up that morning, Adam's arms around him had made him feel…safe. And nothing had ever really made Noah feel safe.

Noah had been certain when Adam left that he'd pass the time in the darkened room staring at the shadows on the ceiling. But as soon as he'd buried his face in Adam's scent, still drunk from his recent orgasm, his consciousness just faded to black.

Noah stirred as the soft comforter slid down and away, leaving him exposed to the frigid air conditioning pumping through the loft. He made a noise of disappointment at the disruption of his cocoon. He rubbed his face in the pillow, still in that space between awake and asleep.

The bed dipped near his feet, and then Adam's naked body blanketed his back, his knees forcing Noah's legs wide as he made himself at home between his legs, his hard cock pressing against the crevice of Noah's ass.

"Adam?" He hated how breathless and nervous he sounded.

Adam's response was a low throaty purr, his fingers threading through Noah's hair, his breath hot against his ear. "I told you I wasn't done with you yet."

Noah's breath hitched as Adam's erection slid between his cheeks, not trying to enter him, just working against him, like Noah was his own personal sex toy. The glide was easy, his cock slick. Had Adam stripped off his clothes and coated his cock with lube before climbing on top of Noah to rut against him?

Noah hardened instantly.

Fuck.

He was so damaged.

He wanted Adam to use him, was already so gone over the panting grunts against his ear, the way his legs were splayed wide, like Adam wanted him as open as possible for him, the way his arms caged Noah in, trapping him beneath him.

Adam bit at his earlobe hard. "You fucking love this, don't you? I can practically smell it on you."

Noah whimpered, managing a wavering, "Yes."

The hand in his hair tightened, craning his head back to slant their lips together. "Yeah, you do. My dirty boy. I can't wait 'til I'm inside you," he growled into Noah's open mouth.

Noah groaned at the thought. He wanted Adam inside him, filling him up, holding him down, taking what he wanted. "You can. Fuck me. It's okay. I want it. I want you."

He canted his hips upward as much as he could, grinding back against Adam's hard length just in case he wasn't getting just how willing Noah was.

Adam chuckled. "You want it so bad. I bet I could make you beg for it." Noah shivered. "Yeah. You'd definitely beg for it. But not tonight, baby. When I fuck you, it's going to be an all night affair and tonight, we both need sleep. Still, when I saw you there, sleeping on my pillow, I knew

I wouldn't be able to sleep without my cum on your body."

Noah moaned, hips spasming at Adam's words, working his cock against the sheet, not even caring how desperate he looked. Adam bit at his throat and shoulder hard enough to make Noah cry out.

"Yeah, be loud for me. Fuck, I love it. I'm going to make a mess of you."

Noah's eyes rolled as a shudder tore through him. Adam forced two fingers into his mouth, working them in and out in time with his thrusts. "Suck," he rasped. Noah did as Adam demanded. "Good boy. That's it. Suck my fingers like you suck my cock. So fucking good for me. You're gonna make me come."

Noah whined around his fingers as Adam started to move faster, worked his thighs wider, so he could get better traction to drive against him. Just thinking about Adam fucking into him with those same long, sure strokes made him crazy, his trapped cock throbbing, his toes curling, his hands fisting the sheets.

Adam came with a harsh shout, spilling between them, sinking his teeth into Noah's shoulder hard enough to leave a mark. He then collapsed onto Noah, breathing hard. He slipped his fingers free of Noah's mouth, using the hand in his hair to crane his head back for another greedy kiss. "Sorry. I can't keep my hands off of you."

Noah flushed, grateful the room was dark. Adam's weight disappeared, and then Noah was being flipped over. He cried out as his aching cock was enveloped in the wet heat of Adam's mouth. "Oh, fuck," he managed, breathing ragged as pleasure shot sparks along his nerve endings. "This is gonna last, like, thirty seconds," he warned.

Adam pulled off him with a pop, grinning up at him. "Then I'm doing something right."

Noah's eyes rolled as the wet suction resumed. "Hnf. Oh."

Noah's heels hit the mattress, unable to keep still. Adam blew him with the same confidence he had in every other aspect of his life, and it was so goddamn sexy.

When he knew Noah's eyes were on him, he'd look up, teasing the tip of his cock as one hand held his weight and the other teased his balls. Noah couldn't stop his hips from bucking upwards, working himself in and out of Adam's mouth. He braced both hands on the bed, letting Noah fuck into him, that perfect suction never wavering.

Noah's hands contracted in Adam's hair. "Oh, fuck. I'm so close. Hnf. Yes. Oh, my God, just like that. Yes. Yes. Oh. Fuck. Oh… Fuck." Heat shot along Noah's spine. "I'm gonna come," he warned, trying to pull free.

Adam pinned his hips, taking Noah deeper, swallowing around his cock, the muscles of his throat convulsing around him. Noah gasped as he came, flooding Adam's mouth. Adam still didn't stop, just kept sucking, like he was trying to pull every last drop from Noah, until he hissed and pushed at his shoulder.

Adam finally collapsed beside him, chest heaving, a ridiculous grin on his face. "Sorry."

Noah stretched his limbs until they popped, giving Adam a rueful smile. "You don't look sorry."

When Adam gathered Noah into his arms, he didn't

protest. "I'm not sorry at all. What was I supposed to do with you all naked and warm in my bed?"

"I can see your dilemma," Noah deadpanned. "In the future, I have no problem being woken up like that."

"In the future, huh?"

Noah flushed. "Well…if there's another—"

"Oh, there's going to be another…and another…and another. I told you, you're mine now. Deal with it."

"What did your brothers want?" Noah asked.

"They saw our pictures online."

Noah frowned, craning his head to look upwards at Adam's face. "We have pictures online?"

"Oh, yeah. Apparently, I'm a lot more interesting now that I have you as my boyfriend."

"I think you have that backwards," Noah said, trying to understand why anybody would think them having breakfast was picture worthy. Though, maybe it was just those girls.

Adam scoffed. "Nope. It's you. You're just too cute for me to let you outside. Those big brown eyes. Those fucking freckles. It's too dangerous out there for you."

"One, I can take care of myself. Two, I'm dating a murderer. How much more dangerous could it get? I could be one of those fucking weirdos who dangles off towers and bridges for YouTube likes, but I'm not. For me, I think I've hit maximum danger levels." Noah placed his hand over the butterfly on Adam's chest.

"I just don't like the idea of you being free out in the world where anything could happen to you," Adam said sleepily. "You could get hit by a bus, or a plane engine could drop on your head, or you could be kidnapped by a vicious biker gang."

Noah snickered. "Were you drinking at your dad's house?"

"Definitely not."

"Your brothers were mad because there are pictures of us online?"

Adam sighed, his arms tightening around him. "No, they're mad that I'm dating the son of somebody I killed. They said it makes things messy."

Noah's heartbeat spiked, a shock of fear ricocheting through him. It was a gross overreaction given how little time they'd spent in each other's presence but Noah couldn't stop the strange sense of panic welling inside him. "What did you say?"

"I told them to fuck off and that you weren't going anywhere and they could deal with it."

"You told a group of psychopaths to 'deal with it'?"

"I told my dumbass brothers to deal with it. Then I talked to my dad who said he'd talk to them," Adam clarified.

"But your dad is okay with this? Us?"

"My dad trusts my judgment. My brothers don't. He knows I wouldn't do anything to hurt the family and I promised him you wouldn't either."

Noah had no interest in harming anybody in the Mulvaney family, but there seemed to be an underlying threat in Adam's casual statement. Maybe Noah was just being paranoid.

"What do we do with the stuff we found tonight? The hard drives?" Noah asked, needing a change in subject.

"I gave them to Calliope to try to decrypt. It's going to take some time, though, especially since we didn't get the whole hard drive from the laptop. But if anybody is going to find something, it's her. I also have her working on figuring out who our mystery guy was at Gary's house tonight. In the meantime, I think maybe we should try to rundown the weird key. It could be nothing, but it could be everything."

"I have to work tomorrow," Noah said, heart squeezing at the thought of dealing with another night of Gary's physical and verbal abuse.

"Why not just quit?" Adam asked.

Noah frowned. "Because I have bills to pay."

"You could work literally anywhere else and make more money."

Adam wasn't wrong. He had worked other places, better places. But those places hadn't let him park his trailer in their parking lot. He'd been willing to take a shitty job for a place to park. But now that he knew the truth, he wasn't leaving until he made Gary pay for what he'd done. He couldn't. "I need to keep close to him. As long as I'm watching, he can't surprise me or anybody else."

Adam carded his fingers through his hair. "If he hurts you, I'll put him through a meat grinder. Alive. Slowly."

"If he hurts me, I'll help you," Noah promised before a yawn overtook him, jaw cracking loudly in the quiet. "Can we go to sleep now?"

Adam kissed the top of his head. "Yeah. But I'm the little spoon tonight."

"We'll look ridiculous," Noah mused.

"To who?" Adam asked.

With that, he flipped over, shoving his ass back against Noah, who snorted, shaking his head. He leaned forward and rubbed his nose against the spot between Adam's shoulder blades, dropping a kiss there and letting his eyes fall shut, surprised when, once more, he started to fall asleep.

ELEVEN
ADAM

"Are you sure you have to go to work?" Adam asked, leaning across the center console to give Noah his biggest puppy dog eyes.

He didn't want Noah to go. Waking up with Noah in his arms had been like waking up and finding somebody had left him a chocolate cake. The best kind of sweet surprise. They'd spent the morning trading lazy blow jobs before getting in the shower where they'd gotten each other off once again. Adam had taken Noah to lunch afterwards, without the fanfare this time. And now, he had to drop him off to get changed for his shift. But he was having a hard time letting him out of the car.

Noah just snickered, unfazed. "Yes. We can't all live off our trust funds."

They were parked in the lot of Gary's club, just outside Noah's rusted little Airstream trailer. At night, it was hard to notice anything but the flashing sign and the neon outline of a ten-foot naked woman in a cowboy hat. But in the harsh light of day, *The Landing Strip* looked like the last stop in some post-apocalyptic wasteland. Its garish brick-red paint peeled from the moldy walls in strips, the film on the windows bubbled and warped. Even the lot itself was a minefield of potholes and broken wheel stops.

Adam did not like the idea of Noah living there. Even the strip mall that had once held a bail bondsman, an attorney, and a gun store had long since closed up shop, leaving Gary's as the sole survivor. How bad did a place have to be for a bail bondsman to leave?

Still, Adam grinned, nuzzling behind Noah's ear. "I mean, several people could live off mine. But you're the only one I'm extending the offer to."

Noah moaned as Adam's tongue traced the shell of his ear. "As much as I'd love to be your sugar baby, I can't just quit the day after we break into Gary's house."

"He's not going to notice we were there," Adam assured him. "A broken picture doesn't equal a home invasion."

Noah tilted his head, letting Adam's mouth explore the column of his throat. "I can't risk it. He already accused me of stealing his backpack full of cash and guns."

Adam chuckled. "To be fair, you did steal his backpack full of cash and guns."

He threaded his fingers into Noah's hair, turning his head for a kiss that lingered. He couldn't keep his hands off him. He wanted to taste every part of him, touch every part of him, crawl inside him and live in his skin.

When Noah whined into Adam's mouth, their lazy kiss turned dirty, his hand sliding up Noah's thigh to run his thumb along the rigid outline of his dick in his jeans. "Fuck, you're already hard," he growled against his lips. "I can take care of that for you if you just quit your job. I have a whole list of things I want to do to you. Unbutton your pants and we'll start right now," he vowed.

Noah ground himself against Adam's palm briefly, but then tore his mouth away. Adam was undeterred, biting at his jaw, his ear, any place he had access to.

"No. No. No," Noah said, pushing his palm into Adam's face and physically pushing him back to his side of the vehicle. Adam licked Noah's palm as he said, "You cannot seduce me to get what you want."

Adam frowned. "Why not?"

Noah gave him an exasperated look. "You know, you don't have to tell anybody that you're a rich kid. You've clearly never heard the word no."

Adam scoffed. "Of course, I have. I mean, never in reference to sex with me, but I'm familiar with the concept."

Noah rolled his eyes. "You're so weird. I'm getting out of this car now before I let you convince me to do something stupid, like quit my job and be your full-time rent boy."

Adam huffed out a sigh. "I don't see what's so wrong with being my full-time rent boy. I would offer you a very generous compensation package."

Noah's gaze dipped to Adam's crotch. "I'm very familiar with your generous 'compensation package' but I'm afraid I'll have to decline your offer at this time."

Adam groaned. "Fine, but I'm picking you up after work and you're coming home with me."

Noah swayed forward and smacked a kiss on Adam's pouting lips. "I'm off at ten. Could you try to drive a less conspicuous car to pick me up? People are going to think I'm banging a drug dealer and try to roll me in the alley."

The idea of Noah getting beat up caused a strange feeling to fill his chest. "I will disembowel anybody who so much as messes up your hair."

Noah pretended to swoon. "Who says romance is dead?"

Adam narrowed his eyes at Noah. "I feel like you're making fun of me, but I can't tell."

Noah smiled big enough for tiny wrinkles to form on his nose and at the corners of his eyes. "If you're ever unsure, just ask. But, in this particular case, I'm definitely making fun of you. But in a good way."

"There's a good way to make fun of somebody?" Adam asked, dubious.

"Of course." Noah grabbed the handle on the door, but it wouldn't give. "Can I get out, please?"

"No."

"Adam."

"Fine. Have a good night, I guess."

Noah kissed him once more. "You're ridiculous. Try not to miss me too much."

"Impossible."

Noah climbed from the car, giving Adam one last wave before bounding up the tiny staircase to his door and disappearing inside. Adam didn't like Noah living in that flimsy trailer. He wondered if he could convince him to just move in or at least buy him a nicer trailer. That thing looked like it cost less than a month's rent on Adam's place. Though, he honestly had no idea how much his rent was. His father's bookkeeper paid his bills.

He pulled out of the lot and was just heading onto the freeway when his phone rang.

Calliope.

He jabbed the button on the steering wheel, saying, "Tell me you've got something I can work with."

There was a sigh of disappointment all around Adam before her voice poured from the Bose audio system. "Hello, Calliope. How are you? I'm well, Adam. Thank you ever so much for asking. And you?" Her voice was saccharine.

Adam sighed. "Hello, Calliope. How are you?" he asked dutifully.

She gave a put upon sigh. "Terrible. The store was out of my favorite Arctic Fox hair color—Poison in case you were wondering." He wasn't. "*Then* I broke a nail trying to open my Diet Coke, found a screw in my tire, found out my ex-husband died, and got a paper cut opening my mail just to find out it was some company asking about my car's extended warranty."

Adam blinked. One of those things was not like the others. "I'm sorry to hear your ex-husband died?" he asked.

She scoffed. "Me too. I thought the son of a bitch died five years ago. Guess I should have checked for a pulse before I left."

Adam had no idea whether she was joking or not. It really was a crap shoot with Calliope. "This is why I never ask how you are," he said, voice flat. "In case *you* were wondering."

Calliope gave a delicate sniff. "You're a rude and ungrateful child. Your father should have quit while he was ahead."

Adam laughed. "You know you don't mean that. Do I not buy you all the best Funko Pop dolls for your collection?"

Calliope gave a deeply bothered sigh. "I suppose."

Adam shook his head, changing lanes to avoid getting stuck behind a minivan with a stick figure family getting eaten by zombies. "Calliope?"

"Yes, Adam?" she said, as breathlessly as if she thought he was about to propose.

"Did you find anything?"

There was the sound of a chair spinning. "No. Well, nothing related to Noah's pervert party guest list. This Gary is no choir boy. He's been in and out of prison for numerous petty crimes. Has a couple of domestic violence collars. The Secret Service is investigating him for money laundering, and his club has received numerous violations from the health inspector."

"Yet, he has NSA-level encryption software."

"All the most depraved losers do," Calliope said.

"There has to be something on those hard drives. Something that proves what a piece of shit he is."

"Proves to who? We know he's a perv. You said Noah was one of his victims. Why not just put him down and be done with it?"

Adam shook his head. "Because he wasn't the only one."

There was a pause. "What?"

"Noah says there were others. Some participated, some only watched, but they're all equally guilty."

"Can't you just torture the information out of him?"

"Yeah, obviously. But with these guys, it's hit or miss. Some of them sing at the first sign of a scalpel. Others, they'll let you carve them like a Thanksgiving turkey and never give up a single thing. I can't believe I'm going to say this but—in this one particular case—torture is a last resort."

"I suppose," she said begrudgingly, then, "Poor Noah."

Poor Noah. Noah was strong. Tough. Had somehow managed to endure unspeakable things and still move on with his life with his psyche still somewhat intact, all without the help of anybody. No friends. No family. Nobody at all.

Something started to scratch at the back of Adam's brain. "Noah's dad, Wayne Holt. He was a school teacher, right?"

"Yeah, for a while. That's what put him on your dad's radar. He'd been repeatedly let go from various schools and, somehow, landed at Our Lady of Sorrows where he stayed and flourished for almost a decade. Your father was introduced to him by a friend of a friend, and it set off Thomas's spidey senses. Why? What are you thinking?"

"I'm thinking: What do a Catholic school teacher and a ten-time criminal loser have in common other than the obvious? Where did they meet? Were they childhood friends? How did they become close enough for Wayne to offer up his son to Gary?"

"That's the other thing," Calliope said, her voice growing hesitant.

"What is?"

"I'm still looking into it but something keeps bugging

me. We vetted Holt for weeks before we sent you in to take him out. There was nothing that said anything about him having a child. Nothing. No birth certificates listed with him as the father. No sign of him having a child enrolled in school, which is pretty weird when you take into account him not only surviving but thriving in a Catholic school."

"What are you saying?"

"I'm saying I don't think Noah is Holt's son."

"What?" Adam said, his pulse kicking up a little.

Calliope let out a shaky breath. "I think Holt might have kidnapped him or maybe even bought him."

It made sense, so much sense that it was actually shocking none of them had considered it earlier. They'd never looked any deeper into how they'd missed the fact Holt had a child after he was dead, afraid they might call attention to themselves with their inquiries. "But Noah went into the system. Foster care. Wouldn't they have run his fingerprints or DNA looking for relatives?"

"It would have only triggered if Noah was old enough to have been fingerprinted at some time or if he was born in the States. You know as well as I do that the only thing bigger than sex trafficking is child trafficking. If Holt bought him, there would be no paper trail."

"No way to find his real family," Adam said, frustrated.

"Now, that's not true. DNA has come a long way. If we submit his DNA to some genealogy websites, they might help us track down familial matches. We could work our way backwards. I would just need a sample."

"Yeah, okay. In the meantime, I want a deep dive into

Wayne Holt's past. I want to know how he and Gary know each other. Wherever they hooked up might be where he found the others Noah mentioned."

"Yeah. I'll keep digging, but I'm gonna have to take a bath in hand sanitizer when I'm done. I hate this part of the job."

"I know."

"Oh, the other guy? Your surprise guest at Gary's? Yeah. Name's Conan Greevey. He's the head of all the city's youth sports programs."

Adam scrubbed a hand over his face, navigating the heavy rush hour traffic on autopilot. "Christ. Yeah, okay. You know what to do."

"Deep dive into his life, too?"

"Yep. Any luck running down what kind of key that was?"

"It's just a key to your garden variety padlock. It could be to a storage unit? A garage? A diary? Hell, it could be a padlock for a gate. I'm looking through his finances to see if he paid for any kind of storage or warehouse space but don't get your hopes up."

"Just let me know."

"I will. Are you almost there?"

"Where?"

There was a long pause. "Adam. Please, tell me you didn't forget to pick up the twins from the airport."

He'd definitely forgotten to pick the twins up from the airport. "Of course, I didn't. But I still don't understand why they can't just Uber? They're adults."

"Your father is a stickler for appearances. You know that."

"Yeah, yeah. Hey, Calliope?"

"Yes, Adam?"

"Can you…maybe send their flight info to my phone? You know, just to make sure I have it right."

"It's already done."

Adam grinned, shooting across three lanes of traffic to exit the freeway. The airport was in the other direction. He was going to be late. Hopefully, their flight was delayed. "Thanks. You're the best."

"I know."

TWELVE
NOAH

Noah had just racked his hundredth bin of dishes into the sanitizer when Pedro nudged him. "Boss wants to see you."

A shock ran through Noah's blood, his pulse accelerating. Was Adam wrong? Did Gary know? Was there some super hidden camera they hadn't noticed, or had the mysterious stranger seen them? He took a deep breath and let it out. He couldn't go in there freaking out. He wiped his hands on his apron and left the back of the house.

There was a guest performing, so the house was rowdy. The music was a mix of classic rock and modern hip-hop, all with a throbbing bass beat that made Noah's head pound. Or maybe that was just his fear. When he made it to Gary's door, Bailey frowned from where she sat perched on the knee of a high roller. He shrugged. He didn't bother knocking. Gary wouldn't hear him anyway.

"You wanted to see me about something?" Noah asked, infusing as much boredom into his voice as possible.

Gary flicked his gaze up and down Noah's jeans, t-shirt,

and stained apron. "You find my backpack yet?"

"What?" Noah asked.

Gary sneered, his body spilling over his desk chair. "My backpack, you little shit. I know it was you."

If Gary knew it was him, he wouldn't be calling Noah into his office; he'd have beat his ass in the parking lot like he'd tried to do the other night.

He relaxed somewhat, knowing this wasn't about his recent home invasion. "Dude, I didn't take any backpack. Why do you have such a hard-on for the idea of me being the one who did it?"

Gary's expression grew smug, as if he had somehow put Noah in checkmate. "Because Bianca saw you in my office."

Fucking Bianca. She was one of Gary's latest hookups, a barely legal dancer with a pill problem and delusions of grandeur. She was certain she was going to fuck her way into becoming the queen of Gary's crumbling stripper empire. Hell, maybe she was right. But she was annoying as shit, a relentless gossip, and a huge fucking snitch, always starting trouble for the others. Everybody hated her. Except Gary.

"I wasn't even working that night," Noah reminded him.

"You were working the night before, though. You could easily have taken it then."

He had taken it then. Gary was right.

"You were the only one anybody saw near my office."

Noah didn't miss a beat. "You told me to drop my updated time card on your desk, remember? After I forgot to punch out the other night?" It was a blatant fucking lie, but Gary had a massive drinking problem and a memory like Swiss cheese. "Did you not see my time card right on your desk?" He hadn't because none of this had ever happened, but he could see Gary furiously trying to search the depths of his memory for any hint that it was true. Time to drive home his point. He infused as much hurt into his voice as he could manage considering how much he hated the man. "Have I ever stolen shit from you?"

Gary's gaze jerked to Noah, examining him shrewdly for a long while before looking momentarily mollified. "No, I suppose not."

While Noah's outward expression never changed, inside the knot tied around his stomach loosened. "Can I go now? It's almost time for my half hour."

Instead of dismissing him like he usually would, Gary leaned back in his office chair, the components groaning in protest. "Who's your friend with the fancy car?"

Fuck. Once more, Noah gave a confused look. "Huh?" he asked, trying to buy himself more time.

Gary narrowed his eyes. "There was a Land Rover parked outside your tin can the other night. When you were fucked up. You banging a drug dealer or a gang banger, kid?"

Noah couldn't help but laugh. "You know any drug dealers who drive a mom car or who would openly admit to being gay? Much less park their eighty thousand dollar vehicle outside my trailer?"

Gary didn't answer, scowling. "So, who was he?"

Noah shrugged, honestly baffled by this sudden line of interrogation. He'd never enquired about a single hookup from Noah's past. "Just a friend."

Gary scoffed. "A friend?"

"Yeah, a friend. Like you and my dad were friends," Noah said flatly.

Gary's spine stiffened, his fat fingers flexing on the arm of the chair. "What's that supposed to mean?"

Noah did his best to school his features into a mask of innocence. "Just that you and my father were friends." Gary studied Noah, like he couldn't quite figure out if he was full of shit. Might as well test the perimeter a little bit. He sighed, doing his best to at least appear sorrowful. "Can I ask you a question? About my dad?"

Gary hesitated until it was almost awkward before finally saying, "Yeah. Sure, kid."

"I've been thinking about my dad a lot, and I don't have anything of his. Do you know what happened to his stuff after he died? After I went into the system? Like, did they just throw it all away?"

Gary's cheek twitched like the question had come with an electrical jolt. He cleared his throat, then sniffed, running a hand over his graying stubble. "Some of it ended up in the trash, some things were thrown away. He kept most of his stuff in storage, but I didn't have the key or any claim to it, so I'm sure it was auctioned off."

Could Adam's key be the key to his father's storage unit? He filed that information away for later. "That sucks. It's not fair, you know? My dad was a good man, dedicated his life to being an educator. I have nothing to remember him by. And the more I think about the person who killed him, the angrier I get, you know?" He threw a hand up in a frustrated gesture. "One minute, he was there, the next, gone. But it's weird. So many of my memories of him are just…gone, too? Like he took them with him. I really don't remember much of being a kid. That's weird, right? I know my dad and I were close. Shouldn't I remember more?"

Gary shifted in his seat. "Eh, everybody deals with shit different, you know? You and your dad were tight. He was a good guy. He really loved you."

Yeah, too much, Noah thought, doing his best to control the shudder wanting to roll over him.

Gary was sweating now, tiny beads of perspiration forming over his lip and hairline. Flop sweat. He was lying through his yellowing teeth. "I sometimes remember little flashes, but I don't even know if they're real or, like… dreams. Did you and my dad ever take me fishing?"

Noah was really walking a fine line. If Gary put together Noah's current line of questioning along with the broken picture of the cabin, there was a very good chance he would no longer think the broken frame was an accident.

But Gary just frowned like he couldn't remember exactly. "Yeah, that sounds familiar. Your dad and I used to head out to my family's old cabin in the woods. I think we brought you along once or twice."

Once or twice. Noah's stomach rolled at the confirmation. Deep down, he'd known he'd been in that cabin, had been molested in that cabin by his father and Gary. Maybe the details were fuzzy, but the nauseating way his stomach sloshed whenever thoughts of that cabin crossed his mind told Noah all he needed to know.

"We should go sometime," Noah offered. "Like, pour one out for my dad."

Gary sat forward, steepling his hands on his desk. "I don't have that cabin anymore. Sold it a long time ago to buy this place."

He's lying. Noah had no proof, just gut instinct, but something told him Gary was full of shit, that he definitely still owned that cabin in the woods. "That's too bad."

"Yeah."

"Can I take my thirty now?" Noah asked, suddenly eager to get out of there and away from Gary's bullshit.

"Yeah, kid. Go ahead."

Noah made a beeline for the picnic table out back. Roxy—who was actually a forty-five year old single mom named Jeanette—sat smoking a cigarette beside Bailey, who laid out on the wooden bench. "You two shouldn't be out here alone. Especially on a night with a featured dancer. It always brings out the real nut jobs."

"What did Gary want?" Bailey asked.

"He's still on his bullshit about his missing backpack. Apparently, Bianca is running her mouth again." Noah sprawled across the top of the table, slipping his phone free and doing a double take. "What the fuck?" he muttered.

Bailey sat up at his confusion, snagging his phone, eyes immediately finding the source of Noah's confusion before blowing wide. "Does your Instagram say you have ten thousand notifications? How often do you check this thing?"

Not that often. He'd only opened the account four months ago after Bailey whined about it for an hour. She'd wanted to tag him in a photo she'd taken. He had all of four pictures. Bailey didn't ask permission before she opened the app. "Who's Adam Mulvaney?"

"The model?" Jeanette asked.

Noah frowned. "You know him?"

Jeanette blew out a smoke ring, then waved it away. "I know of him. One of my gentleman friends is on some kind of foundation board with his father. People love to talk about the Mulvaney boys. All talented. All beautiful. All A names. Are you and him a thing?"

"According to Instagram, they are. You have, like, almost nine thousand new followers in a day."

"It's no big deal," Noah mumbled, trying to reach for his phone.

Bailey ducked him easily, holding it out of the way. "Oh, my God. This says you're Adam Mulvaney's boyfriend. That you were spotted having lunch together at Moe's. Is that true?"

Noah's eyes went wide. "Where does it say that?"

"Uh, TMZ, Business Insider, lots of places."

Business Insider? Why? "How do people even know me? Adam literally only told them my first name."

Bailey scoffed. "That's all it takes. Between internet sleuths and Facebook's auto-tagging, it's not that hard to find somebody on social media," Bailey said before handing his phone back to him. "I can't believe you're dating Adam Mulvaney. Do you know how many of us work in this shithole hoping we'd all get that million dollar meal ticket?"

Noah rolled his eyes. "Shut up. You love Leah. You

wouldn't leave her for a sugar daddy."

Bailey sniffed. "Maybe not, but I might for an engagement ring and a billion dollars.

"Well, we've known each other less than seventy-two hours"—If Noah didn't count their mutual stalking—"so I wouldn't worry about buying us a wedding present just yet. Given my history, I think we all know I'll fuck this up before the week is out."

"I don't know. That pic of you two in the diner looked pretty intense. He looks at you like he wants to eat you."

Adam definitely appeared to like the taste of Noah—told him so each time he swallowed him down—but he didn't need to feed Bailey's imagination anymore.

The notifications from his social media accounts were so overwhelming it took him a long time to realize he had a text from Adam.

It simply read: **I miss your face.**

Noah smiled like an idiot before typing out a message. **I get off in three hours.**

Adam was typing a response almost immediately. **With any luck, we'll both get off tonight. Send me a picture.**

Noah glanced down at his dirty clothes. His hair was greasy from sweat. His face was probably shiny. **I'm not camera ready.**

Adam: You're always hot.

Noah rolled his eyes but once more smiled, then snapped a pic of himself lying on the table under the yellow street light illuminating him from overhead, sending it before he could change his mind.

Adam's reply was almost instant. A pic of him slouched down in the driver's seat of a vehicle. **I can't stop thinking about all the things I want to do to you.**

Noah's face grew warm. **Don't you dare start dirty talking to me when I'm on a break that ends in like ten minutes.**

Adam: Buzzkill.

Noah tried and failed to hide his grin. He had never understood those people who met a guy and became instantly consumed by them. Men, to Noah, were a means to an end. Get off and get out. The years of abuse he'd suffered, no matter how much he suppressed it, still affected the way he responded to men and not in a good way. He was one big trauma response wrapped in a blanket of kinks and insecurities. He almost always chose men who were likely to treat him like garbage because it was easier to walk away as soon as he got what he needed from them.

But now, there was Adam, a literal killer masquerading as a spoiled rich kid. Neither of those things should be attractive. But Adam's dominating personality was just what Noah needed when things got to be too much. When he was talking dirty and pushing Noah to his limits, his brain just went soft in the best ways.

Yeah, Noah was gone on Adam and it had only been two fucking days. Was that a problem? He was surprised to realize…it wasn't. Not yet.

Noah watched as Adam pulled into the parking lot at ten after ten, driving the white Rover from the other night. He seemed to have an endless supply of vehicles at his disposal. But given Adam's net worth, he probably rarely had to worry about things like car payments or insurance.

Noah popped open the door and hopped up into the passenger seat, desperately hoping their destination was Adam's place so he could use his fancy shower with the awesome water pressure and massaging jets. He almost felt bad putting his sweaty self on Adam's leather seats.

When Adam leaned towards him, Noah said, "I'm warning you, I smell like French fries and—"

Adam snagged him by the shirt, dragging him in for a kiss that made Noah's whole body tingle, murmuring, "I love French fries," against his lips.

Noah let himself get swept up in the kiss but was unable to shake the feeling he was being watched.

"Wow, dinner and a show," a low voice drawled, filled with humor.

Noah jumped at the unfamiliar voice in the backseat, jerking around to see two strangers, mirror images of each other. "There's two of you," he mumbled.

They were eerily identical, even the expressions on their faces. They both wore jeans, boots, and t-shirts that showed off their colorful sleeve tattoos. The casual outfits still somehow seemed trendy and reeked of money, especially their trendy thousand-dollar haircuts.

"Well, he can count," one said.

"That's a step up from your last hook up," laughed the

other.

Adam huffed out a breath through his nose like he'd been dealing with them for too long. "Fuck off. This is why I didn't want to bring you two with me."

The one on the left snickered, making his eyes comically innocent. "Come on, we just want to meet your new special friend. It's all over the 'gram."

Adam cut his eyes to Noah, who had gathered by now that these were two of his brothers. He racked his brain, thinking back to his research. The twins. Adi and Avi or something like that. One was a clothing designer and the other an architect. Wildly successful, just like all of the other Mulvaneys.

"These are my brothers, Asa and Avi. They're assholes, but you'll get used to it. Eventually."

They pulled from the lot, and Noah was relieved to see them head towards the highway and Adam's loft.

"We'll drop you at your place," Adam said, not sounding like it was a suggestion.

"No. We want to hear about your little side project."

Noah watched as Adam glanced in the rear-view mirror, scowling at his brother. "What side project?"

"Whatever side project you have Calliope working on."

Noah shot a startled glance at Adam, who placed his hand on the console, palm up. Noah took it, threading their fingers together. Had he ever held hands with a boy? No, definitely not.

"Calliope runs her mouth too much," Adam muttered.

Asa's laugh was deep and rich, almost melodic somehow.

"I mean, technically, she only mentioned it to Dad, who mentioned it to Atticus, who told August, who then told me, and I told Avi, obviously. The only one not in the know is Aiden, but you know him. He's always a lone wolf."

Adam shook his head, seemingly irritated. This clearly wasn't the first time he'd dealt with this level of…whatever this was. Noah didn't understand the whole brotherly love thing and wondered how his life would have worked out if he had a big family, somebody who could have protected him. But that would have just created a larger victim pool for his father.

"It's none of your business."

"Well, you letting your boyfriend walk free after he tried to kill you, even though he knows our secret, is our business. But we haven't held that against you. Even if it could get us all thrown in prison."

Noah's mouth ran dry. "I'd never tell anybody anything. I didn't know what my father was. I didn't remember..." He trailed off.

"Remember what?" Avi asked.

Adam looked like he was about to rupture a blood vessel. He was clearly furious about his brothers' prodding, but they were right. Noah did know their secrets. It was only fair he shared his. He sighed. "I was one of my father's victims. I blocked it out, I guess. After Adam showed me the video, it all started rushing back in weird flashes. There were others. More than a few of them. They watched. Participated. Filmed."

"They filmed?" Adam asked, sounding surprised by that information.

Truthfully, Noah was surprised, too. He hadn't meant to say it, but as soon as Adam pointed it out, he realized it was true. They'd definitely filmed it. "Yeah, I think they did."

"You want some help?" Avi asked, his jovial personality replaced in an instant by that same lifeless stare Adam got when he didn't have to pretend to be somebody he wasn't.

"Not yet," Adam said. "Once we see how big the ring is, how it works, whether we can identify the targets…I'll take it to Dad."

Asa nodded. "We've never had a family project before," Asa said, affect flat.

"How do you guys do that?" he asked.

Adam frowned. "Do what?"

"Just turn it off like that?" Noah asked. "One minute, you guys seem completely normal, and the next, it's like somebody flipped a switch."

Asa and Avi exchanged glances before Asa shrugged. "Practice. From the time Dad took us in, we learned to act normal. We can't process emotions like fear, anxiety, sadness. They don't exist for us. We had to learn to fake it. Not just fake it but…believe it."

"But you can experience other feelings? Like happiness?" Noah asked, twisting in his seat to look back at the brothers. Maybe if Adam could experience other things, one of those things was love?

They looked at each other for a long time, and Noah had the creepy feeling they were communicating somehow. Finally, Avi said, "Yeah. We can be happy, sad, jealous, angry, surprised. Psychopathy doesn't mean we feel nothing. It just means we don't form attachments in the same way others do."

"Right." Noah's voice sounded more disappointed than intended. "How did your father teach you to fake emotions?" he finally asked, refusing to dwell on Adam's inability to form attachments.

Asa seemed almost eager to talk about the process, while Avi and Adam remained silent, though not uncomfortably so. "There's a professor—Dr. Molly Shepherd. Our dad met her after he donated money to his alma mater. She was guest lecturing. She had spent thirty years researching psychopaths like us and used her own son as a case study. That's where our dad got the idea and the techniques he employed to teach us to be more…human."

"This is all so interesting," Noah managed, squeezing Adam's hand. "Why are you willing to tell me all of this?"

Once more, Asa and Avi exchanged meaningful glances. "Can't hurt now. You already know too much. Besides, our father will do whatever it takes to protect us, to protect what he created. So, if you betray us, he'll probably kill you."

Asa said it so casually it took a full moment for the threat to penetrate Noah's brain. "Oh," was all he could think to say.

Never ask a question if you can't handle the answer. That was what his father used to say. It seemed like solid advice in that specific moment.

THIRTEEN
ADAM

Adam's blood boiled at his brother's casual threat. Were they trying to intimidate Noah? Scare him? Make him leave? Noah's thumb began to lazily stroke the side of Adam's hand, as if he could sense his agitation and wanted him to relax. Maybe he could. Maybe that was Noah's superpower. He had too much empathy and Adam had none at all. Was that a bad thing? To Adam, it felt like balance. Did Noah feel the same?

"I think you're making our baby brother mad," Avi said, amused. "He doesn't like when you threaten his new toy."

Asa snickered. "Atticus said this one is different."

"Well, we know that. When have you ever known Adam to bring home any of his playthings? Hell, when was the last time he even saw the same boy twice? Yet here he is, all tied up in knots over this one in just…what? A week?"

Two days. Just two days. But it felt like more. It felt like he'd met Noah a million years ago and they'd been separated all this time. And now, he was back. Back where he belonged. With Adam. And that was how it would stay, no matter who tried to get in their way. But Adam kept that to himself. He wasn't allowed to threaten his brothers.

One of his father's many rules. Never turn on family. What if they turned on him first? It felt like they were threatening Noah, like they wanted to make Noah so scared of them that he wasn't willing to risk life with Adam. His jaw clenched and relaxed, clenched and relaxed, his whole body flushed with…something…at the thought of Noah leaving him. Noah could never leave him. Never. He belonged to Adam. No matter how wrong it was. Or crazy. Or possessive. Noah was his.

Noah's thumb stopped stroking and his hand squeezed Adam's hard, pulling him out of the rage spiral currently consuming him. Asa and Avi had their creepy twin thing, so they were only talking out loud to piss Adam off and to make Noah uncomfortable. Brother stuff. That was what his father called it. He said it made them seem normal. Siblings teased each other. Siblings had banter.

His siblings were going to need a ride the rest of the way home if they didn't shut the fuck up because he was going to dump them on the side of the highway. They had it coming. Even his father would see that, once he explained it. They could call an Uber.

Noah craned his head around to give Adam's brothers a hard look. "I don't know if this is, like, your attempt at intimidating me, or if you're just trying to piss him off, but if I tell you I'm suitably terrified, can we please move past whatever the fuck this is?" he asked, gesturing between them.

The twins blinked at each other, then at Noah, their confusion obvious. Adam squeezed Noah's hand this time, giving him a smile he hoped conveyed how…proud of Noah he was. He was so soft in some ways. His skin, his features, the way he melted into Adam's arms and his brown eyes went hazy when he let Adam take control. But he wasn't a pushover. He wasn't one to back down, even if it killed him. That was a necessary trait to navigate a life with Adam.

"What do you know about Noah's case? Get us up to speed," Avi finally said.

Adam's shoulders sagged, all the tension leaving his body. He gave them what background he had before adding, "One of the men Noah remembered hurting him was his father's best friend, Gary. He owns the strip club where Noah works."

"You work for the man who molested you?" Asa asked.

Noah nodded. "I didn't know he molested me when I started working there. I needed a job and a place to park my trailer. He seemed surprised to see me. It had been a long time. Looking back, he definitely tested me to see if I remembered anything about when I was a kid. Since I didn't, he eventually caved."

"That's smart. Getting in with him like that. That takes balls," Avi said, sounding impressed, though begrudgingly. "Have you learned anything about this Gary guy since you started working there?"

Adam glanced at Noah, his face half obscured in shadow. When he didn't seem interested in answering, Adam did it for him. "We broke into his house last night and scored a key and half of an encrypted hard drive Calliope's trying to crack. But that's it. She's trying to track down where the key came from, but it's most likely a dead end."

"Why half a hard drive?" Asa asked.

"We were interrupted while I was cloning it. It was an almost three hour download," Adam said, eyes flicking to his brothers in the rear view mirror.

"Christ, that's a lot of kiddie porn. Sick fuck," Avi noted. "Who or what interrupted you?"

"A stranger," Noah said. "I'd never seen him before."

"Conan Greevey," Adam explained, squeezing Noah's hand. "Calliope ran him down quickly. He wasn't trying to hide. Runs the city's youth programs, which means, given his association with Gary, he's definitely ending up on our list."

Adam didn't feel the need to clarify for anybody which list he referred to.

"These pieces of shit really are everywhere," Noah said, voice sounding a bit hollow.

"Did Gary seem suspicious tonight?" Adam finally thought to ask.

Noah shook his head. "No more than usual. He interrogated me about the backpack again. I asked him about the cabin."

Adam cut his eyes to Noah, mouth forming a hard line as his pulse picked up. "That was dangerous."

Noah shrugged. "I was subtle about it. He claims he sold it years ago, that it belonged to his father. But I think he's fucking lying. I think he still owns it."

"How many of them do you remember?" Avi asked Noah.

"What?" Noah mumbled, turning to glance at Avi once more.

"The men. How many do you remember? Four? Ten? Thirty?"

Adam heard Noah swallow audibly and wanted to tell his brother to back off and shut the hell up, but Noah needed to decide if he wanted to answer or not. He made the rules outside the bedroom, that was what Adam had promised.

When Noah did finally speak, his voice was strained. "I don't remember exactly. I don't want to," he clarified, as if he thought they might suggest he dig deeper into his memories. "My father and Gary definitely…touched me… but there were also men who watched. Two or three of them. I have nightmares about hands on me. Voices giving instructions. I think if I see their faces, I can probably tell you who…participated."

"Besides, even if these men didn't touch Noah, they definitely touched somebody else's kids. They deserve whatever happens next," Adam said.

"Did Calliope have anything helpful to add?" Asa asked, voice droll.

Only that Noah might not be Wayne's son and could potentially have a whole other family out there. Part of Adam wanted to forget all about that. To just pretend he didn't know it. If Noah had a real family out there, he might leave Adam behind. But he wasn't that selfish. He wouldn't deny Noah a chance to know a real family. But he also wasn't going to get his hopes up. He'd get the DNA sample from him first, then tell him if there was something to tell.

"We'll figure out who did this and we'll make them pay," Adam promised.

"Yeah, I know," Noah said, turning to give him a reassuring smile.

"Well, when you do figure it out, we want in," Asa said.

Adam didn't answer. He had no problem with his brothers helping and would likely need them if there were several child abusers as Noah suspected.

They dropped the twins at their place before heading to Adam's. Noah didn't talk much once they were gone, just fidgeted in the passenger seat, seemingly tense with the twins no longer controlling the conversation. Had they said something that made Noah question this thing between them? The idea of Noah leaving, changing his mind about Adam, was like a knife in his throat, making it hard to swallow. Noah was his. Just his. If Noah didn't feel the same, Adam didn't know what he'd do.

Asa had called Noah Adam's new favorite toy, but that wasn't true. Adam had never had a favorite anything, didn't form attachments to people or objects. He held a connection to his family because that was what society expected and they had a common goal. Their union kept all of them safe and allowed their father's experiment to continue. He'd always imagined if he could form attachments it would be to them. He'd protect them, would mourn the loss of their absence, but losing them didn't cut into him like the idea of no longer having Noah in his life.

Societal conventions said Adam shouldn't tell Noah any of these things, shouldn't tell anybody that he'd somehow fallen for a boy he'd only known for a few days, unless one counted the two weeks of stalking he'd done post death threat. But Adam had already told him, had already made his intentions clear, right? Noah understood what he was to him. He had to know. He had to feel it, too. Maybe this was all too intense for Noah. Maybe meeting his brothers had finally made Noah understand who Adam was deep down inside.

He white-knuckled the steering wheel the whole way back to the loft, casting furtive glances at Noah, who had abandoned Adam's hand to tangle his fingers together in his lap, watching the world go by through the passenger side window. He didn't seem afraid or even bothered, but there was a tension in the car that hadn't been there just moments ago, a thickness to the air between them that almost felt like he could reach out and touch it. It kicked up his baser instincts, the ones responsible for his survival, and Noah was now a thing necessary for Adam's survival.

Once parked in the garage, Adam opened Noah's door. He took Adam's hand and gave him a hesitant, almost nervous smile. The knot in Adam's stomach loosened somewhat. When they stepped onto the elevator, Noah slipped his hand back into Adam's, and the wave of relief was so overwhelming, it took his breath away. But that relief quickly turned to a need to claim, to make Noah understand who he was to Adam.

As the doors closed, Adam shoved Noah up against the

wall, gripping his face in his hands and kissing him as the car lurched into motion. He swallowed Noah's surprised squeak, some feral part of him wondering what other kinds of sounds he could pull from Noah if he applied just the right amount of pressure. He felt the moment the tension left Noah, his whole body relaxing against Adam, letting him kiss him any way he wanted.

That was the thing about Noah; he wasn't weak or frail. He wasn't some meek little timid mouse who was too afraid to speak up. And that made his total submission just so much hotter. It made Adam want to do dirty things to him, made him want to pin him down and make him scream or whimper or moan. It made Adam want to invade him, every fucking part of him, until there was no telling where he stopped and Noah started.

"I want you so fucking bad," he growled, releasing Noah's face so he could bite along the shell of his ear.

"Let me shower and you can do anything you want to me," Noah promised breathlessly before his tongue plunged back into Adam's mouth, giving as good as he got.

They tumbled from the elevator, into the hallway, Adam shoving him up against every available surface to kiss and lick and tease over whatever bit of Noah he could get to, only stopping to fish his key from his pocket. Once inside, he trapped Noah up against the door. "I want to be inside you. Now."

Noah moaned. "Shower…"

Adam wrapped his hand around Noah's throat. "Now."

Noah shoved Adam away. "No. No. No. Shower first.

Then sex. That's not up for debate." When he saw Adam's sullen expression, he rolled his eyes and smiled. "You can shower with me," he coaxed, giving him another lingering kiss. "You can even wash my back."

Before Adam could reply, Noah began stripping, leaving a trail of clothing behind him in a way that shouldn't have been sexy but somehow was. Adam picked up the fallen pieces like breadcrumbs, dumping them in his hamper, entering the bathroom just as Noah stepped under the shower head, eyes closed, face tipped into the spray.

Adam slowly peeled off his own clothes, not in any attempt to seduce but just because he was loath to take his eyes off Noah long enough to complete the task. Once naked, Adam just stood there, bottom lip trapped between his teeth, his eyes following the water as it ran over Noah's skin, clinging to every muscular curve. Noah was fit but without the washboard abs and bulging biceps of the rich kids Adam usually partied with. Noah's body had been carved from labor, not the gym, and he couldn't get enough of it.

Adam stepped in behind Noah, who glanced up over his shoulder. Droplets of water clung to his lashes, and his tongue darted out to taste the water on his lips. Adam wanted a taste, too. He cupped Noah's face, giving in to temptation.

The thought had him groaning into Noah's mouth, his hands sliding around to grip his ass and pull him close enough to feel his hard cock press against his hip.

Noah broke the kiss, grabbing the washcloth and holding it out to Adam. "Help me?"

Adam's nostrils flared at Noah's breathless tone. "Seems

a waste when I'm just going to dirty you up again." Adam sulked before catching his mouth once more, nipping hard enough to draw blood, then sucking on Noah's wounded lip.

Noah tilted his head to give Adam access to his throat. "Promises. Promises."

Adam laughed, spinning Noah back around and dragging him up against him. Noah dropped his head against Adam's shoulder, eyes floating closed as he began to wash him.

He took his time, using the soapy cloth to explore Noah's body, drawing the rough cotton material over one nipple while his fingers teased the other, floating lower over his belly, wrapping his cloth-covered fist over Noah's cock, jerking him slowly. "Adam…" he groaned, face tipped just right for him to watch Noah fall apart.

He pressed his lips to Noah's ear, even as he let the cloth work along his body, scrubbing every fold and crevice before pressing his erection against the curve of Noah's ass. "This was your idea. I would've had you bent over the mattress by now, my fingers already deep inside you, working you open so you're nice and ready for me." Noah's eyelids fluttered, lips parting as his breaths quickened. Noah was always so responsive. "Do you feel how hard you make me? I want to be inside you so fucking bad right now. I want to breed you, mark you… I want my scent on your skin. People need to know…"

"Know what?" Noah whispered.

Adam's hand closed around his throat, gripping just tight enough to pull a shuddery sob from him. "That you're mine. Just mine. That you fucking belong to me." Adam dropped the washcloth, encircling Noah's cock with his soapy hand. "You like that, don't you? Like being mine?"

Adam needed the words, too, needed Noah's confession, but his only response was a stilted nod and a broken sob. The sound shot straight to Adam's dick. He wanted to tease Noah, make it good for him, but he was two seconds away from just pushing him up against the shower wall and impaling him right there.

"You want me inside you?" Adam crooned as he licked the water from the shell of his ear. "You want me to fuck you? Fill you up? Make you take it? All of it? All of me?"

Noah's hips flexed as he tried to work himself into Adam's loosened fist, giving another little whine of frustration when Adam didn't give him what he wanted. He tightened the hand at Noah's throat until he could feel his pulse thrumming beneath his fingertips.

"I asked you a fucking question," he growled into his ear, tone menacing.

Noah shivered against him. "Fuck. Yes. You know I want that, too. Stop teasing me and fuck me already."

Adam blew out a breath at Noah's panting words, fingers squeezing his throat just a tiny bit tighter. "I need to hear it. I need to hear you say it. Tell me."

"I want you to fuck me. Fill me up," Noah promised, still trying to work his way in and out of Adam's clenched fist. "Make me beg."

Adam's teeth sank into Noah's throat. "Is that what you want? To beg?"

Noah didn't answer, just whimpered.

Adam couldn't take it anymore, he dropped to his knees on the tile, biting Noah's ass cheek hard enough to make him hiss in pain. Adam tongued over the imprints from his teeth. "Open your legs."

He made a low rumbling noise in his chest when Noah did as he was told without hesitation. Adam skimmed his fingertips over his balls before trying to spread him open. Noah was too tense. Adam bit him once more, then soothed over the spot. "Open up for me, baby. I want to taste you."

This time, when Adam touched him, he opened easily. Adam took advantage, burying his face in the heart of Noah, teasing his entrance, licking and sucking at it until Noah's legs were shaking.

When Adam pressed his fingertip into Noah, he moaned. "Fuck."

When Noah tried to push back, Adam pulled free, standing once more. Noah gave another frustrated sob, but Adam just wrenched the water off and pulled Noah out of the shower. He used a towel to roughly dry them both before he slapped Noah's ass hard enough to leave his handprint on his skin. Noah moaned.

That was something Adam would definitely need to explore more later. "Bedroom. Now. And you better run because I plan to fuck you wherever I catch you."

Noah grinned then took off running. Adam counted to five before taking off after him at a dead run, catching him just as he reached the bed and tackling him, pinning him to the mattress. He kept a hand on Noah's chest while he reached for the lube still sitting on the bedside table. He spread Noah's legs, sitting back on his heels to look at him before slicking up two fingers and pressing them to Noah's hole.

He didn't know what he wanted to see more—the way Noah's body made room for him or Noah's reaction to the invasion. Adam moved over him, weight braced on his palm just beside Noah's head. He tried to turn away, to look at the wall, but Adam wasn't having it. "Look at me." Noah slowly dragged his gaze back to Adam's, his expression so vulnerable it took Adam's breath away. "You feel so good."

Noah shivered, pushing himself down on Adam's fingers, his hands fisting in the comforter beneath him. He couldn't wait anymore. He needed to be inside him. He sat up, then froze. Noah frowned. "What's wrong?"

"Condom?"

Noah's tongue darted out to lick over his lower lip. "I'm negative. On PrEP. You?"

Adam nodded, voice strained as he said, "Same."

"I don't want anything between us," Noah finally said.

"Thank fuck. Me neither." He moved to the edge of the bed, slicking up his cock before crooking his finger. "Come here."

Noah's eyes widened as he realized what Adam wanted, but he didn't protest, just stood and slid a leg over until they were face to face, gripping Adam's cock and pressing it to his hole. Adam groaned as he was enveloped in the tight heat of Noah's body.

FOURTEEN
NOAH

Noah sucked in a sharp breath as Adam breached him, the thick head of his cock working past the first tight ring of muscle with a slow, steady push that robbed him of thought. He squeezed his eyes shut, wincing at the flash of pain, waiting for his body to relax.

He tried to focus on anything but the burn. The feel of the wood floor beneath his feet, Adam's hands squeezing his ass, the sound of his strained breaths as he forced himself to wait for Noah's body to adjust.

When he opened his eyes again, Adam was staring at him with such intensity it robbed him of breath. Nobody had ever looked at Noah the way Adam did. It was too much. Noah kissed him, had to do something to distract himself before he did something stupid like blurt out, "I love you," to a stranger.

Adam said Noah was his and looked at him like he meant it, like it was something he couldn't fight, like he needed Noah to know that he wasn't going to let him go. Ever. That should have scared him, but it didn't. It just…overwhelmed him, because if Adam changed his mind, it might fucking kill Noah. He had nobody. Nobody but Adam.

It made no fucking sense. They didn't even know each other, but he wanted to be Adam's, wanted his heat, his passion, hell, even his violence. But, buried deep down, Noah wanted Adam because he knew he would burn the whole fucking world down for him and never feel a shred of remorse.

His cock leaked between them at that thought. Adam's protection was a heady thing. Knowing that it was Noah he wanted to protect made his chest ache in the best kind of way. He buried his face against his throat, eyes rolling at the pleasure shivering over his whole body as Adam drove into him. "Fuck me. Hard," he begged.

Adam growled, hooking his arms under Noah's legs and standing, forcing him even deeper. Noah hadn't thought it was possible to be this full. When his back hit the wall, he hissed at the rough brick biting into his bare skin, but then he didn't think about anything else. He couldn't. Adam was giving Noah just what he asked for, pounding into him relentlessly, driving all thoughts away and leaving behind only feeling.

"Oh, fuck. Yes, that's it," he heard himself say. He wrapped his fist around his cock, jerking himself in time with Adam's thrusts, realizing after just one stroke that it wasn't going to take long to get him there.

"I'm going to come," Adam snarled as he watched Noah.

"Oh, fuck. Do it," Noah rambled. "Please. I'm so fucking close. I want to feel it. I want to feel you come inside me."

"Beg for it," Adam demanded. "I need to hear you."

Noah let his head fall back, too close to orgasm to worry about being embarrassed. "Come for me. I need it. I need you. Please, Adam. Please. Please."

Adam's hips stuttered and ground against Noah, and he dropped his forehead to Noah's as he throbbed deep inside him. That was all it took. Noah spilled his release between them, working himself until he was shivering from the overstimulation.

"Put your legs around me." Adam shifted his grip, folding Noah into his arms. He could only hang on as he walked them back to the bed, lowering Noah onto the mattress and following him down, hovering over him to ask, "You okay?"

Noah nodded. "Yeah. I think so. Are you?"

Adam grinned, then dropped a kiss on Noah's nose, his cheeks, his eyelids. Each kiss was so fucking gentle, it made him ache. "Yeah, I kind of want to stay inside you forever."

"I'm okay with that," Noah assured him. "But I think we might eventually start to get hungry.

Adam sighed, slipping free of him, leaving Noah feeling empty and disconnected until Adam kissed him once more.

"Did you mean it?" Noah asked, after a minute or two.

"Wanting to stay inside you forever? Definitely. Forever and ever and ever," Adam said.

"No. When you said I was yours. Did you mean it, or is this, like, a…thing you do."

Adam propped his chin on his hand to look down at Noah, brows knitted together. "A thing I do?"

"Yeah, it's hot. Don't get me wrong. But if you don't

mean it…if this is just your game, tell me now. I'm fine with it," he lied. "Whatever this is. Letting it play out until you're sick of me—"

"Stop," Adam said, covering Noah's mouth with his palm. "This isn't a game. I don't play games. If I didn't mean it, I wouldn't say it. Honestly, if I said half the things I think when I look at you, you'd run screaming into the night."

Noah's pulse hammered in his throat. He pulled Adam's hand from his lips. "Like what?"

Adam searched his face like he was truly uncertain whether what he said next would send Noah running. "Like I want to stitch my body to yours. Like I want to live inside your skin. Like I would handcuff you to the radiator if you tried to leave me."

Noah smiled despite himself. "You don't have a radiator."

"I don't want to be like this."

Noah frowned. "Like what?"

"This," he said, sounding frustrated. "Crazy. Possessive. I know my brain doesn't work the way it's supposed to, but it never really mattered before because I knew why I was put on this planet. My dad said the world needs people like me to maintain order. Balance. But I never thought I'd meet somebody and feel the way I feel when I'm with you."

"I like that you're possessive."

Adam scoffed. "You won't be saying that when you're chained to the bed."

Noah lifted a hand to cup Adam's face. "I like the idea of being chained to your bed."

Creases formed on Adam's brow, his expression almost

pained. "I won't let you go."

"I'm not trying to leave," Noah said. "But you don't get to leave either. You don't get to walk away when you're done with me."

"I will never be done with you," Adam promised.

Noah shook his head. "You can't promise that. We're strangers. You know nothing about me."

"I know you're mine. I know it. Deep down, in that part of my brain that doesn't care what is right or how society dictates how people choose a mate. I chose you. I want you. Just you. My brain has picked you, and now, I can't undo it. You're trapped. With me. For life."

Noah's heart hammered in his chest. "Nobody has ever picked me. Most people don't even notice me—"

"Bullshit," Adam said, shaking his head.

Noah gave a half smile. "It's partially my own fault. I never wanted to be noticed. In foster care, nothing good ever comes from standing out. That's just the way it is."

"That's my fault."

It wasn't a question, just a blanket statement of guilt, like he knew he should feel bad, even though he wasn't capable.

Noah sighed. "I'd already been through the worst things in my life. I was just lucky enough not to remember. I don't know if I'll stay lucky, though. I've been having nightmares, flashes of memories. I keep them out of my head with pills and booze, but, eventually, they're going to break free. And I don't know who I'll be after that happens. So, you should be careful of the promises you make."

Adam dropped his head, kissing Noah softly. "The thing

about being raised in a house full of psychopaths? We're pretty accepting of other people's crazy. I think I'll be alright."

Noah didn't know what any of this meant long term. Maybe Adam would tire of him, maybe he wouldn't. It was all lip service until they both just did the hard work of staying, of making it happen. There were people in arranged marriages who stayed together for years. Who was to say Adam and Noah couldn't make their relationship work off of kinky sex and a shared understanding that neither of them would ever be mentally sound?

"I'm hungry," Noah said, needing to break the tension.

"Do you like Greek food? There's a twenty-four hour place that delivers."

Noah nodded. "Yeah, that sounds amazing."

Adam jumped up, padding naked down the stairs, probably to find his phone. Noah rolled over and buried his face in Adam's pillow, inhaling deeply. This was definitely an upgrade from the trailer.

They ate sitting cross-legged on Adam's bed, both of them sharing bits of food with the other. There was plenty to choose from as Adam had ordered what looked like half the menu to the house. After the dishes were cleared away and they were both stuffed, they lay in bed, in the dark, Noah's head on Adam's thigh as he combed fingers through his hair.

"Can I ask you something?"

Noah startled as Adam's words broke the silence. Between

his full belly and recent orgasm, he was practically in a food coma, lingering somewhere between sleeping and awake. He blinked his eyes open, struggling to adjust to the darkness. It was a moonless night and not even the glow from the kitchen downstairs could penetrate the shadows of the loft.

"Sure," he mumbled, snagging Adam's free hand and playing with his fingers.

"How'd you find me?"

Noah's heart rate shot up. It was only a matter of time before Adam's curiosity got the best of him, but still, Noah hesitated to say it out loud, though he had no reason to hide his detective skills. "Does it matter?"

"Yeah, of course, it does. We're so careful at covering our tracks. It would be good to know if we're missing something," Adam reasoned.

Noah sighed. "Yeah, but you have to remember, I had something others didn't… I saw you."

There was a long silence. "What?"

"I saw you running away. Before I found my dad. I didn't get a good look. You left the front door wide open. I went to close it and you were taking off down the stairs. You turned around and glanced back over your shoulder for just a second."

"There's no way you could have found me off a split-second glance over my shoulder. You were ten." Adam sounded breathless but skeptical.

Noah laughed softly. "The cops didn't think so either. They grilled me for hours, trying to get information out of me. They were frustrated by my limited details. When I told them you were a kid, they didn't believe me. They said no kid would leave a crime scene that clean." When Adam didn't interrupt, Noah shook his head. "You're gloating over that, aren't you?"

"A little. Yeah. It's nice to know my attention to detail is appreciated. My brothers seem to think I'm reckless." There was a story there, but Noah wasn't sure he wanted to probe further just yet. "So, how did you go from barely being able to describe me to hunting me down in a warehouse?"

"I didn't, at first. For eight years, I just focused on survival. Foster care sucked. I blamed you. Fixated on who you were, why you did it. Figured maybe you were some street kid or a former student of my dad's. Thought maybe you were a junkie. When I aged out of the system, I went to the cops to ask about my father's case. By then, it was a cold case. It took forever to even get somebody to return my calls."

Noah didn't know why talking about this made his stomach dip, but when Adam laced their fingers together, he felt like crying.

"Keep going," Adam said.

Noah sighed. "They had CCTV footage that they'd pulled from the bank and a corner store. I begged the detective to let me watch it. She told me it was useless because there were no faces, just people's backs and side profiles. She eventually caved. I guess the idea of closing a decade old case won out. The bank footage was useless, but then, I saw you. On the footage from the corner store. You'd changed your clothes and you'd even obscured your face from the camera, but I just knew it was you. Something about the way you walked just clicked in my head."

"Even if you saw the back of my head, I still can't figure out how you put it all together."

"Your jacket."

"My jacket?"

"Yeah. Do you remember it? You weren't wearing it when you were in my house so you must have changed as soon as you left."

"Yeah, I shoved my black hoodie in my backpack, which was stashed in the alley, and threw on a jacket I'd stolen from a photo shoot. But there were hundreds of those jackets sold."

"I know. I went directly to the designer's boutique and asked. The girl behind the counter looked at me like I was crazy when I asked about credit card receipts from over ten years ago. But when I refused to leave, she called over the manager who'd worked there for twenty years. He essentially told me the same thing, but when I showed him the jacket, he took one look and told me it was a knockoff."

"No, it fucking wasn't."

Noah snickered at Adam's tone. "That's what you're worried about? That somebody thinks you're rocking fake couture?"

"I'm just saying, that manager is a fucking idiot," Adam said, tone sulky.

"*Anyway,*" Noah said. "When I asked the manager why he thought it was a knockoff, he pointed out the red outline on the back of the jacket. He said the real ones didn't have that red lettering, that they'd shelved it after the Paris show because of some kind of dispute between the label and the designer."

"Well, shit."

"Yeah. I knew it was a long shot. But it was all I had. I tracked down photos of the Paris show—which took months, by the way—and as soon as I saw your picture, I knew. It was you. You killed my dad. But I also knew I couldn't go to the police. You were Adam Mulvaney. Son of billionaire Thomas Mulvaney. I couldn't accuse you of being a murderer. They'd think I was insane. Shit, I thought I was insane. That's when I started following you."

Adam squeezed his hand. "How long did you follow me for?"

"Six months or so. Long enough to start to see the massive discrepancies between where you went and where your social media said you were. That's a neat trick. Calliope?"

"Yeah, she's great at manufacturing alibis."

"I knew you were the man who killed my father before I started following you. I realized you were a serial killer after about four weeks. I didn't think it was a family affair at that point, but I did think your father was covering for you."

"You're kind of amazing," Adam said.

"No. Just determined."

"There are a lot of cops determined to put to rest about a hundred homicide cases. But you are the one who somehow put it all together. Off a jacket. But…maybe don't tell my dad that unless he asks."

"Yeah, deal," Noah said, jaw cracking around a yawn. "Can we go to sleep now?"

"Only if you come up here."

Noah wiggled himself up beside Adam. "Better?"

"Uh-uh, roll over."

Noah rolled his eyes but did as he was told. "You could have just said you wanted to be big spoon," he teased.

Adam kissed just behind Noah's ear, voice low. "In the morning, I'm going to fuck you awake. This just makes it easier."

Noah's cock hardened at Adam's statement. "I'm totally on board with that…but could we make it afternoon?"

"We'll see."

FIFTEEN
ADAM

Adam stayed awake long after Noah's breathing had slowed and he began to snore softly. He hadn't been lying about fucking Noah awake, but it wasn't the whole truth either. It was easier to steal the hair Calliope needed to run his DNA when he couldn't ask questions. Luckily, Noah slept soundly and didn't even notice when Adam plucked the strands from his head and slipped them into a tiny baggy, stashing it in his bedside table, before drawing the covers up over them both and letting himself drift to sleep as well.

The sun was high in the sky when Adam woke the second time, Noah still tucked beside him. He buried his face in Noah's throat, his hand curving around his hip to palm over his soft cock, stroking him just enough to get him hard but not enough to wake him. Not yet.

Adam rubbed himself against Noah's ass lazily as he played with him, loving the sighs and tiny whimpers he made even in his sleep whenever Adam did something right. He released Noah long enough to grab the lube, slicking his fingers, and sliding down between Noah's cheeks, groaning as he slipped two inside, pumping them in and out of his tight passage. He worried Noah's ear between his teeth, pulling free and slicking his cock before snugging it up against Noah's wet hole, sliding home in one smooth motion.

Noah's gasp of surprise turned into a low moan, his hand reaching back to grip Adam's hip.

"Morning," Adam murmured, turning Noah's head so he could kiss him deep as he rocked in and out of him lazily.

"Oh, fuck," Noah rasped, voice sleep soaked, lids still at half-mast.

Adam took Noah's cock back in hand, working him in time with his thrusts, using his panting breaths and tiny half bitten cries to gauge just how close he was and adjusting accordingly.

Adam had wanted to draw it out, savor it, but his resolve lessened when Noah's whimpers turned into frustrated whines as he tried to work himself into Adam's fist faster. "Adam," Noah groaned.

Adam chuckled, pulling free of Noah, flipping him onto his back, catching his knees over his elbows, practically bending him in half as he slammed back into him. They both moaned as Adam fucked into him in hard, deep strokes.

He wasn't going to last much longer. The tight heat of Noah's body was too good. "Touch yourself," he ordered.

Noah did as Adam commanded, working his cock without any real finesse, eyes locked on where they were joined together. Somehow, that was even hotter to Adam, knowing Noah wanted to watch him disappear into his body, as desperate for it as Adam was.

"Come for me," Adam said, eyes locked on Noah's cock. When his expression grew pained, like he was too in his head, Adam slapped his face hard twice, then locked his hand around Noah's throat. "Don't think about it. Just listen to me and do what you're told. Come on, baby. Let me hear you. You know how much I love listening to you fall apart."

Noah's eyes rolled back, his lips parting. "Oh, fuck. Harder. Squeeze harder. Please. Please, Adam. I'm so close. Please."

Adam snarled, giving Noah what he asked for, tightening his grip on his neck and giving in to his need to fuck Noah the way he wanted, driving into him, fire running through his blood as he could feel his pleasure building.

When Noah finally cried out, spilling over his fist, Adam was right there, too, giving a few more aborted thrusts before burying himself deep, filling Noah up. God, that would never stop being hot.

He collapsed, pressing his face against Noah's neck.

"Morning," Noah said with a breathless laugh. "It's a good thing I don't have a job that requires me sitting all day. I think you broke me."

"It's a good thing you don't have a job that would question the bruises already forming on your throat," Adam said, kissing said bruises.

"That's hot," Noah said, arms coming up around Adam in a loose hug.

Adam had never really been hugged before—not without it being some kind of learning exercise his father had created—but found he liked Noah's arms around him, liked Noah's everything, really.

"What time do you work today?" Adam asked, pulling back to look at him.

"Five, why?"

Adam grinned. "Just want to know how many times I can fill you up before we have to shower."

Noah blushed. "You need to feed me first."

Adam sighed. "Fine. Shower, then breakfast. Then sex. Then lunch. Then sex. Then another shower. Then work."

Noah rolled his eyes. "I'm only willing to commit to food and a shower. The rest is to be negotiated on a case by case basis."

Adam made a sulky face. "This is why you're going to end up chained to my bed."

Noah shoved Adam off him with a snort. "You're ridiculous. I'm starving."

Adam's phone began to vibrate across his nightstand. He almost ignored it until he saw it was Calliope. "Hello, Calliope. How are you?" he asked, voice full of mocking.

This time, it was Calliope who got right to it. "I found your creep's cabin. Noah was right. He didn't sell it."

Adam had called Calliope after he'd ordered dinner last night, but he hadn't anticipated her finding the cabin so fast. That was what he got for underestimating her. "Where is it?"

"About forty-five minutes outside the city. Just close enough to use it as often as he wants."

"Gross. Any news on the key?" he asked.

There was the sound of nails tapping over keys. "Not yet. I'm still going through financials. I'll let you know."

"Shoot me the address of the cabin?"

"It's already done, sweet cheeks."

"That's why I love you." Adam disconnected, finding Noah watching him with an amused expression. "What?"

"You seem to genuinely like her."

Adam stopped short. "Yeah. I do. I like most people when I think about it. I find them fascinating. Like opening up a car and seeing how the engine runs. If you watch a person long enough, you start to see all the pieces that make them go."

"What are my pieces?" Noah asked.

Adam looked at him for a long moment. "You're soft." When Noah bristled, Adam cupped his face. "Not in a bad way. You're like candy. Sweet. Soft on the inside with a hard shell around you."

Noah snorted, but he seemed hurt, like he thought maybe Adam didn't really see him at all.

"The boy I met in that warehouse, the one with the stars on his cheeks, that's the real you. The you who might have stayed soft and gentle if you'd had different parents. But circumstance has made you build a wall around yourself, made you push back against anybody who even slightly wronged you so that they didn't see how vulnerable you were. You want affection, but you fear it. You want love but are afraid it will be taken from you if you let anybody get too close. You've numbed yourself to kill the pain of the life you've lived so far, but it's made you so…impervious to touch that you need it rough just to get off."

The color had drained from Noah's face, and when he spoke, he sounded almost on the verge of tears. "Jesus. You could get a job as a carnival psychic."

Adam pulled Noah close until they were almost nose to nose. "I like all your pieces. I like you soft and I like you tough. You see all my pieces, too, you know? You see things about me even my family doesn't. Letting somebody see you isn't a bad thing if you can trust them."

Noah swallowed hard. "And you trust me?"

"Yes. Do you trust me?"

Noah nodded. "Yes," he said, voice thick.

"Good. Then there's nothing to worry about."

"What did Calliope have to say?" Noah asked after a few minutes.

"She found the cabin. It's forty-five minutes outside the city."

"We need to go. Like now. We need to see what's in there."

"We're going to go. But first, shower, then we'll grab food on the way. Calliope already sent me the address."

Noah just kept nodding, looking spooked. "Yeah, we need to go."

Adam didn't know what else to do so he just leaned forward and kissed his forehead. What did you say to somebody who was about to relive the worst time of their life?

"What's Calliope look like?" Noah asked around his

breakfast burrito once they were on their way out of the city.

Adam shrugged. "I don't know. I've never seen her."

Noah froze with food stuffed in his cheek, looking like a chipmunk. "Wuh?"

"Yeah. My father knows who she is, but we don't. It's safer that way. For her. She has a family, children, hell, maybe even grandchildren. I don't even know how old she is or what she looks like or even her real name. I just know she loves romance novels and Funko Pop dolls."

Noah frowned. "But you gave her the hard drive."

"No, I left the hard drive at the drop point. She goes there to retrieve it later."

"And you've never been curious enough to stake out the drop point? See what she looks like?"

Adam scoffed. "Uh, no. My dad made it very clear that we are never to break that confidentiality. Ever. He has a way of getting his point across."

Noah munched his breakfast burrito thoughtfully for a few minutes. "But isn't that dangerous? For you? Like, wouldn't it be safer if you all knew what she looked like? Mutually assured destruction or something?"

Adam shrugged. "Like I said, she and my dad are friends. He knows who she is. She understands what my father is trying to do. His end game. I'm pretty sure she lost somebody a long time ago. She feels the need to be a part of this, to right the wrongs or whatever. My father is very… careful about who knows our secret."

"And now, I know your secret," Noah said, voice full of apprehension.

Adam gripped Noah's hand. "I'll never let anybody hurt you. Especially my family. If it came down to it, I know where all the bodies are buried…literally. If they hurt you, they have to take me out, too, and despite what my brothers think, I'm too valuable. My father would never eliminate a research subject."

Noah crumpled up his wrapper and tossed it into the empty bag at his feet. "Is that what you are? A research subject?"

"My father would never say it that way. He looks at each of us as his…creations. He thinks he Frankensteined us into becoming useful members of society. While Dr. Shepherd wanted to study psychopaths to better understand her son and how to keep him from becoming a danger, my father wanted us to harness that danger, point it at the right target. But to do that, we have to be able to move seamlessly between who we are and who the world perceives us to be. His money makes it possible for us to operate as two people."

"He adopted all of you to turn you into weapons?" Noah asked, sounding more curious than concerned.

"'Look like the flower but be the serpent underneath,'" Adam quoted. When Noah frowned, Adam clarified. "Shakespeare. *Macbeth*, specifically. In order to right the wrongs of the justice system, we have to look innocent to the world as a whole."

"Is that why you have a snake tattoo?"

"We all have them. Even my egghead brother Atticus. My father made each of us get one after our first kill, so we'd never forget our purpose."

"Does it bother you? That your dad thinks of you like that?"

Adam shook his head. "No. My dad loves us. He's proud of his creations. He calls us works of art. He sculpted each of us into the killers we are. He really believes we're not a flaw in the genetic fabric of society but a necessary evil. We can do what others can't. If anything, I sometimes wonder if it bothers him. That he found us, saved us, educated and trained us, loved us…and we can never love him back. Not like he loves us."

"You don't feel love at all?" Noah asked.

Adam glanced over at Noah's taut expression. "Not in the way others can. I'm not wired that way. Sometimes, I wonder if I could still be me if I had the ability to empathize or feel guilt and remorse, but I think my father's right. My brothers and I have our place in society."

Noah fell quiet, folding his arms across his chest to stare out the window. Adam had said something wrong, done something wrong, but he didn't know what. He'd made Noah sad. Maybe just Adam's past had upset him or maybe the thought that Adam and his brothers didn't have a normal upbringing. But neither did Noah.

"What did I do?" Adam asked.

Noah's gaze darted to him. "What? Nothing," he said, a little too quickly.

"Please, don't lie to me."

There was sorrow in Noah's eyes. "I'm not," he lied again.

"I can't fix what I did if I don't know what it was. Please, just tell me."

Noah opened his mouth and closed it, swallowing audibly, shaking his head, like he was fighting with himself. "You can never love me," he blurted.

Oh. That. Adam reached out and took Noah's hand. "I don't know what love feels like. I don't know what empathy or guilt feel like. But I know this: I want to fuck you and fight with you and fight for you and make up with you and make out with you and eat Greek food naked with you. Is that enough?"

Noah blinked rapidly before looking away. "Yeah. Yeah, that's enough."

Adam still couldn't shake the feeling he'd done something wrong, but the terrain was getting treacherous. The two lane paved road they'd taken once they were off the highway had given way to a dirt road, which led to a barely-there dirt path that was little more than a trail created by tire treads taking the same route again and again.

Adam was almost certain they'd somehow taken a wrong turn as trees beat their branches against the side of his father's Rover. Then they were suddenly there, the cabin just before them, sitting in a barren spot in the middle of a circle of trees. The trees were a distance away but uniform, like they'd all decided it wasn't safe to get too close, like even they knew the place was poison.

"Do you want to go in with me?" Adam asked.

Noah's gaze shot to his. "I have to. I have to know. There could be something in there that could identify the others."

Adam nodded, but he didn't like the sudden stiffness in

Noah's body language. He handed Noah a pair of nitrile gloves and, after a cursory glance for cameras, they exited the car, walking towards the entrance as if they had a right to be there.

There were three locks on the front door. What cabin in the woods needed two additional deadbolts? They exchanged glances before moving around the cabin. The windows were blacked out. Whatever was going on in there, they clearly didn't want an audience. They checked each one for a point of entry, hoping for just one unlocked window, but Gary was clearly a careful monster. Adam picked up a rock and cracked the pane of glass, reaching in and unhooking the latch, sliding it up and carefully brushing away the shards.

Adam went in first. The smell hit him like a fist, making him wince. Sweat and booze and nicotine. Even in the minimal light, Adam could see it was a bedroom of sorts. He helped Noah inside, then held a finger to his lips, reminding Noah to be quiet so he could listen. When there was nothing but silence, Adam went to the wall and pushed the light switch up.

A dirty quilt lay over a bare mattress pushed in front of a deeply scarred wooden headboard. There was an ashtray on a crooked bedside table and a dresser with two missing drawers. Somebody had taken the mirror and propped it up on a chair, angling it towards the bed.

Adam shook his head, gesturing for Noah to follow him. They ignored the closed door across from where they stood, first checking the kitchen and living room. Both looked mundane. The pantries were bare and the couch sagged, but there was nothing incriminating to justify three locks and blacked out windows.

"Maybe you should stay here," Adam said when he backtracked to the closed door, noting the locks—plural—were on the outside, though neither were latched.

Noah swallowed hard, but then straightened his shoulders, his mouth set in a grim line. "No. Open it."

Adam pushed the door open, letting it swing wide. Part of him had hoped they'd find nothing more than another stained mattress, but he'd been wrong. For as dirty and disgusting as the rest of the cabin appeared, this room was pristine, the average boy's childhood fantasy come true.

A bed shaped like a car dominated the center. There was a rug with tracks trailing through an imaginary town and small matchbox cars scattered across the room beside a toy box overflowing with stuffed animals and games. But there were two things that stood in stark relief to the idyllic room. Restraints on the bed and cameras set up in the four corners of the room.

Noah's reaction was swift, the contents of his stomach splashing across the hallway floor before he began to shake violently. Adam gripped Noah's shoulders. "Noah, look at me."

Noah's gaze remained unfocused, likely trapped in a vivid memory he couldn't escape. Adam tried shaking him, but he just swayed on his feet. Out of options, he slapped him hard. Noah's panicked gaze darted to Adam, like he couldn't remember where he was or what was happening to him.

"Baby. Listen to me very carefully. Focus on my voice

and breathe." Noah stared at him, mimicking Adam's deep breaths. "I need you to go outside and get in the car. Can you do that for me? I need to clean this up."

Noah looked at the vomit covering the floor like he didn't know how it got there. Maybe he didn't. "Go. I'll be right behind you. I promise. Here. Take the keys."

When Noah didn't reach for them, Adam took his hand and dropped them into his palm, curling his fingers around the steel. "Go. Go."

Once Noah was outside the room, Adam set about fixing the mess they'd made, grateful there were paper towels still sitting on the counter, though, from the looks of the place, they weren't used for cleaning. When he was done mopping up Noah's vomit, he removed the trash bag and replaced it before tying up the used one and dropping it outside the window to take with them. But he didn't leave, not yet.

He needed to check for the footage. If Gary was recording, he had to be editing somewhere. It didn't seem practical to do it in his home, not this far from filming. Adam went through the house, slower, more methodically, taking his time to open every door and closet. He found it in what looked like a linen closet. A sophisticated setup, similar to those used by high-rise buildings, though Adam hoped the resolution was better.

Adam had no choice but to snatch the entire hard drive. He had no way of cloning it or even downloading what was there. He just had to hope whatever they already had would be enough to identify the other players, so Adam could just kill Gary before he became a problem.

With his findings in hand, he made his way back out to the Rover, throwing the garbage bag in the back along with the hard drive. Noah just sat, staring straight ahead, his fingers twisted together in his lap, tears streaking his face. As soon as Adam slid into the driver's seat, Noah said, "I'm sorry."

Adam frowned. "What? Why?"

"For puking all over the place? For freaking out? All of it? We just had sex for the first time last night and you're cleaning up my vomit. Jesus."

Adam blinked, trying to see the correlation between those two things but missing the point entirely. "We're going home and you're not going to work tonight. I don't give a fuck what Gary thinks at this point. Something on one of these hard drives is going to give us what we need, and if it doesn't, I'm going to start cutting off pieces of him one at a time until he gives up their names. You're not going back there." When Noah opened his mouth, Adam shook his head. "This isn't up for negotiation. You're done with that place."

"But my trailer…"

"You can move in with me."

Noah shook his head. "No. I'm not giving up my trailer, even if we move in together. I'm not. That's not up for negotiation either."

Adam's eyes widened at the renewed panic in Noah's voice. "Okay. Call out sick tonight. I'll have a tow company take your trailer to my dad's house. He has a garage that fits 14 cars and three boats. I'm sure one small Airstream won't be a problem. But once the trailer is out of there, so are you. Deal?"

Noah deflated, all the fight seeming to leave him at once. "Yeah, okay. Deal."

SIXTEEN
NOAH

Adam had to pull over for Noah to throw up three more times on the way back to the city. Each time, he'd fall back into the passenger seat and Adam would hand him a wet wipe from the center console like he was a suburban soccer mom. It would have been funny if Noah could pull himself out of…whatever was happening to him.

He tried to push the memories back down, but he couldn't. Every time he so much as blinked, he was right back in that fucking room with all those people. The dam walling off all those memories had finally ruptured and Noah was drowning.

He couldn't escape it. Hands touching him, men hurting him, the sound of his own cries and the laughter that followed… It felt like it came from everywhere, like he was trapped in some house of mirrors where a threat lurked in every pane of glass with no way of knowing which threat was the real one.

He could smell that room, not as it was now but as it

had been back then. The stench of cigarettes, sweat, stale beer, and men's cologne…sex. He shouldn't have known that smell back then. It wasn't right. It wasn't okay. Nobody should have had to endure that. But above it all—the strangers, the pain—the thing that was ripping him apart on the inside was his father's voice. At first cajoling, promising toys and ice cream, then angry, then furious when he wouldn't stop crying.

How had he buried that? How? What magical part of his brain had covered that up for years? When did he start to forget? How did he make it go back? He needed it to go back. He couldn't stop crying. Not huge wracking sobs, just an endless stream of tears rolling down his cheeks against his will.

Once they were back at Adam's house, he wouldn't even let Noah call his job. Adam made the call, telling whoever was on the other line that Noah was sick and wouldn't be in, his tone leaving no room for questioning. He removed Noah's clothes and put him to bed but set up his laptop on the blanket beside him, putting on cartoons like he was a child. He felt like a child. He felt like that child. The child his father had handed over to be tortured and abused.

Holy shit. He *was* that child. That was him. His father did those things to him. He'd let others do those things, too. Had recorded them. Somewhere, there were videos. Videos other people could see. His stomach heaved but there was nothing left to throw up. Adam had left a metal trash can beside the bed anyway. Just in case.

Noah had known all these things had happened to him,

had seen previews of what was to come, had filled in the blanks after seeing the video Adam handed him that night. But it wasn't real to him, to his brain, just a concept, a thing that he only understood in abstract, like outer space. It was out there, somewhere, but he wasn't likely to ever experience it. But now, there he was, floating through his memories with no oxygen, just waiting to die.

He tried to focus on the laptop. *Darkwing Duck*, Noah noted absently. But his real focus was on Adam's voice. He paced downstairs on the phone, his voice strengthening and receding like waves as he approached the stairs only to walk back towards the kitchen. He was mad, arguing with somebody about the logistics of torturing Gary for the information they sought versus waiting to see what Calliope could find on the hard drives.

The conversation went back and forth, his anger growing to rage, his voice ratcheting higher with each passing minute. Then Adam was just gone, the door slamming shut behind him, leaving Noah alone without so much as a goodbye. Part of him expected it. Who the fuck would want to deal with something like this? Noah didn't and he was equipped with the necessary emotions to process it. But Adam wasn't. He didn't understand how Noah felt. He literally couldn't. That wasn't Adam's fault.

In the silence, the voices in Noah's head—the laughter, the orders—only grew louder until Noah thought he might scream. He threw the covers off, padding down the stairs in his underwear, heading to the most logical place for Adam to store medications. His bathroom. He had to be quick. He didn't know when or if Adam would return quickly. He wrenched open the medicine cabinet, making a noise of frustration when he saw nothing but Advil and a box of condoms. There was nothing in the drawers or under the sink either.

He went to the kitchen next, opening every drawer and cabinet except the one over the refrigerator. That would be the last resort. Adam had to have alcohol there somewhere. When he opened the freezer, he gave a triumphant cry. A bottle of top shelf vodka, still sealed. Noah didn't think twice about cracking it open, taking two heavy pulls, letting them burn their way to his stomach, praying that this would put the lid back on his memories like it had before. He took it back to bed with him, clutching the frigid glass to his chest as he continued to watch cartoons, truly having no interest in anything heavier than *Rugrats* and *Teenage Mutant Ninja Turtles.*

The more he drank, the more he enjoyed the cartoons of his childhood. By the time Adam's apartment door swung open, Noah was well and truly drunk. There was a strange rustling sound as Adam walked back upstairs, stopping short when he saw the vodka bottle. "I see you found my brother's stash."

Noah shrugged, body numb. "Which brother? You have, like, twenty."

Adam snickered. "Archer. Our degenerate gambler. A role he takes a lot of pride in." He set his two plastic grocery bags on the bed, scooting the laptop out of his way to sit. "How drunk are you?"

Noah held his thumb and forefinger about an inch apart. "Pretty drunk. You left me."

Adam didn't flinch at the accusation in his words. "I was mad. Blackout mad. I knew I couldn't control it, and you were already stressed enough, so I went and drove around and listened to some angry music. Then I called my dad and asked him what I should do about you."

"Do about me?" Noah echoed, wondering if that only sounded harsh because his brain was pickled.

Adam sighed. "Not…about you. For you? I don't know how to help you through this. I *want* to help you."

Noah's eyes filled with tears at the sincerity in his voice. "What did he say?"

Adam sneered. "A bunch of shit about recovered memories and you needing to process them with a trained therapist and that I wasn't qualified to deal with what you're going through."

Noah's heart shriveled in his chest. "Oh."

Adam scoffed. "Yeah, oh. So, I hung up on him and called Calliope."

Noah swiped at the tears on his cheek, wondering how he had any left. "What did she say?"

Adam pulled out his phone, reading from it like he'd made some kind of list. "She said to wrap you in a…blanket burrito? To buy your favorite things to eat. To hold you if you wanted it. To leave you alone if you didn't. She said if you wanted to stay in bed all day and cry, I should let you, but that I shouldn't leave you alone to deal with this. So, I stopped at the store and then came back as fast as I could."

Noah's chest ached. Adam had called two people to find out what humans did when other humans were hurting. Was that romantic? What the fuck did Noah know? It felt sweet. "What's in the bags?"

Adam brightened up a bit. "I didn't know what you liked, so"—he upended the bags in the center of the bed—"I got a little of everything."

A small laugh escaped as a pile of candy appeared between them on the bed. So much chocolate—the cheap kind and the expensive stuff Noah could never afford—plus Blow Pops, Ring Pops, Twizzlers, Swedish Fish. It was every kid's fantasy come true.

"If you don't like any of this, just tell me what you want and I can have it delivered here in an hour. Anything. And if you're hungry, we can order from anywhere you want."

"This is good. I like all these things. Except the Swedish Fish. Those are all yours." To prove his point, he grabbed a chocolate bar and unwrapped it, taking a bite, surprised to find he was hungry and the sugary treat hit the spot.

Adam took the bottle of vodka from Noah's lap, but he didn't put it away, just took a swig before setting it back down between them.

"You're not going to lecture me on drinking my problems away?" Noah asked.

"No. If this is what you need to cope, then I'll keep you safe while you do it."

Noah's heart ached, and his chin wobbled for the thousandth time that day. "Thanks."

Adam nodded. After a minute, he said, "My parents

abused me when I was little, before my dad adopted me. It was bad. Netflix documentary level bad. But even back then, I knew I was different because the others felt sad and scared and cried. But I just felt rage."

"You remember all of it?" Noah asked, both sad for Adam and a little jealous that he'd escaped the torment of having to feel the way Noah did.

"I remember it all in that hazy way people remember things that happened a long time ago. But I don't feel any kind of way about it. I can't. I'm not built that way. But you are and I'm not going to judge you for how you get through it, you know?" Adam asked with a shrug before adding, "Besides, I tend to kill my problems, so there's that."

Once more, Noah smiled in spite of himself, just a little. "Can we order pizza?"

Adam met his gaze. "We can fly to Chicago and eat pizza at Lou Malnati's if it will make you smile," he promised.

Noah somehow both laughed and sobbed at the same time, his brain unable to process two separate but equal feelings at once. "I don't want to put pants on," he finally managed.

Adam leaned into Noah's space. "Good. I like you without pants."

He was close enough to kiss Noah but then hesitated, like he wasn't sure if he was allowed to touch him. He cupped Adam's face and closed the distance, pressing their mouths together in a chaste kiss. Adam looked relieved. Noah felt a little bit relieved, too. "I'm sorry about all this."

"Don't apologize. I want you here, with me, always." He scanned Noah's face, smirking. "Even covered in snot and vomit."

Noah wasn't even offended. He was sure he looked and smelled awful. "If you keep feeding me candy and pizza on top of this vodka, there's a very good chance you'll be cleaning up my puke again before morning."

"Whatever it takes," Adam promised, taking another swig from the bottle before using an app on his phone to order the pizza. "Let's go watch this on the big TV downstairs. You can bring the blanket and your emotional support vodka."

Adam bagged up the candy and took the comforter, too, stating his fear of Noah falling down the stairs. He wasn't wrong. Noah clung to the railing, his steps wobbly. Once downstairs, Adam turned cartoons back on and wrapped Noah in his blanket burrito before sitting on the end of the couch and patting his leg for Noah to join him.

Noah knew he expected him to lie down on the couch with his head on his leg like they'd done last night but, instead, he just crawled into his lap fully burritoed. Adam seemed surprised, but when Noah rested his cheek against his chest, Adam just tucked him beneath his chin.

"Is this okay?" Noah asked hesitantly, even though he knew Adam would never say no to him.

"This is perfect."

The next morning, Noah woke to a room filled with sunshine and groaned, certain his head would crack like an egg at the slightest touch. He felt like he had to peel himself off the sheets just to roll over. Beside him, Adam sprawled naked, face down with a pillow over his head. Noah had no recollection of why or how Adam lost his clothes. He couldn't remember much of anything after he'd eaten his body weight in pizza.

Noah's underwear was still on. If he'd had any kind of sex with Adam, it was either unreciprocated—which seemed unlikely—or Noah had put his underwear back on afterwards—which seemed even more unlikely given his inebriated state last night.

Adam could just like sleeping naked. Noah definitely didn't mind it. Adam in clothes was hot, but Adam naked… His body was art.

Noah couldn't stop himself from running a hand along the sleek expanse of his back, trailing fingertips down his spine, following the generous swell of his ass down one hairy thigh before moving back up to start the process over again. He loved touching Adam, and his chest felt full at the knowledge that, somehow, Adam's fucked up brain had taken one look at Noah and decided his equally fucked up brain was what he wanted.

Yesterday had been one of the worst days of his life but Adam had chased his demons away. For now, at least. It was like he'd had a vivid nightmare that, upon waking, disappeared, leaving a lingering sense of dread. It wasn't over. At some point, Noah was going to have to face what happened to him, but not today. Today, he just wanted to enjoy the peace, hungover or not.

He rose, kneeling between Adam's splayed legs before

blanketing his body over him. Adam didn't even stir. Noah slid his hands beneath his chest, resting his cheek between Adam's shoulder blades. The warmth of his skin bled into Noah's, thawing the chunk of ice lodged in his belly for the last however many hours. That was where he stayed, letting the steady rise and fall of Adam's back and the reassuring thud of his heartbeat lull him back to sleep.

Noah dozed there for a while before he felt Adam begin to rouse. His arm rose up to take the pillow off his head, squinting as the light hit his face. He tossed the pillow then reached both arms behind him to cup Noah's ass. "Morning."

He loved Adam's sleep-soaked gravelly voice.

Noah placed kisses wherever his lips fell along Adam's skin. "Morning."

He gave Noah's ass a gentle squeeze, then rolled, dumping him beside him on the mattress. Before Noah could even be mad, Adam's mouth was on his, kissing him slow and deep in a way no two people should ever kiss before brushing their teeth. Especially after last night, but Noah didn't care.

"Are you feeling better?" Adam asked, kissing his cheek, then his ear and his shoulder. There was no heat to it, no promise of something more.

Noah gave a hesitant nod. "Yeah. I think so."

"Good," Adam said before rolling onto his back, stretching with enough force for Noah to hear his joints crack. "Wanna shower with me and go get breakfast before I head to my dad's?"

"You have to go to your dad's?" Noah asked, that feeling of unease creeping closer.

"I dropped the hard drive for Calliope last night when I was getting the candy rations. She downloaded it this morning. It's every bit as horrific as we thought it would be. But it's…recent. She's trying to identify the victim and has isolated the faces of those who participated, and she's running them through facial recognition programs. My father doesn't anticipate any problems running down their identities. He wants to put together some sort of strategy for eliminating them. We've never gone after this many people in one go. If we're not careful, somebody might start putting the pieces together."

Noah waited for the horror to overtake him once more, but it didn't. There was only that vague sick feeling of too much pizza and vodka. "I want to go with you."

Adam twisted onto his side, one hand propping up his head and the other resting on Noah's belly. "What? No. I don't want you triggering yourself again."

Noah shook his head vehemently. "I'm fine. I'm good. There's still a chance that some of those men could be the same men…from when it was me. Those impulses don't just go away with age, and after a decade of not being caught, I imagine these guys are pretty cocky, like you said."

Adam studied Noah's face like he was searching for the right answer. "My whole family is going to be there. Well, minus Aiden. I don't know if you're ready for six of my family members at once."

Noah shrugged, propping himself up, mirroring Adam's pose. "If I'm yours—just yours—like you say I am, aren't I going to have to meet them all eventually?" A thought struck Noah like a physical blow. "Unless you've changed your mind."

Adam frowned, then leaned forward to press his forehead to Noah's. "Nothing is going to change my mind."

Noah flopped backwards. "You didn't sign up for my mental breakdown."

"I didn't sign up to be a member of a family of killers either. I didn't sign up to drag my brother Archer out of a thousand bars or the twins out of kink clubs or sit through a handful of boring lectures about cell regeneration in rats or quantum physics," Adam said. "I did sign up for you. I chose you. Mental breakdown and all. Eventually, you're going to see that I have my own kind of breakdowns...and mine sometimes end with a body count."

"But only people who deserve it, right?" Noah asked.

Adam nodded. "The code is non-negotiable. My father would put one of us down for breaking it. He says once we cross that line, we can't go back."

"Put you down? Kill you?" Noah asked, that icy feeling in his belly returning once more.

Adam didn't seem even remotely fazed by the thought of his father killing him for breaking some arbitrary code he'd created.

"We're only useful to society if we follow the code. If we turn our backs on it, then we can't be trusted. We become the monsters. My father will act accordingly. And my brothers will help."

"Jesus."

Adam grinned. "Still want to meet the family?"

Did he? Part of him had no interest in meeting four more people who would treat him the way Asa and Avi had, but he also needed to know. He needed to figure out who had done those things to him and probably other children. If that meant putting himself in the Mulvaney family's cross hairs then that was what he needed to do. He wasn't leaving Adam—not ever—and if Adam came with a family of psycho killers…so be it.

SEVENTEEN
ADAM

By the time Adam and Noah left the house, it was well past noon. Breakfast became brunch as they both nursed mild hangovers, though Noah was far worse off than Adam. He kept his sunglasses on, even in the shade of the patio, nursing black coffee like *he* was the psychopath.

They were receiving plenty of furtive glances from other patrons, but it was hard to say whether it was simply because they recognized Adam as a Mulvaney or if they were just observing two clearly hungover individuals. Either way, they kept their distance, and Adam did his best to focus on Noah and whatever he needed.

Apparently, what he needed was a stack of pancakes taller than he was and greasy bacon barely cooked. Adam ordered French toast coated in syrup and powdered sugar, though he spent more time watching Noah take down the intimidating amount of food than he did actually enjoying his own.

"Why are you just staring at me?" Noah finally asked, his tone suspicious, pancake-filled fork frozen halfway to his mouth.

Adam smirked at him. "I like looking at you?"

Noah smiled like he couldn't help himself. "I look like shit today."

"Still pretty, though," Adam countered, watching a blush spread across Noah's cheeks.

"Are all psychopaths this good at flirting?" Noah asked, his tone suggesting he was only half kidding.

"Honestly? Yes. That's why people always talk about how charming serial killers are. We're very good at pretending to be people. But it's all acting. Most of the time, we don't mean a thing we say. But, in this case, I'm telling the truth. I like the way your face is put together. Your brown eyes, your freckles, your lips. It makes me happy to look at you."

"Oh, my God, stop," Noah said around a laugh, covering half his face with his hand. "You're embarrassing me."

"I know. You're turning pink," Adam said, leaning back to better look at him.

Noah removed his sunglasses, dropping them on the table. Adam saw the cameras come out then, knew people couldn't resist photographing and recording the two of them and how in love they appeared.

Adam wished he was capable of loving somebody. If he could love anybody, it would be Noah. Just Noah. But he couldn't. He could only protect him and spoil him and give him lots of pancakes and orgasms. He hoped that was enough. He hoped Noah never changed his mind because, the truth was, he wasn't letting him go. He couldn't. But he'd already warned Noah of that. He just hoped he'd taken the warning to heart.

"Be prepared for another onslaught of followers and tags on Instagram," he murmured, without looking over at the amateur paparazzi.

"Why do they only catch us when I look like death and you look hot?" Noah asked.

"One: you always look hot, and two: because I have a habit of feeding you when you're sad."

"Will you still want me when I'm fat and happy?"

Adam gave him another smirk, popping an entire piece of bacon into his mouth at once, chewing and swallowing before he said, "We'll get fat together."

Noah laughed. "I could be down with that, but I think your fans would cry."

Adam's smile faded as he leaned in close. "Fuck them. Fuck everybody but you. Yours is the only opinion that matters. So, don't change your mind about me. Okay?"

There was no missing the threat in Adam's tone, but Noah's gaze was solid when he said, "I'm not going anywhere."

Adam reclined once more. "Good."

They finished eating and Adam paid the check. On the road, Noah synced his phone to the Rover's sound system, sharing his love of eighties music with Adam, pleased when he was familiar with the songs.

"My dad was big on eighties music. He was raised on it, so we were, too," Adam said.

Noah smiled. "My foster mom, Leslie, loved all things eighties. Her clothes, her makeup. Her hair was blonde and teased into a wave on top of her head. It was the same as it was in her high school yearbook picture. She taught me all about pop music and hair bands. Michael Jackson and Tiffany. Poison. Bon Jovi. I loved being at her house. It was always a party. Cake for breakfast, surprise road trips to the beach, skipping school to stay home and watch movies on the couch."

"Why didn't you get to stay with her?" Adam asked.

Noah looked out the window. "She died. Drug overdose. She was addicted to pills. Oxy, morphine, fentanyl. She had bipolar disorder but nobody knew until later. They said she was self medicating. I was too young to really notice how all over the place she was, barely twelve. I just thought she was fun, you know?"

Adam took Noah's hand and squeezed. Adam really had made Noah's life so much harder when he killed his father. Maybe Thomas should start paying closer attention to the collateral damage they left behind. It wasn't the kids' fault their parents were monsters.

When they pulled into the driveway of Adam's house, Noah's eyes bulged at the palatial estate with its enormous garage and sprawling gardens. "This is one person's house?"

Adam chuckled. "It is now. For a while, it housed me and my brothers, three very specialized nannies, four housekeepers, a chef, a martial arts instructor, the occasional weapons expert, and, once, even a professional knife thrower."

"Your dad ran a boarding school for assassins," Noah mused.

Adam had never thought about it. He'd definitely had a bizarre upbringing, but, like Noah said, it wasn't something he noticed until it became obvious. "Something like that, yeah."

Adam took Noah's hand before he pushed open the front door. They only made it about ten steps in the door when Noah's footsteps slowed, his head on a swivel, as he seemed to take in the vaulted ceilings and ornate furnishings.

Adam dragged him along.

"It seems weird that you can just walk into a place this big without having to knock or talk to a person at a check-in desk. What does your electric bill look like? How do you even find your way around this place? Is there a map like at the mall or like the one in the Harry Potter books? Doesn't it freak you out? Like, somebody could be living in this place for weeks and you probably wouldn't even know it. Like, that doesn't freak you out? This place looks haunted. Do you think it's haunted? Have you ever seen a ghost?"

Adam grinned at Noah's rambling, not bothering to answer the questions as he didn't seem to need Adam's contribution to the conversation.

"You have two swimming pools? Who needs two pools in one house? Your dad lives alone. Does he just get up in the morning and look at one pool and be like, 'Nah, not this one,' and go to the other? Two kitchens, too? And a kitchen outside? What does somebody do with an oven outside? Decide to bake a turkey poolside? Is that a golf course?"

Adam laughed. "There's a bowling alley, too. And a shooting range."

"Shut up," Noah marveled.

"You're welcome to use any part of the house any time

you want. It's my house, too."

Noah shook his head. "No, thank you. This place is too big. It gives me anxiety, like I'd get lost and be doomed to wander the halls forever trying to find the exit."

Adam wrapped his arms around him from behind as they looked out over the bigger of the two swimming pools. "How did I never notice how weird you are?"

Noah craned his head back to look up at him. "Your dad has a shooting range…in his house…and I'm the weird one? Maybe you're just a spoiled brat."

"Oh, I definitely am. It's my job. Adam Mulvaney, spoiled youngest son of Thomas Mulvaney. Former model turned unrepentant playboy. Bedding actors and rich boys, wrecking cars, and spending money on dumb shit."

"Sounds like a really hard life," Noah mused.

Before he could respond, a voice rang out. "Adam."

He spun around at his father's voice, bringing Noah with him. His father wore a pair of tailored pants and a white oxford shirt, with the sleeves rolled up to reveal muscular forearms. Even in his fifties, Adam's father was striking, with silver black hair, gray eyes, and tan skin. He stopped short as his gaze fell to Noah.

"Dad. This is Noah."

Thomas flicked his gaze to Noah, then back to Adam. "You didn't tell me you were bringing somebody with you."

"I told Atticus. And it's not just somebody. It's Noah. I told you about him."

His father shot another irritated look at Noah then turned on his heel. "Let's go. You've wasted enough time.

NECESSARY EVILS

You were supposed to be here an hour ago."

Adam stood, blinking, shocked at his father's rudeness. What the hell was his problem? His gaze cut to Noah, who seemed sad at his father's casual dismissal but looked almost like he'd expected it. Still, he squeezed Adam's hands that were still wrapped around his waist.

"We should probably get in there. Unless you think I should wait out here?"

"No. You have every right to be here. I don't know what my father's problem is, but it's his problem, not ours."

The meetings always took place in the locked room downstairs, accessible only with the keypad at the door. His brothers were already gathered. Asa and Avi perched on the large table, and Archer, August, and Atticus sat in the chairs. There were several pictures tacked up on the board, faces only.

When they entered, all eyes went to Noah. None of them looked surprised, so Atticus must have already broken the news that Adam was bringing him.

"Oh, are we allowed to bring strangers down here now?" Atticus asked. "You would never let Kendra down here and we were together for three years."

"Kendra would have had us all on TMZ getting carted out in handcuffs," Adam snapped. "Besides, Noah already knows about us."

Archer gave Noah a calculating once-over. "How is that, by the way? How is it this stranger knows all our secrets?"

"I'm great at connecting dots," Noah said, giving Archer the same cold stare he was getting.

"He's not a stranger," Adam snapped.

"You've known him for less than a week. That's the definition of stranger," August said drolly.

Adam's skin began to crawl, heat flaring in his belly and radiating outward. "We've known each other for weeks."

"You've been stalking him for weeks," August clarified. "Hardly the same thing."

"If you count the time I stalked him, we've been in each other's lives for almost two years," Noah countered, gaze defiant.

Archer snorted. "Two years? You've had a tail for two years and you never noticed? Are we really just going to sweep that under the rug?"

"Enough. Let's just get to work identifying these men," his father said, seeming far more impatient than usual.

"Of course, the baby gets away with murder," Asa said.

"Don't you all get away with murder?" Noah quipped.

Avi snickered. "We'd have been strictly clean up crew for a year if we'd had that sort of fuck up."

Adam's whole body flushed hot as his rage built. "They're going to be cleaning your blood out of the fucking carpet if you don't shut the fuck up," Adam promised.

"Adam. Enough!" his father shouted.

Adam shot a startled look at his father. He never yelled. "He started it," he mumbled, flicking off Atticus.

Thomas raised a hand, expression taut. "Not another word unless it's about that board."

Adam fell into a padded leather office chair, pulling Noah down into his lap, earning another disgusted sound from Atticus, who glared at Noah like it was Noah who'd harmed

Atticus and not the other way around.

"These are the players we've identified so far. Conan Greevey, who was already on our radar according to Calliope." His father paused and gave Adam a stern look. "And this guy is Paul Anderson."

"He's a cop," Noah said, voice dull.

"What?" Adam asked. "Do you remember him?"

Noah gave a stilted nod, voice trembling. "He was there. In uniform. My father used to say if I didn't behave, Officer Paul was going to take me to jail."

Adam's rage was a living, breathing thing inside him, a wolf pacing its cage, looking for somewhere to direct its anger.

Thomas nodded. "He's a detective now, about to be made captain."

Noah's only response was a forced exhalation of breath, like Thomas's words were a physical blow. Adam tightened his grip on Noah, as if he could somehow absorb some of his pain through touch.

"If cops are actively participating, it makes sense why their little pedo ring has never been found out," Atticus said.

"You want us to kill a cop?" Asa asked. "Isn't that risky?"

August shrugged. "Being a cop is a dangerous job. Accidents happen, convicts want revenge. We can stage the crime scene, frame the narrative to read any way we like. A dead cop is probably a much easier sell than most."

"Conan Greevey, on the other hand, has friends in high places. He rolls with city council members, district attorneys, the archdiocese."

"The man in the lower left corner is a priest," Noah said.

"He liked to make me call him Father…during. Was into role playing. He wore his collar."

"Christ," Thomas said, writing the word priest over the man's head with a sharpie.

"So, we've got a cop *and* a priest and a youth sports director with friends in high places. This is way bigger than we thought. You get that, right?" Adam asked his father. "This could become a problem."

Archer spun in his chair. "It's only our problem because you made it our problem."

"Yeah, we're not your boyfriend's personal hit squad," Atticus added. "I think we should scrap the whole project."

Adam exploded from his chair, taking Noah with him, stomping towards Atticus. Noah jumped in front of him, hands on his chest, scrambling to walk backwards as Adam continued to advance on his brother. Atticus had this ass whooping coming for years, the smug piece of shit. Atticus was now also on his feet, calmly removing his glasses like he found Adam tedious.

"Adam. Adam!" Noah shouted. "Stop." He did stop, looking down at Noah with a frown, nostrils flaring, chest heaving. Noah cupped his face. "Stop. They're just trying to piss you off. Don't you see that? Stop letting them bait you. Breathe, baby."

Adam took in a deep breath and let it out, the cool touch of Noah's palms on his cheeks soothing the heat burning through him until the throbbing red rage faded back to just mild irritation.

"I told you," Asa said, talking not to Adam but to the

others.

"Told them what?" Adam growled.

"That Noah has superpowers," Avi snarked. "That he somehow keeps you from raging out or, at least, from staying enraged."

"So, you were being a dick to Noah as some kind of test?" Adam asked, his anger trying to make a comeback.

His father raised a hand. "I needed to see how Noah reacted to you at your worst. Asa and Avi said I didn't have anything to worry about but I needed to put it to the test. I asked the others to be deliberately provocative." He looked directly at Noah. "I'm very sorry we were rude to you. Please, forgive us. It's very nice to meet you."

Noah looked around the room, gaze finally settling back on Thomas. "It's nice to meet you guys, too."

EIGHTEEN
NOAH

After the dust settled, Adam returned to his seat with Noah perched on his lap. He was hyperaware of the others' heavy stares. The only one not watching him was Adam's father, Thomas, who was not at all what Noah expected. He'd seen photos of the man in newspaper clippings and magazines, but they somehow failed to show just how young and hot Adam's dad actually was.

He certainly didn't look old enough to have children in their early thirties, but Noah supposed it was because he hadn't actually created any of them, just raised them. Raised them to be killers.

Noah watched as he pushed a button on a strange boomerang shaped object in the center of the table. Noah half-expected a strange futuristic 3D model to appear over it, but it was just a speaker.

"This is your friendly neighborhood oracle speaking, how may I service you today?" a voice chirped in surround sound.

"Hi, Calliope," Asa and Avi said in unison.

"Hello, boys. I see Adam didn't leave you at the airport. I'm assuming you're all calling from the Batcave."

Noah's lips twitched. This was much nicer than the Batcave. In addition to their shiny white wall that allowed for scribbling, there was another wall of computer screens and a bar that ran along the length of another. They clearly spent a lot of time down there in their secret room.

"We need some real time information. Can you help?" Thomas asked.

"How dare you question my abilities in front of mere mortals?" she asked with mock offense.

Noah's eyes widened, looking to Thomas, relieved when he only chuckled. "My mistake. We need some information."

There was the distinct sound of a chair spinning. "I'm ready. Shoot."

"Noah was able to identify Paul Anderson and a priest, whose name he can't remember. Can you cross-reference Paul Anderson and Wayne Holt along with Gary and see if there's any overlap? There has to be something. A baseball team. A prayer group. A men's league."

There was a series of clicks, and then she said, "Uh-uh. Nothing. But if it's something like an AA meeting, there would be no record of it."

Thomas's disappointment was palpable. "I just sent you a photo of the priest. Run it against yearbooks from the Catholic school Wayne Holt used to teach at. My guess is that's where you'll find him."

"Hold please," Calliope said, though she didn't actually

put them on hold. They all sat silently while nails tapped over a keyboard. The only other sound was K-pop music playing in the background. Maybe Calliope's kids liked BTS? Or maybe Calliope herself did. The only person who would truly know was Thomas.

Noah had thought he'd be more affected by this after his meltdown yesterday, but, somehow, sitting in a group of murderers made him feel safer than he'd ever felt before. Safe enough to tentatively search his memories for anything else that might help them put the pieces together, but there was nothing concrete. A cop and a priest were easy to remember; they had uniforms that stuck out and jobs that were supposed to protect children like Noah.

But the others… Gary had never done a good thing before in his entire life. He wasn't likely to be running in the same circles as Paul Anderson and a priest. Of course, his father had been a respected school teacher and he and Gary were best friends. I guess videotaping each other in repulsive acts of violence against children guaranteed mutually assured destruction should one of them get caught. Or maybe they just enjoyed reliving the moment.

"Got him," Calliope cried out, triumphant. "Father Patrick O'Hara… Jesus, Thomas. He was the school principal."

"Of course, he was," August said. "These guys somehow always rise to the top."

"I bet they'd all say he's a respected member of the community," Atticus added.

"His victims wouldn't," Noah muttered, bitter.

"Who's that?" Calliope asked. "I don't recognize that voice."

Asa snickered. "It's Noah. We have a guest in the Batcave."

"Yeah, apparently that's a thing we do now," Avi said.

"Hi, Noah!" Calliope exclaimed, like she was meeting a celebrity and not just plain old Noah, who lived in a rotted out trailer.

"Hi," Noah said, face hot.

"Noah made an excellent point," Thomas said.

Had he? Noah couldn't imagine how but it was nice to think that might be the case. Thomas perched his hip on the large conference room table, close to the twins.

"Calliope, look for any lawsuits where O'Hara was named as a defendant. They'll most likely be sealed. The church is really big on keeping those things under wraps and paying to make problems go away. If you don't find that, search for cases against Holt's school and any previous schools O'Hara worked at."

Once more, they all listened to Calliope's frantic tapping. "Nothing for O'Hara specifically, but there was a case against the city's archdiocese. Records sealed. But the complainant was an adult. Not a child."

"Got a name?" Thomas asked.

"Josiah Smithfield."

"What can you tell us about him?"

"Twenty years old, high school dropout, arrested twice for narcotics and once for petty theft. He has been in rehab twice. Oh!" she cried. "Josiah's rehab facility? St. Anthony's, run by the same church that runs Holt's school. Guess who's listed as the social worker? O'Hara. He has a doctorate in child psychology and a bachelor's degree in education. This fucker literally dedicated years to putting himself in the lives of vulnerable children." Calliope's voice was shaking.

Noah didn't blame her. His insides were shaking, too. What kind of monster spent his entire life trying to find new ways to victimize little kids? The same kind of monster who would videotape it and share it with others.

Noah wiped his sweaty palms on his jean clad thighs. "But, this boy…he doesn't fit the pattern. These guys are—what's it called—preferential offenders, right? So, what would O'Hara want with a teen?"

"Good point," Calliope said, followed by a series of more tapping. "Gold star for Noah. Josiah likely first met the man at Sacred Heart in 1997. He was the parish priest and Josiah's parents show tithing records all the way back to the eighties. That could have put him in O'Hara's cross hairs. Maybe seeing O'Hara's name once he was in rehab triggered his memories like Noah. Maybe he couldn't live with not doing anything?"

"Can we go talk to him?" Adam asked.

More typing and then a sound of dismay. "No. He died three years ago. Death record says suicide by hanging."

Noah's stomach churned and, for the first time that day, panic started to bubble inside, vomit climbing his throat until he knew he couldn't hold it back. He lurched for the trash can, barely making it before he lost his breakfast. Adam was beside him in a second, hand on his back. It felt like hours before he stopped but it was probably only a few minutes.

When he finally stopped retching, Adam sat beside him, legs sprawled in a vee. Noah didn't bother trying to stand, just sat between his splayed thighs, letting him curl his arms around him. Not one of them missed a beat, turning back to the board. "Keep looking. He can't be the only one," Thomas said.

"I have an idea," Noah said, wiping his mouth with the back of his hand. They all turned to him expectantly. "The age group they target, younger children—they tend to suppress trauma, right? That's what I read a few weeks ago after I started to remember. Kids with early trauma often act out, have substance abuse problems later, anger issues. Can't you cross-reference children in the preferential age range against prison and rehab records like you did with Josiah? I mean, they won't all be victims, but it would probably narrow our search. Maybe they remember more than I do."

"I can do that, but it will take longer than searching just one name," Calliope said.

"Do we really believe this kid offed himself?" Atticus asked suddenly.

Thomas turned to frown in his direction. "What do you mean?"

"Holt wasn't just a child rapist. He was a killer. He killed the kids he hurt. Not all of them, but a good amount. What if it wasn't just him? What if these men have been eliminating the children who complain? The ones who refuse to keep the secret or, like Josiah, possibly remember later?"

Thomas looked pained. "Calliope, you know what to do. Add children who went missing or who died under suspicious circumstances to the list."

Archer cleared his throat. "You should probably also

cross-reference the sex offender registry with children who came into contact with O'Hara. Some victims go on to become offenders, as we all know."

Noah's insides curdled like milk. He couldn't imagine ever wanting to hurt a child the way somebody had hurt him. But the things these men had done to him had changed Noah. Even when he didn't remember, it had changed him. He'd had a huge hole in his heart, one that he could never fill, not with drugs or alcohol or casual rough sex. He'd spent his life feeling worthless and…tainted…like he had a permanent stain on his soul that only he could see.

Still, Thomas was right. If a person couldn't keep their impulses in check, they were a danger to society. Once a person crossed the line from victim to aggressor, the good of the people outweighed any sympathy for the child the monster used to be. It had to. If not, the cycle continued.

"Get back to me as soon as you have anything, please, Calliope," Thomas said.

"Aye, aye, *Capitan*," Calliope said, then the line disconnected.

The others began to make their way to the entrance, but Thomas approached Noah, holding out a hand to help him up off the floor. Noah took it, noting the calluses on his palms. How did a doctor have such rough hands? Adam rose on his own, hovering over Noah's shoulder.

"Why don't you go join your brothers," Thomas said. "I would like to speak to your Noah alone."

"Why?" Adam asked, tone somewhere between alarmed and suspicious.

Noah felt both those emotions and then some. He found Thomas way more intimidating than Adam and his brothers combined. Who was more terrifying than a man who raised and trained psychopaths? It was like meeting a lion tamer. Noah didn't know if the man was crazy or confident in his abilities. He wasn't sure which he found more terrifying.

"Because if Noah is going to be part of this family, he needs to understand what he's signed on for."

"I just don't understand why I can't come," Adam said sullenly.

Thomas shook his head. "Don't pout, Adam." To Noah, he said, "Why don't we go chat by the pool? It's lovely outside."

Noah's heart plummeted to his shoes, but he simply nodded.

Once they were alone, Thomas glanced at Noah, a small smile on his face. "Are you afraid of me?"

"Yes," Noah answered honestly.

Thomas tilted his head. "But not the others?"

"No."

"Interesting. Why is that?" Thomas asked, gesturing for Noah to sit down at the poolside table.

"Because they don't do anything without your permission. They would only hurt me on your orders. That makes you the scary one."

Thomas chuckled. "You're smart. That's a good thing." He gazed out over the blue waters of the infinity pool, so Noah did, too, watching it spill over the edge into oblivion. "You understand my son can never love you."

It wasn't a question, but Noah treated it as one, a pit forming in his stomach. "Yes. I know."

"Can you help me understand why you want to be with somebody who cannot love you back? I know it's not our money. I observed the two of you carefully. You are genuinely fond of my son. So, tell me, what is it you get from him?"

There was no malice in the man's tone, more a curiosity, like Noah had now become part of the experiment. Noah sighed. It was so much more complex than anything he could put into words. All he could do was share what he could articulate. "He protects me. He takes care of me. He would kill or die for me. He sees me. Nobody ever sees me."

Thomas nodded, seeming to absorb Noah's words. "He takes care of you how? What happened after I spoke with him on the phone yesterday? He was very angry with me for suggesting you should talk to a therapist—you should, by the way. But what happened last night?"

Noah felt himself smile. "He found me drunkenly clutching a vodka bottle and took me downstairs, wrapped me in a blanket, and just held me. We watched cartoons, ate pizza, and got drunk."

Thomas made a noise of surprise. "All on his own?"

Noah shook his head. "No. Calliope told him what to do. But the fact that he cared enough to ask has to mean something, doesn't it?"

"Yes, I suppose it does. You're an adult, Noah. I'm not going to attempt to tell you or my son that you cannot see each other. I truly believe he would come unhinged at the slightest suggestion of it. But being a part of this family means not only keeping our secrets but becoming part of our cover-up. You'll have to lie convincingly enough to pass a lie detector test. You will need to train to protect yourself. Shooting, fighting, all of it. I can't have Adam distracted worrying about your wellbeing. You'll have to think quickly, act quickly, and never, ever hesitate. In this family, everybody pulls their weight."

"I understand," Noah stated solemnly, even though, deep down, he was more than a little excited by the prospect of learning to protect himself. It would be nice to feel safe even when Adam wasn't around.

"Do you think he'll get tired of me?" Noah suddenly asked, choking a little on the words. He wished he had Thomas's crazy confidence when it came to his place in their world.

"No. The opposite, in fact. I think you'll find that my son's attention is a lot like a child holding a kitten. They are excited by it, fascinated with it, want so badly to give it affection, but they don't understand how fragile it is. I don't want Adam's attention to crush you. Quite frankly, I'm not sure he'd recover."

Noah thought about it. "I don't know how Adam feels. I know he can't love me, like you said. But I don't even know what love is. Is it wanting to be in each other's company all the time? Wanting to protect each other? Take care of each other? Comfort each other? The thing about Adam and I…we tell each other exactly what we need from one another. We have to because neither of us have the instincts necessary to navigate it any other way. Like, how is that different than love? Nobody's ever loved me, so I honestly don't know."

"I can see why my son finds you so fascinating," Thomas said, returning his gaze to the view. "And, if I'm being honest, I truly don't know what love is, but I suppose that makes sense."

"Why's that?" Noah asked.

Thomas's intense gaze pinned him in place. "Can I tell you a secret? One not even my sons know?"

Noah nodded, chest tight.

"Nobody's ever loved me either."

NINETEEN
ADAM

As soon as they entered Adam's loft, Noah headed to the bathroom to brush his teeth, while Adam tossed his wallet and keys on the table, staring at the cracked bathroom door. He wasn't sure what Noah might need from him. It seemed his days were becoming more and more stressful and it was Adam's fault.

On the way home, he had grilled Noah pretty hard about what he'd talked about with his father. Noah had answered each of the questions without hesitation but seemed more subdued than he'd been on the way there. Before they left, his dad had pulled him aside and told him to keep a close eye on Noah, to be cognizant of his feelings because he'd had a hard day.

Noah left the bathroom, flipping off the light and walking straight to Adam, wrapping his arms around his neck. Adam returned the embrace, surprised when Noah lifted his legs and wrapped them around his waist, burying his face against his throat.

Adam dropped his hands to cup Noah's ass, shifting his weight before carrying him farther into the room. "What's happening here? What are we doing?"

He nuzzled his nose against Adam's neck. "You're carrying me to bed."

"To bed, huh?" Adam teased, walking towards the staircase. "And what are we going to do when we get there?"

"Slow boning," Noah said, kissing his way along Adam's jaw.

"I'm sorry, what?" Adam asked around a laugh, trudging up the stairs with Noah still clinging to him.

"I want you inside me, but I don't want it rough. I'm not in the mood. I want the feelings stuff. Kissing. Missionary. Lots of eye contact and mushiness. Fuck me but make it romantic-like."

Adam snickered at Noah's explanation but was more than happy to give him whatever he needed.

Once upstairs, he set Noah on his feet, finding his mouth as they undressed each other. Adam liked roughing Noah up but only because that was what he needed and Adam loved watching him fall apart. But if Noah wanted slow, Adam could give him that and was already half hard just thinking about sliding inside him.

When they were both naked, Adam laid Noah down on the bed, then followed him down, blanketing his weight over top of Noah so he could kiss him again, slowly, deeply, thoroughly. He found himself caught up in just kissing Noah—the softness of his lips, the way his tongue darted and retreated, the breathy sighs he released.

Somewhere along the way, Adam slowly started rocking against him, their cocks slotting together in a friction that sent tiny shocks along his spine. He couldn't remember ever enjoying sex as much as he did with Noah. It had always been a means to an end, an orgasm that required far more work than just masturbating.

But everything Noah did was sexy. The way he rolled his hips upward to meet Adam's. The way he gripped his ass like he needed him closer. The way his breathing quickened the longer they lay there, and the tiny aborted noises of frustration when Adam didn't immediately give him what he wanted.

Adam broke the kiss. "You wanted slow. I'm giving you slow."

"I said slow, not glacial," Noah said, tone grumpy.

Adam chuckled, catching Noah's hair in his fist to tug his head back, giving him access to his neck and shoulder. "What do you want, baby?"

"I want your mouth on me."

"Oh, I can definitely do that," Adam promised. He moved down Noah's body, licking over one nipple and then the other, tugging gently with his teeth. "Here?"

"Lower," Noah murmured, breathless.

Adam smiled, biting at Noah's side and earning a barked out laugh as he squirmed to get away. Noah was ticklish. That was good to know. "So, not there?"

"No, not there. You're getting warmer, though."

Adam skipped over Noah's flushed and leaking cock to nuzzle at the seam where his hips and thigh met, the hair tickling his nose but Noah's whine of irritation making it worth it. He gave the other side the same treatment. "What's wrong, baby?"

"Stop teasing," Noah said.

Adam caught his knees in his hands and brought them over his shoulders, using his thumbs to spread Noah wide, tonguing over his entrance. Noah moaned long and low, his hands fisting in Adam's hair, pulling him deeper into the heart of him. "Oh, fuck. More."

Adam gave Noah what he wanted, licking and sucking at him like a starving man, Noah's cries feeding him. He lifted his head, searching for the lube. The tube slapped him in the forehead.

"There. Get back to work," Noah managed.

"Yes, sir," Adam said around another laugh.

He coated his fingers, his mouth closing over Noah's cock as he pushed two fingers into him, eyes rolling as the tight heat of Noah's body seemed to almost suck him in. Once more, Noah's hands found Adam's hair, squirming beneath him as he sucked him, wanting to make him feel good but not good enough to get off. Noah was only going to come with Adam buried inside him.

"I'm ready. Get up here," Noah said, digging his heels into Adam's shoulders to drive home the point.

Adam crawled up his body, pressing his forehead to Noah's. "You sure are pushy when I'm not bossing you around," he said before burying himself in Noah in one thrust.

Noah cried out in surprise, moaning as Adam began to move within him. "Is this what you needed?" He captured

Noah's mouth in a greedy kiss before tearing his mouth away to say, "Fuck, you feel so good. I've wanted to be inside you all day, fantasized about sneaking you upstairs and fucking you up against the wall of my childhood bedroom, coming inside you with my whole family downstairs. Is that romantic?" he mused.

Noah wrapped his legs around Adam's waist, his blunt nails scratching at his back. "I don't know, but it's definitely working for me," Noah promised.

It was working for Adam, too. The tight heat of Noah's body was like a drug, and Adam couldn't get enough. He sank his knees into the mattress, giving himself the leverage to drive up into Noah in a way that had Noah's panting breaths ratcheting higher. "You like that, baby? You like when I go deep?"

"Fuck, yes. More."

"I want to hear you. You know what I want," Adam growled, biting at his earlobe.

"Please, Adam. I want more. I need it. Fuck me harder. Faster. Make me come."

Christ. Noah was far too articulate for Adam's liking. He raised up on his hands, making room between them. "Touch yourself," he ordered, gazing downward to watch himself piston in and out of Noah as he jerked himself in time with his thrusts. "Fuck, yeah. That's it, baby. Make yourself feel good. God, I love to watch you jerk off."

Noah's head fell back, eyes closed and lips parted, as he worked himself faster. Adam knew he was close, close to giving Adam what he needed to push him over the edge.

"Come on, baby. You can do better than that. Don't you want to feel me throbbing inside you as I breed you?"

"Oh, fuck. Yes. I need it. Please, Adam. Please, I want to feel you come inside me. Oh, God, I'm so close. You feel so good."

There it was. The babbling. Adam fucking needed it like a drug. "Who do you belong to?"

"You," Noah swore, eyes flying open to look directly into Adam's. "Only you. Forever. I promise."

Adam's orgasm took even him by surprise, his hips stuttering off rhythm as he came, spilling deep inside Noah. Luckily, Noah wasn't far behind. Two more strokes and he was painting his release between them a second before Adam collapsed on top of him.

"Was that slow boning?" he asked, when he could formulate any kind of real thought.

"I don't know, but it sure was hot," Noah said with a laugh, sucking in heavy breaths. "I don't ever want to move again. Forward my mail, I live in this bed now."

A shock ran through Adam, a strange feeling overtaking him—a weird warmth. "You do live here now. You know that, right? This is your home. We need to get your stuff from the trailer," he said, making a move to sit up.

Noah snagged him back down with a chuckle. "I think we can wait until the cum dries before we rush off to pack my things. I'm not going anywhere."

Adam bristled. "You say that now…"

The idea of Noah trying to leave him stole his breath. Maybe they hadn't known each other long but part of him recognized something in Noah, something deeply ingrained in their DNA. Adam didn't believe in soul mates—was quite certain he didn't have any soul to speak of—but Noah was it for him.

"I will say that always," Noah promised, carding his hands through Adam's hair in a weirdly comforting gesture.

He had never received much affection as a child. It hadn't been offered or needed, but Adam found he loved the way Noah would pet him, like it soothed something within him to touch Adam. "This would be a lot easier for me if I could just chain you to my radiator."

"You're the only person I know who could make a felony sound romantic." Noah grinned. "And, as previously stated, you have no radiator."

Adam flopped down hard enough to make Noah grunt. "Details."

After a few minutes, Noah asked, "What do you want to do for the rest of the day?"

"I don't know, go on a date?" Adam asked. The concept was as foreign to him as advanced calculus. "That's a thing couples do."

"Like, you wanna take me to the movies? Buy me popcorn and hold my hand?" Noah asked, sounding almost as perplexed by the concept as Adam.

"We could go to the movies," Adam said, propping his chin on his hands that rested in the center of Noah's chest. "But once the lights are out, I can't guarantee I won't try to fuck you again."

An almost evil grin spread across Noah's face. "Buy me

popcorn and I'll give you a handjob in the back row."

Adam kind of liked the sound of this whole dating thing. "Deal."

Adam and Noah woke up at the crack of noon the following day. Their movie date had been fun. Neither had any idea what the movie was about but giving each other buttery handjobs in a crowded theater turned out to be a kink neither of them knew they had, but one both were eager to explore further at a later date.

Adam leaned against the counter, his pajama pants slung low on his hips, watching a very sleepy Noah shovel Cheerios into his mouth. He didn't get how Noah could eat cereal with no sugar. They weren't even the Honey Nut Cheerios, just the plain kind. It was weird. How did he live without sugar? Adam took a sip of his overly sweetened concoction of caramel-flavored creamer and sugar with just enough espresso to be able to say he was drinking coffee. He needed sugar to survive.

When the phone started to vibrate between them on the counter, they both froze, Noah leaning forward to see who it was, sighing when he saw the name. "Calliope."

"Answer it," Adam said.

Noah swiped to answer, then put it on speaker. "Hey, Calliope."

"Hi, Noah," she said, sounding absolutely thrilled over a simple greeting.

She never acted that way when Adam answered. Noah seemed to be everybody's new favorite. He was unintentionally charming the pants off everybody in Adam's life. He smiled, sipping his orange juice, letting Noah do the talking.

"What's up? Any news?" Noah asked, taking another bite of his cereal and munching loudly.

"Not about the priest or even your dad, but…I think I found a lock for the key you swiped from Gary's."

Noah's startled gaze shot to Adam then back to the phone. "You did?"

"Yeah, it took some deep, deep digging. Like, a decade of digging. It took forever because I don't think the key belonged to Gary. I think it belonged to your father."

"My father?"

"Yes. While I was cross-referencing all the players like Thomas asked, I came across your father's will."

"My father had a will?" Noah asked, seemingly confused.

Calliope paused. "Yes. But he left everything to Gary… including you."

"What?"

"Holt had named Gary as your guardian. But he was declared unfit to care for you given his record and…uh, lifestyle. So, you were turned over to foster care."

Adam watched Noah try to process that information. "Hey, I know foster care sucked, but if Gary was your guardian, there's a very good chance he would have just found a way to make a profit off a defenseless ten-year-old boy."

Noah nodded, clearing his throat. "So, Gary has whatever

this key unlocks?"

"Afraid not. The key unlocks a small storage unit at a place called Sure-Lock Storage."

"Wouldn't anything in a storage unit have been auctioned off long ago?" Noah asked.

"You would think so, but no. In addition to handing over his meager possessions and his son to Gary, there was a strange little provision in his will. Part of his life insurance money was to go to keeping that storage locker paid for. The key was to be held by Gary and, upon his death, the contents of the storage unit were to be forwarded to the police."

Noah's dad sure did have a hard-on for this Gary guy. What the hell was the deal between them? Were they in love? "Can you send me the address?"

Calliope sighed. "You already have it. Be careful, though. The GPS on Gary's phone shows he was out at the cabin yesterday but only for about twenty minutes. He could be starting to suspect something."

"I'm always careful," Adam quipped, even though they both knew that wasn't true. When they disconnected, he gave Noah a look. "You up for a drive?"

Noah nodded. "Yeah, why not. Let's do it."

Adam checked his phone, finding Calliope had indeed sent the address, but that wasn't all. She'd sent an email marked confidential. When he opened it, there was a link to a DNA profile. Noah's DNA profile along with the username and password. Adam flicked his gaze towards Noah. "Why don't you go get dressed? I just have to email something to my dad."

Noah frowned but nodded. Adam waited until he heard him moving around the bedroom, looking for clothes to borrow. They needed to go get the rest of his stuff. Maybe on the way back from the storage unit. With one final covert glance towards the stairs, he opened his laptop, which sat abandoned on the dining room table. He hadn't touched it in weeks. He preferred to work off his phone.

Once he punched in the information, a profile popped up giving Noah his genetic makeup, his ancestry in percentages, but there was also a button that showed familial matches within the database. There were three. All girls. The three matches were siblings to each other but appeared to be Noah's first cousins on his mother's side.

They lived in Mexico City.

Noah had family. In another country. Adam swallowed the lump in his throat. What if Noah decided to leave him, to go be with a family he'd never known existed? Now that the information was in the database, it was there for anybody to see. Any of them could contact Noah at any moment and tell him about his newfound family.

Shit. He closed out the profile and toggled back to Calliope's email.

> **I fast-tracked Noah's DNA test. I put it on your credit card. I figured you wouldn't mind. I did some checking based on the results and found Josephina Hernandez. She has two sisters, Juana and Veronica. Both have children, but Juana has a son who went missing when he was just two**

years old. I'm pretty sure she's Noah's mother. She now lives in Killeen, Texas with her husband and three other children. Noah has a family.

Texas was much closer than Mexico City. Still, the thought of losing Noah weighed heavy on Adam as he walked up the stairs to dress. He needed to tell him. He had to know. But part of him longed to keep it a secret. Noah's mother had moved on. She had a new life and a new family. Noah was his.

Adam dropped to sit on the end of his bed.

Noah spun, holding up a shirt. "We definitely need to stop and get my clothes. All your stuff makes me look like I'm shrinking." He frowned when Adam didn't immediately respond. "What's wrong?"

Adam cleared his throat. "Calliope had a hunch about your dad. One she followed up on."

Noah crossed the room to stand between Adam's splayed thighs. "And? What could be worse than what we already know about him? My dad was a rapist and child killer. How much worse could it get?"

"He wasn't your dad."

Noah sucked in a sharp breath. "What?"

"You were kidnapped from Mexico City when you were two years old. Either by Holt or by somebody who gave or sold you to Holt. He wasn't your father."

Noah dropped to his knees in front of Adam, looking up at him, face pale. "That's not true."

"We ran your DNA."

"What? How?"

"I took your hair while you were sleeping and Calliope sent it to an ancestry website to see if we could find any familial matches."

Noah blinked rapidly, like he was attempting to process this information, his expression pained as he asked, "Why didn't you just tell me?"

Adam cupped his face. "Because if we couldn't find your family or if it turned out you were put up for adoption or sold by your mom, I didn't think you needed to know that."

"So, you just wouldn't have told me?" Noah asked, not exactly accusatory but close.

Adam swallowed. "Probably not. It would have done you less harm not to know. But you weren't given away or sold. You were taken. You have a family. Cousins. Siblings. A mom. We have their information if you want to get in touch."

Noah's face was hot beneath Adam's hands, his eyes wet with unshed tears. He pushed Adam's hands away and stood, wiping at his eyes with the back of his hands. "What I want is to go see what's in that storage unit."

"Are you mad at me?" Adam asked, unsure if he'd somehow betrayed Noah.

Noah shrugged. "I don't know. I don't know how I feel. I get that your heart was in the right place, but it wasn't your decision to make and you promised me I would be able to make my own choices outside the bedroom. That's what you said."

Adam crossed the room and hugged him, even though he stiffened in his arms. "I know. You're right. I wish I could say I felt bad about it, but I don't. I didn't want to be the reason you were hurt again. Yes, it was selfish and stupid, but I thought I was making the best decision I could to keep you safe. I'll always do the thing that keeps you safe."

Noah relaxed in his arms but didn't return his embrace. "I know."

"Are you going to leave me?" Adam asked, the thought turning him cold inside.

"What? No. I can be mad without leaving you. I'm probably going to be mad at you a lot because you do boneheaded shit like this and then don't even have the capacity to feel bad about it."

"That's true," Adam agreed, dropping his cheek to the top of Noah's head.

Finally, Noah's arms came around him. "You cannot lie to me about the big stuff, Adam. I know people keep things to themselves and hide little white lies, but you can't keep this kind of shit from me. It makes me feel stupid and unimportant."

Adam stepped away from Noah, tipping his chin up. "You are the single most important thing to me. You're the only thing that matters to me in this whole fucking world. Tell me you believe that."

Noah stared at him with wide eyes, swallowing audibly. "I believe you believe that."

Adam kissed his forehead, pulling him back into his arms and holding him tight. "Then I'll just have to prove it to you."

TWENTY
NOAH

Wayne Holt wasn't his father. He chewed on that thought the whole way to the storage unit. He'd suffered unspeakable things because of him, would have endured far worse if his father—Holt, he corrected—had gotten his way and was able to just hand him over to Gary. It made Noah light-headed imagining just how much worse things could have gotten for him, but it also hurt more than he'd imagined it could.

Whatever Holt had done to him, Noah had tried to rationalize it, had found a way to convince himself that his father had loved him despite every hurt and injury he caused, had told himself it was a compulsion he couldn't control. But the truth he could no longer avoid was that Holt had only loved Gary and had thought so little of Noah that he'd not only abused him and shared him with others but had intended to then hand him over to Gary so he could have his turn at doing the same. Noah was a commodity to them both.

And now, there was this new thing… A family. A mother

who had somehow let him get snatched away and sold to a monster. A mother who had a new life and new kids in a new country. Noah knew nothing about who he really was. Had never imagined he might be Mexican. Had never even questioned where his mother might be. Had he asked as a child? Had Holt made up some excuse that Noah had just swallowed as easily as he'd swallowed everything else Holt told him? Were the answers to his questions swallowed up in the abyss that had also taken his bad memories, too?

He gazed at his reflection in the side view mirror. He looked nothing like Holt. His father had been a predator hiding behind the visage of a weak, mild-mannered teacher. Not his father. Shit. Holt had thinning blond hair and sharp green eyes hidden behind thick black-rimmed glasses. Noah had always just thought he looked like every other pasty white kid at his school and had maybe pondered as a child whether he looked like his mother. But Mexican? He hadn't even taken Spanish as an elective. He wasn't racist enough to assume every person of Mexican descent had dark hair and dark eyes, but that was all he ever saw on television. No fair skinned, freckle-faced boys like him.

He tried to shake the thoughts from his head. None of this even mattered. They had bigger problems than unraveling Noah's complicated family history. There were men out there still hurting little boys. They needed to be stopped. Noah needed to stop them.

But no matter how he tried, his thoughts kept wandering right back to his new reality. For better or for worse, Noah had to spend the rest of his life knowing he had a mother somewhere, siblings somewhere, whether they wanted him or not. Adam had said he'd kept the information to himself in case Noah had been given up for adoption and had only told him because he wasn't.

But there was no guarantee his mother wanted him back. She'd clearly moved on. Did Noah want to open up that can of worms? Did she want Noah ruining her rebuilt life? What if her new family didn't even know he'd ever existed? What if she was horrible? What if she was a nightmare? What if she found out the truth of what he endured and thought he was tainted by it forever?

Then there was Adam. He had no doubt Adam could fake being charming. He'd seen it. He'd watched him easily slip the mask on without skipping a beat and had seen it come off just as quickly. But how would Adam take having to share Noah with others? Did Noah even want to be shared with others? He liked the cozy little bubble of their truly fucked up relationship.

"Hey."

Noah startled, looking over at Adam. "Hey?"

Adam tilted his head, narrowing his gaze to really examine Noah. "You good?"

He wanted to say yeah. To just nod and smile and fake it like Adam, but he wasn't like Adam. He was just Noah. "No. No, I'm not good. I'm so far from good I couldn't locate it on a map."

Noah watched Adam process this information, saw the way he appeared to be accessing some inner network, like he was trying to know what a person with emotions might say. Then he reached over and took Noah's hand. "What can I do?"

Tears sprung to Noah's eyes. "Just be here, I guess. Respect whatever choice I make regarding my mother. I don't know how to deal with any of this. I didn't ask for it and I don't want it. You know? I wish I didn't know Holt wasn't my father. I wish I didn't know that he wanted to give me to Gary like he was handing over property. I wish I didn't know that I have a mom and she moved on from losing me. If you had just asked me if I wanted to know all this before you stole my DNA, I might have said no."

Adam's gaze flicked back to the road and then to Noah, squeezing his hand. "I'm not trying to take the blame off me. I should have asked you. That's all on me. But had I given you the option of knowing who you really are, do you really think you would have said no?"

Noah pondered the question but didn't get a chance to answer as Adam continued.

"I mean, what are we even doing here? We're heading to a storage unit to look for information on the men who raped you because you can't live with yourself knowing they might still be out there doing the same thing to other children. Even if what you're doing is ripping you to shreds, even if sometimes the memories are so violent they make you puke and shake and break your heart, you don't hide from the hard things. That's not who you are."

Tears slipped down his cheeks, but he quickly wiped them away. "I think you overestimate me."

"I think you underestimate you. You impressed a room full of killers. Hell, you impressed my dad. Do you know how hard that is? He likes you. Like, really likes you. The twins think you're great and they don't like anybody. I know that we're not the family anybody would want, but we're your family if you want us. But that doesn't mean you can't also learn about your own family, too. If you want. Or when you want. There's no time limit."

"And you'd be okay with that? Me having a family? A mother, siblings…?"

Adam was quiet for a long while. "I know I'm supposed to say yes. A normal person would say they just wanted you to be happy, which I do. But a selfish part of me wants to keep you all to myself. I have a family—people who always have my back—but I'm alone in all the ways that matter. It's just how my brain works. At least, it was, until you. You are the family I'll fight to keep. Nobody else. If you want to meet your real family, I definitely won't stop you and I'll do everything in my power to be whoever you need me to be around them. But the jealous part of me will always want you to pick me…just me, and that's probably never going to change."

"I do choose you. I will always choose you. You're my family, too. And I do feel safe with your family. Safer than I have ever felt, but a part of me wants to know who my mother is, while another part is terrified."

Adam pulled up in front of the storage unit and put the Rover in park. "We don't have to decide anything right now except whether you want to open that door and see what was so important your father wrote it into his will."

Noah stared at the door of the unit. "We've come this far…"

"We have. But I can do this alone. My brothers and I can finish this for you. We've already got blood on our hands and memories that would break normal people. We have no problem eliminating an army of pedophiles if that's what it takes."

Noah's stomach plummeted. He should just say yes. Let Adam do the hard stuff. But maybe he was right. That wasn't who Noah was. "Let's go."

The key slid home and unlocked with a solid click. The rolling door groaned in protest as Adam slid it upwards, revealing…two storage boxes. Just two. Sitting in a large, otherwise empty space.

Noah bit down hard on his cheek before asking, "Do we take them or look at them here?"

Adam's gaze seemed to snag on something in the corner of the unit and, for a second, Noah had the irrational thought that somebody was standing there. He turned slowly, following his gaze over and up, heart stopping when he saw the small camera and the blinking light. "Do you think it's hooked up to something or just there to scare people away?"

"I think it doesn't matter either way. There's clearly something in these boxes worth seeing. Snag one and put it in the back."

"Where are we going?"

"Back to my father's house."

Once they were back in the Batcave, Noah felt much safer. Nobody could touch him there, least of all Gary. But now, he could never go back to his old life. He hadn't ever intended to go back, but having the choice taken away from him made him feel sick. He was like a spy who'd been burned, and now, the only way out was through. They had to kill Gary, or Noah would never be safe. He might not be safe anyway. There was no guarantee that camera feed went to Gary, even if he was the most obvious choice.

Thomas had joined them downstairs, along with August and Atticus. The twins and Archer were missing. Noah wasn't sure about the last sibling, Aiden. There were pictures of the seven of them along with Thomas all over the house, but Aiden disappeared around the time of his college graduation.

There was definitely a story there, but Noah couldn't begin to imagine what it was. The newspapers referred to Aiden as the estranged son, the one adopted as a teen who just never seemed to take to being part of a large family. There was definitely more to his story, but Noah wasn't going to pry. It didn't matter in the grand scheme of things. At least, not at the moment.

Adam and Noah sat cross-legged on the conference room table, the file boxes in front of them, while Thomas and the others stood. Thomas gave a nod and the boys cracked the lids on each box. Noah frowned. Inside was a bunch of loose pictures, but not the kind Noah had anticipated. It looked like a camp of some sort. There were boys playing basketball, soccer, or just sunbathing on a dock. They were all smiling, happy. The photos were stamped with the date July 1990.

There were hundreds of them, scattered across all the other items, but one caught Noah's eye. Ten boys in bathing suits, standing in front of a lake, arms thrown around each other's shoulders. There was something vaguely familiar about it.

Noah sighed. "Well, I have summer camp pictures. What about you?"

Adam seemed equally perplexed. "I don't know what I have. Bank records? Copies of checks. Financial documents, legal briefs?"

Thomas snagged the first folder from Adam's box and handed it to Atticus, who dropped into a chair and started to sort through the papers. The second file went to August, who simply began to flip through the documents like he had a specific target.

"What are you looking for?" Noah finally asked.

August frowned at him. "What do you mean?"

"You're flipping through the pages so fast. What are you looking for?"

"I'm not looking for anything. I'm reading."

Reading? How? Nobody could read that fast. Nobody.

Thomas gave Noah a smile. "My son has an eidetic memory. He retains everything he reads even if he appears to skim."

Noah absorbed that bit of information. "Oh."

August just smirked like he was used to people being impressed by him, but Atticus snorted, rolling his eyes. He was clearly tired of people feeling like August's talent outshined his own. Were all siblings this competitive or just murderous ones?

Noah went to set the photo down when something caught his eye. He squinted harder at the picture, his gaze snagging on one man in particular. It was the eyes. "That's my da—Holt. That's Holt." He scanned the photo and found another familiar face. "And that's Gary."

"They met at summer camp?" Adam asked, taking the photo and flipping it over. "New Horizons, 1990."

"That doesn't sound like a summer camp to me. Sounds like a drug treatment facility," Atticus mused without looking up from his task.

Thomas hit the button on the boomerang and, before Calliope could even say hello, asked, "Calliope, we're looking for a camp program called New Horizons, would have been active in 1990 or so. Holt and Gary both attended the program."

They listened as she worked, Noah frowning at the pictures, flipping back through them before stopping short. "I-Is that the priest? Father O'Hara?"

Adam leaned forward, close enough for their hair to touch. The photo was grainy and the man wasn't even in the forefront, just lingering in the background, watching.

"Yeah, I think so," Adam confirmed, handing over the photo to Thomas.

"Okay, no summer camps," Calliope interrupted, "but I do have a New Horizons Program for Boys that started in 1974 and…still runs to this day."

"What kind of program?" Atticus asked.

More clacking and then a soft exhalation. "It's a rehabilitation program—"

"Told you," Atticus broke in, smug.

"But not for drugs or alcohol. It's a treatment program for juvenile sex offenders run by the church. It's billed as an alternative to prison. If these boys went there, it's because they were ordered there by the courts."

"Wouldn't you have seen that in their backgrounds?"

"Not if the records were sealed or expunged," Calliope said. "Records for juveniles are often hidden so they don't ruin the rest of their lives."

"Can you unseal them?" Adam asked.

Calliope scoffed. "I can now that I know they exist, but it's going to take more than five minutes. I'll call you back."

There was no goodbye, so Noah returned to his file box. Beneath the stack of pictures was a photo album with a pink and blue pastel patchwork bear. Noah's hands trembled, every fiber of his being telling him to just hand over the album to Adam. Instead, he turned the page and came face to face with a photo of himself.

He couldn't have been more than five. He sat on that race car bed from the cabin, wearing a t-shirt and shorts. His eyes were hollow and he stared up at the camera with a pain and desolation that made Noah dizzy. Under the photo were the words: Our Boy.

The album fell from Noah's hands, clattering on the table, capturing the attention of the room. Adam swiped it before Noah could reach for it again, flipping open the cover and then thumbing through it, the muscle of his jaw ticking as he scanned the pages.

"What is it?" Noah asked, voice dull.

"Exactly what you think it is," Adam said, handing it to his father. Noah had to fight the urge to rip the album from Thomas. Hadn't he already been humiliated enough? Did they all have to share in his tragedy? Thomas grimaced as he opened the book, fanning through it, just as Adam had, though with more speed.

"Let me see it," Noah said, voice trembling.

Thomas gave him a sad smile. "No. I won't. There's literally no reason for you to see this."

Part of Noah was grateful, while the other part hated that they got to see him at his worst but he didn't. "How will I know who they are if I can't see their faces?"

Thomas closed his eyes, his face pained. "There are no faces but yours. Please, I know you want to be tough, but you can never unsee this. Just…let us protect you, just this once."

Adam snarled, his own hands trembling, not with fright but with rage. "I want them dead, Dad. All of them. I don't care if it puts us on the map. They all need to die. Screaming. Bloody. Bruised. Writhing in agony. Every fucking one of them."

Noah would usually try to rein in Adam's homicidal fury, but, this time, it felt good. Just. Necessary. Every one of them deserved to die screaming, and he didn't want Adam less angry. He just wanted to watch.

Thomas kept a grip on the album as they continued to excavate the boxes. More photos, more albums, more boys.

Noah might have been the first album, but he was by no means the last. Each with their own disgustingly childish album cover. Noah wasn't permitted to see any of them. He really didn't want to see. It was one thing to know it was him being hurt, it was something else altogether to see another child suffering the way he had.

The boomerang chirped beside Noah's thigh. Thomas reached over and pushed the button. Calliope's somber voice flooded the room. "Incoming," she said.

A screen lit up on the wall beside the white board and a picture of a boy in his early teens appeared. It was a mugshot. "Wayne Holt, arrested at the age of thirteen for assaulting his six-year-old neighbor. Was sent to New Horizons instead of a juvenile detention center because the judge felt he shouldn't ruin a young boy's life after 'one mistake.'"

"Pretty big fucking mistake," Atticus muttered, sounding disgusted.

"That's not all. Paul Anderson was also there that summer, as was Conan Greevey. All under the watchful eye of Father O'Hara, the program director." A series of pictures began to fill the screen, ten total, all men who were around the same age Holt was when Noah lived with him. His stomach rolled. "Noah, do any of these men look familiar?"

"Yeah." He closed his eyes and took a deep breath. "One, six, seven, nine and ten."

"Raphael Nunez, Judd Dunnigan, Julian Keys, David Krebs, and Phil Armstrong. All part of the program. All with expunged records. All went on to have jobs that allowed them to work closely with children," Calliope said.

"I'll send you everything I have on them, but I think we've found our major players."

"Not all of them," August said. "I have at least three more names that you didn't list who are somehow tied to this. They were selling the content. VHS tapes, then DVDs. There's payment information, emails, IP addresses. Many of them are overseas but most are right here in the US. This is a much bigger operation than we imagined but, from what I can gather, it's all run by those men you mentioned, all under the direction of Father O'Hara."

"Yeah, curiously, nothing to incriminate Gary or Holt, except maybe the use of the cabin."

Noah frowned, trying to put the pieces together. "That's why he sent this to Gary. He was handing over the keys to the kingdom. He wanted to be able to burn it all down once Gary died. Why?"

"Who knows? We're never going to understand whatever twisted bond these two shared. But I think we have more than enough to agree these men all need to be eliminated, no?" August asked his father.

Thomas nodded. "Yeah, but once we kill one, the others are going to go to ground."

Adam met Noah's gaze and gave him a gentle smile before he looked at his brothers. "Then let's take them out all at once."

TWENTY-ONE
ADAM

Noah gazed out the window the whole way home, humming along to the radio but making no attempt at conversation. Adam was learning that Noah needed time to process things, to chew on them before he could fully digest whatever horror appeared in their lives. Even though Noah didn't engage Adam in conversation, he held his hand, fingers threaded together, palms touching, letting Adam know it wasn't anything he'd done.

In the elevator, Noah wrapped his arms around him and rested his head just under Adam's chin. But, just like the last time they'd been to Adam's father's house, Noah turned on him almost immediately, his hands sliding up Adam's chest, beginning to unbutton his shirt. "I want you. Now."

It wasn't a question. Adam didn't protest, letting Noah shove his shirt off his shoulders to pool at their feet. He was already hardening behind his zipper. "Yeah, baby? Tell me."

Noah's gaze flicked to his, his tongue darting out to lick over his lower lip. "I want you to fuck me."

Adam's grin was feral, his hand clamping around Noah's throat, walking him backwards until his back hit the banister. "You always want me to fuck you," Adam said, leaning forward to lick over the seam of Noah's lips. "I want you to open your mouth and tell me exactly *how* you want it. I want to hear the words." He leaned down, trailing his tongue along the path of his jaw. "You want it nice and slow and deep? Or you want me to fuck you until you forget your own name?"

Noah moaned. "Definitely that one. I want it hard. Rough."

Adam growled low in his throat. "How rough?"

"Make it hurt," Noah begged.

"That's a very dangerous ask," Adam teased against the shell of Noah's ear. "Because I love the way you sound when you're choking on my cock, your nails clawing at my thighs as you grow desperate for air." Adam kept his hand firmly around Noah's neck as he pulled back to look at him. "And you're just so goddamn pretty when you cry."

Noah's pupils blew wide, swallowing hard beneath Adam's palm. "I trust you. Do it. I want to feel you every time I sit down. I want it to look like a crime scene when you're done with me. Please, Adam."

Christ. The sound of his name on Noah's lips was hotter than any touch. He really was perfect in every possible way. And he was all Adam's…in every possible way. He loved that, no matter how brutal it got, Noah always knew Adam would take care of him, knew he would always give him what he needed.

He gently kissed Noah's cheeks, his nose, his eyelids,

grazing their lips together before pulling away to clamp his teeth onto the shell of his ear. "Say it again," he rasped.

"Please…"

"My name, say it," Adam demanded.

His name was a sigh on Noah's lips, like he was the answer to every one of Noah's questions about life. It made Adam crazy, made him want to do evil things to the people who harmed Noah. Things so depraved most people wouldn't utter them out loud. "You know I'd fucking tear the world down for you, don't you?"

Noah smiled sweetly, crooning, "I know, baby." Adam's cock throbbed as much from the endearment as the way Noah's smile turned bloodthirsty. "But, right now, the only thing I want you to tear apart…is me."

Adam was never letting Noah go. Never. He couldn't. He knew that now. He couldn't live without him, and he knew—in that deep, dark ugly part of himself he wasn't supposed to ever acknowledge out loud—that he'd never let Noah live without him either. But that was the thing of it. Noah didn't want to leave. Adam knew that on a cellular level. Noah felt safe, protected, loved. Even if that love was dangerous.

Adam released Noah's throat, gripping his jaw and rubbing his thumb across his wet lower lip. "You want my cock in your mouth? Wanna take it nice and deep, make it wet for me so I can bend you over and fuck you right here?"

Noah whined. "Yes," he said, breathless.

Adam tilted his head, dropping the mask completely. "Then take my cock out and show me."

Noah's hands were sure as he freed Adam's already straining

erection, wrapping it in the warmth of his hand. But he didn't let him sink to his knees just yet. He tugged Noah's jaw down, capturing his lips in a dirty open-mouthed kiss before pushing him to his knees. He collapsed at Adam's feet, so close his breath rustled the pubic hair at the base of his cock, but he didn't do anything else. He waited, nose grazing his groin and the dip of his hip bone.

Adam fisted his hand in Noah's hair, forcing his gaze upward, slapping his face hard. Noah's lashes fluttered, his eyes going soft. Fuck. He really was perfect.

"Harder," Noah begged.

Adam didn't ask if he was sure. That was the thing about Noah; he knew just what he wanted and he didn't mind asking for it. He slapped him harder, the crack of his palm echoing throughout the space, leaving a partial handprint on his cheek. "God, you're so fucking good for me. Always willing to get on your knees for me, bend over for me."

Noah gave a shuddery breath. "Yes."

Adam pushed two fingers into Noah's mouth, cock throbbing as Noah sucked obediently. "*Just* for me," Adam warned. Noah's moan vibrated over Adam's skin. He pulled his fingers free, guiding Noah's head to his dick. "Show me how good you can be."

Noah swallowed him down in one go, head bobbing as he took him deep, drawing almost completely off before sinking down once more until his nose grazed the skin of Adam's belly. The suction and the tight heat of Noah's mouth had goosebumps breaking out over his whole body. His hand twisted in Noah's hair, holding him still so he could fuck into his mouth. Noah melted, jaw relaxing as he let Adam use him. His eyes rolled as he forced his cock into the back of Noah's throat, the muscles of his throat convulsing violently around him, constricting him in the best way. Noah gagged, his hands sliding up Adam's thighs to grip his hips. Adam kept him there until tiny panicked cries rolled along his cock and Noah's blunt nails dug into his skin. When he finally pulled free, Noah swayed on his knees, drawing in great sucking breaths, tears rolling down his bright pink cheeks, saliva coating his lips and chin. Adam held him still, smearing his cock across the mess, before reaching down and pulling him to his feet.

"Turn around." Noah did as Adam asked without question, almost like he was in a trance. He dragged Noah's jeans and underwear out of the way, growling in frustration when the zipper wouldn't give fast enough. "Grab the banister. Don't move your fucking hands unless I say so." When Noah didn't answer, Adam brought his hand down on his ass hard enough to make Noah hiss in pain. "Did you hear me?"

"Yes," Noah ground out.

Adam spit in his hand, wrapping his fist around his cock and pumping it a few times before swiping his damp fingers over Noah's hole. "This is going to hurt."

"Good," Noah murmured.

"Bend over a little more. Yeah, stick your ass out. Good boy. There you go. Now, spread your legs for me."

Noah did as Adam commanded, the picture so obscene he could have come just from that alone. He gripped Noah's hip hard enough to leave bruises. This time, it was Adam who hissed, biting his lip hard enough to draw blood as he sank into the tight grip of Noah's body. "Jesus."

Adam fucked in and out of him twice, the friction just this side of painful. When he pulled free, Noah whined, but Adam dropped to his knees, burying his face between Noah's cheeks, licking over his hole, spitting on it before pushing two fingers inside. Then he stood, plunging back into him.

Noah gasped at the sudden invasion, but then moaned. Adam fucked him hard and fast, each thrust driving Noah up onto his toes. He wanted it hard, wanted it to hurt. And Adam wanted to give Noah what he needed—knew, sometimes, that was the only way for Noah to chase his demons away. Noah was grunting and whining with each thrust, his fingers white knuckled around the iron bars of the elevator railing.

Adam hoped Noah wasn't expecting a long drawn out affair because the tight heat of Noah's body was driving him closer and closer to orgasm with every movement, even when he would stop to coat his cock with more saliva before driving inside. "I'm so fucking close. You want me to come? Fill up that greedy little hole?" Noah whimpered but didn't say anything until Adam spanked him once more, hard enough to make him cry out. "Fucking answer me when I ask you a question."

Noah moaned. "Yes. Yes. It's what I want. Fill me up. Please. I want to feel it."

That was all it took. Adam gripped Noah's hips, grinding against him, knees almost buckling at the waves of pleasure cresting over him as he emptied himself inside until he shivered.

He pulled free of Noah's body, turning him before shoving him back up against the wall, dropping to his knees to take Noah's leaking cock into his mouth. He slipped his hand between his legs, fingers slipping behind his balls, following the trail of wetness before plunging two fingers back inside Noah's sloppy hole.

Noah moaned long and low, his hips seeming to move against his will as he fucked into Adam's mouth with abandon. "Oh, fuck. I'm gonna come. Just a little more. Please. Please. Harder. More." Adam fucked into him with three fingers, finding his prostate and massaging over it with purpose. Noah's knees almost buckled. "Oh, fuck. Oh… Oh, God. Adam. Fuck. Yes. Just like that. So good."

Then Noah spilled onto Adam's tongue. He swallowed every bitter drop, sucking until Noah pushed him off. Adam fell back onto his heels, looking up at Noah with a grin. "Feel better?"

Noah smiled, sinking down to the floor. "Yeah, I feel fucking amazing. You?"

Adam gave a breathless laugh. "Yeah, I'm…I'm good."

"You good down there?"

They were lounging in Adam's sunken tub, Noah tucked between Adam's splayed thighs, his wet head resting on his chest. Noah's head lolled on his shoulders, looking up at

Adam with a sleepy smile. "I'm okay, just tired. This has been a lot."

"Yeah, anybody who said killing is easy has clearly never had to plan a mass homicide," Adam teased.

"How will you do it?"

Adam had no idea. He wasn't usually the one planning these things. He was more of a soldier. Thomas would have an idea. Maybe they would all just make multiple kills on the same night. It sounded like a lot of work. Definitely risky. Truthfully, he couldn't wait to sink his blade into Gary. Granted, they wouldn't have the kind of time together he'd like, especially if he had multiple targets, but watching these men die bloody would have to do. "That won't be the hard part. The cover-up is going to be the issue."

"Yeah. Won't twenty dead people trigger a huge investigation?" Noah asked, sighing when Adam began to soap up his torso.

"There will definitely be an investigation. But we're used to that."

"You guys just cover up the bodies and move on? You don't worry about getting caught?"

Noah's knees fell open as Adam's soapy fingers dipped below the waterline, but there was no promise in it. Noah was just touch starved and Adam loved feeding him.

Adam exhaled. "We're careful. Nobody would ever suspect a bunch of rich kids are murderers. It's too ridiculous to even comprehend for most people."

Noah was right, though. The fallout had never really been anything any of them had taken into consideration, but since meeting Noah, Adam knew they wouldn't make that mistake again. But before he could explain that further, his phone began to vibrate along the side of the tub.

When he saw it was Calliope, he swiped the phone to answer and jabbed a wet finger on the speaker button. "What's up?"

There was a long pause before Calliope asked, "What's with the echo? Are you in the bathroom? Tell me you didn't answer the phone on the toilet, Adam."

Adam snickered. "If I had, would I admit it?"

"No, probably not. But it does sound like you're in the bathroom."

"Adam and I are taking a bath," Noah supplied, shifting so the water sloshed around them.

"Aw. Hi, Noah," Calliope said with that same sunshiny voice she seemed to save just for him.

"Are you ever going to stop saying hello to me like I only have six days to live?" Noah asked.

Calliope's voice didn't lose its sparkle. "I'm just so happy Adam finally found somebody. That's all."

Adam scoffed. "You do know that not having a relationship was my choice, right? I had plenty of offers. It's not like Noah took pity on me."

Noah snickered, reaching back to pat Adam's cheek. "Nobody thinks that, baby. Look at you."

Adam tipped Noah's neck to the side to suck the water from his skin before pressing a kiss to the spot.

Calliope cleared her throat. "Keep it in your pants, boys."

"We're not wearing pants," Noah pointed out with

another breathy sigh.

"Your metaphorical pants," Calliope said, exasperated.

Adam rolled his eyes. "Yeah, yeah. What's up?"

"Nothing good. I tried calling your father about this but he's got that gala tonight. I've been going through all the paperwork you found in the storage locker and attempting to piece together exactly what these men have going on, but obviously the data stops when Noah's father—" She stopped short, as if realizing her mistake. "When Holt died. But the server at the cabin revealed some things. Some bad things."

"Yeah, we're well aware of that," Adam said, voice grim.

"But you aren't," Calliope said. "That's what I'm trying to tell you. When I went through the video the first time, I was simply looking to isolate faces and identifying marks that could tell us who those men were."

When she didn't continue, Adam prompted, "Are you pausing for dramatic effect? Because, I promise, we're riveted."

There was the sound of a deep breath and a slow exhalation, like she was gathering herself. "I decided to go through it again, hoping to find anything to help me identify the victim. We still don't know where he is. Maybe he's at home, but maybe he disappeared like so many of Holt's victims. You know?"

Noah stiffened against him. "And did you? Find him, I mean?"

"No. Not exactly. When I went through the video a second time, I paid more attention to what was happening before those men arrived, trying to find a picture I could use to run facial recognition software against the missing person database. But I went back all the way to the beginning. The boy was just sitting in the corner, running a toy car over his leg…" Once more, another deep breath. "Gary and another man were talking just out of frame. The mic picked up everything."

"What did you hear, Calliope?" Noah prompted gently.

Maybe that was why Calliope liked Noah better. Adam had never considered what it must be like for people who could empathize with the victims. Noah and Calliope were the same. Two people willing to wade into the worst parts of humanity despite the toll it was clearly taking on both of them. Especially Noah.

"They were auctioning off ten spots. One night only," she said, choking on the words. "They sold him to those men. They might not all be part of the circle, or maybe they're all part of a larger circle. I don't know how it works or what the fuck they're doing to those boys, but they appear to have expanded their empire far outside their initial group."

Noah shot to his feet, water cresting over the side of the tub onto the tile below. "When are we going to just kill these fuckers?" he snarled.

Adam followed Noah from the tub, wrapping him in a towel before grabbing one for himself. "I appreciate the added information, but we already knew these men are scum. That's why they're all going to die. One at a time or all together. Their time on this planet is limited. We're not the cops. We don't need physical proof to know they're guilty."

"That's not the point," Calliope said. "They're selling children. Trafficking them. There could be living, breathing victims out there who need help. They could still be living with their abuser, like Noah was. We have to find a way to figure out who these kids are. Not just this boy, but all of them."

Adam examined Noah. His skin looked ghostly white and his eyes were hollow, strain etched across his beautiful face. "How do we do that?"

"I think the information on the hard drive you cloned holds the key to everything. I don't think it's just chock full of kiddie porn. I think Gary is keeping records, maybe even recordings of the auctions, like Holt did before he died. I think it's insurance of some kind. I could mine through the data on what I do have of the hard drive you took from Gary's house, but I can't crack it. It's fucking Fort Knox. I need the encryption key."

"Encryption key?" Noah echoed.

"Yeah. It's a string of letters and numbers, like a super complicated password," Calliope said.

"And you can use the encryption key to crack the hard drive and figure out who the victims are?" Adam asked.

"It would still take a lot of work. I only have a fragment of the drive, but it might be enough with the key."

"And you want me to go torture Gary to get you this encryption key?" Adam asked, fire shooting through his blood at the prospect of finally getting a little alone time with the piece of shit who hurt Noah.

"Pretty please," Calliope said.

"Why not just go get the full hard drive from Gary's house?" Noah asked.

"I'm not opposed to that, but I would still need the encryption key to get any information," Calliope said.

"And I'll get it for you," Adam promised.

"We already have it," Noah said.

Adam frowned. "We do?"

Noah smiled for the first time in hours. "Yep. I think I know why Gary was so desperate to get that backpack back. It wasn't the guns or the drugs. It was the crumpled up paper I found in the small inner pocket. It was just a string of nonsense, so I tossed it back in the bag. The encryption key is in your dad's garage behind a fake panel under the bench in the kitchen."

"*This* is why I like Noah better," Calliope said. "In case you were wondering."

"So, I don't get to torture Gary?" Adam said, voice huffy.

"Not yet," Noah muttered. "But soon."

"How fast can you go get it?" Calliope asked.

Adam toweled his hair. "I can go now."

"*We* can go now," Noah clarified, then gave a jaw cracking yawn.

Adam shook his head. "No. You're exhausted. You get some sleep. I'll run and get the encryption key, drop it at the meetup spot, and be back in an hour." Noah chewed on his bottom lip until Adam tugged it free and kissed him. "It's going to be okay. Let me do this."

Noah nodded. "Yeah, okay."

"Perfect. Text me when you make the drop," Calliope said before disconnecting.

"Get some rest, baby. I'll be back soon."

TWENTY-TWO
NOAH

Noah did go to bed, and he was exhausted, but it was impossible to sleep. He couldn't stop his racing thoughts. No matter what he did, Calliope's words kept creeping back into his head. *"They could still be living with their abuser, like Noah was."*

Like Noah.

There were dozens, maybe even hundreds, of kids who were just like him, victims of the worst kind of abuse. The kind that stained a person's whole life, even when they didn't remember it. What were those children's lives like? Had they been lucky enough to forget, too? Had they even lived long enough to talk about it? Were they spiraling like Noah had before he met Adam?

Calliope was right. They needed to find these kids and, somehow, make sure they got some kind of help or, at the very least, justice. If Noah had known Holt was not his father but his abuser—if he'd remembered the abuse and torture he'd endured sooner—he would have thanked Adam for killing the man. Even if foster care had sucked. Even if he'd spent years living in a constant state of uncertainty. Holt being dead would have been worth all of it.

Noah couldn't imagine a world with Holt still in it and felt a wave of relief every time he remembered the man was dead. He scrubbed his hands over his face. What if the fragmented hard drive showed nothing? They'd only managed to get half of it at most. Noah knew nothing about computers, but he knew the whole drive had to be better than half.

Noah sat up, throwing off the covers. He could go get it. He still had the key. He could slip in and out without Gary even knowing he had ever been there. Then Calliope would have the whole drive, not just pieces of the puzzle.

As quickly as inspiration stuck, it evaporated, disappointment replacing his excitement. Even if he could get to Gary's house, he didn't know anything about cloning hard drives or any other technology outside a cell phone. Adam had taken care of that part. He didn't even fully understand what cloning was, but he assumed it was like taking a photocopy.

Noah flushed at his own stupidity. He didn't need a photocopy. Gary was already onto them. Noah just needed the original. He could take the laptop. There was no way Gary wasn't putting it all together, even if he hadn't installed the cameras in the storage unit. Noah didn't have to be careful anymore, and even he could steal one fucking laptop. Hell, he'd stolen Gary's backpack right under his nose.

If he took the laptop, Calliope would theoretically have

everything. Even if the boys' names weren't on it, there had to be something to help them unravel this fucking mess of victim and abuser. He took a deep breath and let it out, just as Calliope had done earlier. He was doing it. Even if it was a bad idea. Even if it was the worst idea ever. Those kids deserved some kind of justice.

He grabbed his phone, looking at the time. Midnight. Gary would definitely be at the club at that time of night. Noah dropped his phone back onto the side table and stood, shoving his legs back into his jeans and throwing on a t-shirt. Once he had his phone and wallet, he ordered an Uber and went to meet it out front.

He slipped into the icy interior of a Lincoln Navigator, shivering as the leather seats grazed his skin. He was grateful the driver didn't try to make conversation. It already felt like there was a hornet's nest in Noah's stomach. Was he really doing this? Yes, he was, and Adam was going to fucking kill him.

But Adam wasn't the boss of him. At least, that was what he told himself. Still, Noah pulled his phone out, firing off a text before he could think better of it.

Can't sleep. Going to get the hard drive from Gary's. Be back soon. Love you.

He hit send before he realized what he'd typed. He stared down at those last two words. It was true. He did love Adam, but he'd never said so. For a number of reasons. They barely knew each other. It seemed insane to declare his love after just a couple of weeks.

But more than that, it was because he knew Adam couldn't

reciprocate. And saying *I love you* only to hear nothing back would break something in him, even if that wasn't fair to Adam. Thomas had warned Noah, and he'd said it didn't matter. And it didn't in a big picture kind of way.

Adam protected him, comforted him, gave him what he needed as long as Noah gave clear, concise instructions. Adam did everything he could to show Noah that they belonged together. He knew it, too. He did. On the most basic, fundamental level, Noah knew there was nobody else for him but Adam. They were…bonded. Even if that bond was formed through blood and trauma. Or maybe because of it.

But Adam would never have butterflies over Noah, would never ache from missing him, wouldn't long for him when they were apart, would never get that breathless, caught up feeling that came from just knowing that person was near. Part of Noah envied him, while the other part hurt for him. Those things were both a blessing and a curse.

Noah looked down at his screen at the photo of the two of them that Adam had turned into Noah's wallpaper. They looked so normal, so in love. In the picture, Adam was lying beside him, their heads slotted together, both making stupid faces. Adam didn't look like somebody who couldn't love Noah. Adam looked like he did love Noah and Adam never pretended with him.

Noah once more took a deep breath and let it out.

"Everything okay?" the driver asked.

Noah's head bobbed. "Yes, I'm fine. Just tired."

The driver once more went back to ignoring him, and

Noah watched the world pass by in a swirl of headlights. The truth was, it didn't matter if Adam loved him or not. Noah wasn't going anywhere. The chemicals Adam's brain denied him—the ones that released endorphins or dopamine or whatever it was that tricked people into thinking they were in love—were the same ones that told Noah nobody else mattered, nobody but Adam.

Hell, Adam hadn't even needed those chemicals to choose Noah. He just had. He'd looked at Noah and decided he was his person. The one he'd kill for, die for, choose over any other, including his own family. So, that had to be better, right? Making the decision to do those things without the chemicals. It felt better to Noah. It felt like love. So, that was what Noah would call it. Adam loved Noah in every way he could.

Fifteen minutes later, they pulled into Gary's development. Noah asked the Uber driver to stop a block from the house, choosing to approach on foot. Once he saw the drive was empty, he strode to the front door, key from the other night in hand, unlocking the door and entering like he had a right to be there.

Once inside, he headed directly into Gary's office, stopping short at the wall of boxes. Moving boxes. Neatly taped and stacked on top of each other in the corners of the rooms. Noah's heart galloped in his chest. Where the fuck was he going? Did Gary think they were on to him? Had he alerted the others?

Noah shook the thought away. People fucking moved all the time. Maybe he was just being paranoid. He needed to concentrate on the task at hand. He had a job to do. He needed to get that laptop. He weaved his way around the boxes, dropping into Gary's office chair, relieved to see the key still beneath the tray in the top drawer where Adam had returned it. He put the key in the lock. It gave with a soft click. But when he opened the drawer, it was empty.

Fuck.

Acid sloshed in Noah's stomach, frustration making his chest tight. He slammed his fist onto the desk, fury and frustration overwhelming his system. Goddamn it. Maybe it was all too late. Maybe the whole thing had already blown up in their faces.

No.

Laptops were portable. He couldn't imagine that Gary would bring it to the club with him. Not after his backpack was stolen. It had to be there somewhere. Adam kept his laptop on the dining room table. He rose, slipping between the stacks of boxes to the hallway. He tried to keep his search orderly, working room to room. He didn't check the boxes. He found it hard to believe somebody would pack a laptop away.

Unless he had. Unless he didn't use it that often. Shit. Was it packed away? Lying at the bottom of one of the many boxes? The laptop certainly wasn't anywhere obvious. Noah had scoured the rooms. Even Gary's bedroom. And nothing.

Fuck it.

He went to the kitchen, relieved to see the silverware hadn't been packed. He grabbed a small paring knife and made his way back to the office. He sliced the first box, lip curling when he saw it was nothing but old file folders and bank statements. He tossed the box aside before moving on to the next. He was done with orderly. Each box that produced nothing was tossed aside until Noah was surrounded by paper and upturned boxes littered the floor.

Noah jumped as his phone started to vibrate in his pocket, his heart rate skyrocketing before he realized what it was. He pulled it free, glancing down at the screen. Adam. He swiped to answer it but froze at the sound of a gun being cocked.

He whipped around to find Gary standing there, a fifty caliber Desert Eagle in his hand. It was huge, so big it made Gary's hands seem small in comparison. Of course, he'd have a gun that big. So fitting.

Gary sneered. "You always were a little street rat."

"Hey, Gary," Noah said, voice coming out chipper with just a hint of fear, even though his heart was in his stomach and blood was whooshing in his ears. "I thought you'd be at the club."

Gary snorted. "Clearly. Drop the phone and kick it to me."

He did his best not to lose his composure as he did as Gary asked, watching as the man pocketed his phone. Would Adam come to look for him when he didn't answer his call? He must have seen Noah's text, right? Maybe he was already on his way. Noah just had to keep Gary talking long enough for Adam to find him.

"How'd you know I was here?"

"Silent alarm. Rudimentary, but it's only temporary. After

you stole my backpack and then broke into my house, I knew I needed something short term until I move. My new house has a much better, more sophisticated alarm system. Can't be too careful, right?"

"I guess not," Noah muttered. If he lived through this, Adam was never going to let him do anything alone ever again.

Gary gestured to his desk chair. "Have a seat."

Noah was grateful Gary hadn't put a bullet in his head with that cannon he was holding but couldn't help but wonder why. He was somehow both terrified and numb at the same time. As if, once more, his brain was trying to keep him removed from how fucked he was. He couldn't let Gary know. He needed to play it cool until Adam came for him.

If Adam was coming for him.

Please, let Adam be coming for me.

"Sorry about the mess," Noah quipped, a slow smirk spreading across his face. "I might be a street rat, but you're kind of a pack rat."

Gary took two steps into the room, eyes glinting with hatred. "You have always been far more trouble than you were worth."

Noah leaned forward, resting his forearms on the desk. "Then maybe you and Holt should have left me in Mexico."

Gary's eyes widened, mouth opening and closing before he seemed to regain his composure. "How did you figure that out? That's not even in those records you stole from me. It's also not on the hard drive you took from the cabin."

"I submitted my DNA to one of those ancestry sites.

You'd be amazed at what you can find on those things. Like the fact Holt wasn't my dad. Or how I have a whole other family in Texas. A real family. One you deprived me of."

Gary took his time with that bit of information. "You really are a nosey little bastard. Where's my backpack? I want it back."

Noah eased back in the chair, rocking slowly. "What for? Seems like you make plenty of money and you clearly don't need any more guns. What could possibly be so interesting about that ugly black backpack?" Noah queried.

"None of your business."

"Could it be that random string of letters and numbers I found rolled up in the pocket? The encryption key."

Noah had thought to shock Gary again, but his physical response was troubling. He flushed an almost purple color, beads of sweat erupting on his forehead and upper lip. "You don't get it, do you? You fucked everything." He shook his head. "This whole thing"—he gestured around with the gun—"just got out of hand."

"This whole thing?" Noah echoed. "You mean your pedophile ring? What's the matter? No longer just an intimate gathering of depraved rapists? Too many people crash your party?"

Sweat was actively rolling down Gary's face. Noah wondered if he might be on the verge of a heart attack. "It wasn't like that. We cared about those boys. We tried to be gent—"

Noah slammed his fist down on the desk, startling Gary. "Don't. Don't you dare say you were…" Noah sucked in a breath through his nose, trying to pull himself together. Now wasn't the time to piss Gary off. Noah needed to stay alive.

Besides, Gary had a date with Adam and his brothers. "I've got a hard drive and two boxes full of records that say otherwise. Did O'Hara teach you all of his tricks for abusing kids? Did he think of all of you as his protégés? Keep the tradition going?"

Gary wiped at his brow with the sleeve of his black button down shirt. "He taught us that our impulses were natural. Showed us books and…other things that proved we weren't crazy or perverts. That it's just evolutionary."

Jesus fucking Christ. "Do you really believe that shit? Really? Like, deep down, do you hear the things you're saying and think it makes sense, or do you just use it as an excuse for all the suffering you've caused? These are little kids. Do you know how many lives you've ruined? If your intentions are so pure, why is it so many kids have ended up dead once you're done with them?"

Gary sniffed as if the topic of dead children was somehow more distasteful than abusing them. "You'll never understand. The outside world…polite society, they'll never understand. We didn't kill all of them. Just the troublemakers. The ones who swore they would talk no matter how many times we tried to persuade them otherwise. We didn't want to do that, but there are too many power players in the mix now. It just keeps growing, and the higher up the food chain the members go, the more dangerous it becomes if we get caught. But you…you turned out fine."

"Fine?" Noah snapped. "What you did to me was so traumatic I blocked it out entirely."

Gary blinked sweat from his eyes. Noah couldn't help but wonder if he was on something or if he was truly afraid of what might happen to him if he couldn't get that encryption key back from Noah.

"You were our first," he said. "Did you know that? Wayne and I were down in Mexico. He knew some people down that way who could…find us what we were looking for."

Noah frowned, heartbeat hammering against his ribs. "So, somebody arranged for you to kidnap me?"

Gary scoffed, shaking his head. "No, that's the thing. Your father saw you—"

"Stop calling him that," Noah snapped, like it was he who had the gun, not Gary. "That man was never my father."

"Fine, Wayne saw you and was instantly in love. You were so pretty. You were playing in the street with some older kids. And he just walked right up and held out his hand…and you took it. Just walked right off with him like it was fate."

Noah's vision began to go fuzzy at the edges. This time, it was him beginning to sweat. Was Gary rewriting history? Had Noah truly just walked away with Holt? How had nobody noticed?

"It wasn't planned," Gary continued wistfully, like he was enjoying his stroll down memory lane. "We honestly thought we'd get caught almost instantly. But…somehow, the stars aligned. A little cough syrup and a short ride in the trunk and we made it back to the States with you without any issues at all. Then you were ours. A child completely off the grid. Nobody knew you existed."

Noah's blood ran cold. He swallowed hard as his memories beat against the wall he'd built around them. He'd been the perfect victim. They could do whatever they wanted to him. And they had. "You're monsters."

Gary looked surprised by that response. "We spoiled you rotten. You never had to go to school. Wayne taught you himself. You got cake for breakfast and all the toys you could play with. All you had to do was ask for it, and we happily complied. Was the trade-off really that bad?"

Noah swallowed the bile climbing up his throat. "Yes. Killing me would have been kinder."

"You're being dramatic," Gary chided.

Dramatic. He wasn't dramatic enough. "So, why did you have to hurt the others if you had me? Your perfect victim?" Noah couldn't hide the disgust in his voice.

Gary shrugged. "You got old. Well, for us. We had offers on you. Lots of them. You've always been beautiful. Those freckles alone would have made us a fortune, but then somebody murdered your father—Wayne—and everything went to shit. You were supposed to be mine. Wayne left you to me. Left it all to me. Even the rope I needed to hang all the others, so I could keep them in line. Mutually assured destruction is a powerful motivator."

Noah's head hurt. His heart hurt. But he had to keep him talking. "How many are there now?"

Gary's brow furrowed. "How many what?"

"How many others are out there who are just like me?"

Gary shrugged once more. "I don't know anymore. I

just procure the boys and provide the use of my cabin so nobody is disturbed. Partake from time to time. We all have our parts to play."

If Noah had held the gun, Gary's brains would be painted across that room. But he didn't. "And who exactly do you answer to?"

Gary scoffed. "I think you know the answer to that."

He did. "O'Hara. Your mentor. He runs you all around like his chess pieces and you just go and do his bidding. You're pathetic."

"Yet, you're the one with the gun to his head," Gary reminded, his voice growing cold.

"He's not the only one."

Noah let out a sigh of relief at Adam's voice. He stepped forward out of the shadows, a much smaller gun trained on Gary.

Gary's eyes went wide but he didn't lower his weapon. "Who the fuck are you?"

Adam pressed the gun to Gary's temple. "I'm the guy who killed your boyfriend. Now, drop the gun." Gary hesitated. "Do it now and I won't fillet you before I kill you. Make me take it from you and I'll make sure you die screaming."

Gary lowered his arm, the gun slipping from his fingers, head swiveling back and forth between Noah and Adam, like he couldn't quite get the pieces to fit. "You couldn't have killed Wayne unless you've been swimming in the fountain of youth. You would've just been a kid."

"I was sixteen. But I'm not anymore. And I promise you, I'm going to enjoy killing you far more than I did Holt."

Noah's tongue darted out to lick over his lower lip. He wanted nothing more than to watch Gary take a bullet. But then inspiration struck.

"Wait!" he cried. "I have an idea."

Adam arched his brow. "I'm listening."

TWENTY-THREE
ADAM

"Why are we standing in an empty storage unit?" Atticus flicked his gaze to the center of the room, lip curling in disgust. "Well, almost empty."

Adam rolled his eyes as he watched his brother remove a silk handkerchief from his pocket and wipe his hands, as if just standing in the damp, musty unit was enough to make him dirty.

"Yes, I'm just dying to know why that guy"—August pointed at Gary, tied to a folding chair—"is not currently dissolving in an acid bath?"

Gary began to thrash around in the chair, frantic noises coming from behind the gag in his mouth.

"Shut up," Asa said, bored. When Gary didn't take his advice, Asa picked up a booted foot and upended the chair. "This one's going to be fun. He looks…juicy."

Avi ignored the man flailing on his back to study Adam. "So, why are we all here?" he finally asked, exasperated. "And why isn't Dad here?"

Adam shrugged. "Don't ask me. Noah's the one who called the meeting."

Most people would have wilted under the gaze of five stone cold killers, but Noah just continued to lean against the wall, hands in his pockets. Maybe after having a gun pointed at his head for twenty minutes, he lacked the ability to look frightened.

Noah looked positively serene as he addressed Adam's brothers. "Thomas isn't here because he chose not to come. If I had to venture a guess, I'd say this is a test of some kind, but I don't have time to worry about that now."

August looked amused, Archer bored, Asa and Avi intrigued, and Atticus, as usual, looked like he'd smelled something bad. But Adam found it hard to tear his gaze away from Noah. He looked so sure of himself. It was sexy.

Noah flashed a quick smile in his direction. "Adam said the only way to kill these men is to do it all at once. That prospect seemed less difficult when we were looking at six or seven major players. Now, there could be as many as twenty major players. Politicians. Police. Priests. High value targets that are going to draw a lot of attention."

"And that changes things how?" August asked.

Noah tilted his head, examining August with the same shrewd gaze he was receiving. "Well, the original plan was for each of you to take out a target on the same night, at the same time. You can't do that with twenty people. As soon as word hits that one is dead, the others will start scattering like roaches."

Asa cocked his head. "Go on."

"Adam said Thomas would probably make you take out the targets one at a time, but that's not very efficient."

"Alright?" Atticus said, frowning like he was hoping Noah would get to the point.

"So, we kill two birds with one stone. We make Gary here call up the major players and get them to agree to meet them somewhere desolate, say Gary's cabin. Then you lock them in, set it on fire, kill the stragglers as they run for their lives. That takes them out all at once and the fire will hide the evidence. It ain't sexy, but it will work."

As far as plans went, it was more than a little risky. It was madness if Adam was being honest. But it could be done. Quickly if need be. Adam knew just the place. Not Gary's cabin, but somewhere equally as desolate.

"Damn," Asa said with a laugh. "That's fucking cold, bro. I like it."

"No way. These guys all deserve to suffer," Avi said, once more kicking Gary's fallen chair.

August snickered. "You just like butchering people."

Avi gave him the finger. "I'm not the one who has a kill playlist on Spotify."

August bristled, giving an offended scoff. "You know all the screaming and begging gives me a migraine."

Adam shook his head. He liked guns. They were clean. Efficient. Portable. And left very little mess if you knew what you were doing. Which he did. He didn't kill for fun. He did it because he knew it needed to be done. Because his father said it was what they were born to do. But his brothers…they weren't like him. They didn't just like it, they fucking reveled in it. All but Aiden. Aiden was a lot like Adam. More a soldier than a monster.

But, in this particular case, Adam was willing to forgo guns and knives for fire and flames if that was what Noah wanted. There was some divine justice in watching them all burn. It wasn't like they didn't have it coming. He just had to convince his brothers to skip the gore and theatrics for a clean kill.

Adam sighed, looking at August warily. "You don't always have to use blades. You could just put a bullet in the ones who try to run. I know for a fact you're an excellent shot," he reminded, trying and failing to keep the bitterness out of his voice.

August rolled his eyes. "Are you seriously bringing this up *again*? I shoot one of your targets, and you harp on it forever. I did you a favor. You froze up."

"I was thirteen," Adam shot back.

"You wouldn't have made it to fourteen if I hadn't stepped in. So, you're welcome."

"Enough!" Atticus shouted. "Can we save the witty banter for later? What Noah is proposing is most definitely the smarter plan."

Avi shrugged, pouting. "I guess. Can we at least hurt this one?"

Noah frowned. "Are you guys really disappointed that you can't stab somebody when the alternative is to just set them on fire?"

Asa nodded. "No offense. It's just a little…hands off for our taste. We take pride in our work."

"Look, I don't care how you take them out, but we need to do it all at once and Gary is the key to doing that," Noah said. "Can we all at least agree on that?"

Adam's brothers all looked at each other before Atticus nodded. "It will work. We just have to get this one to make the call without signaling the others."

Adam looked down at the man, still making distressed noises from behind his gag. "Oh, Gary here knows the alternative is a slow, painful death versus a nice quick bullet to the head."

"He's going to play ball," Noah assured them. "Right, Gary?"

The man frantically bobbed his head. Atticus nodded towards the twins and they grabbed the back of the chair and set it upright. Gary's eyes darted from person to person.

Adam was surprised when Noah approached the man, dropping down onto his thighs until they were nose to nose. "How does it feel to be scared?" he asked, tone chilling. "How does it feel to know you're going to die?"

Gary didn't respond, just stared wide-eyed at Noah. As did the others. This Noah had been born of so much pain and trauma and had come out stronger for it. His brothers seemed fascinated by Noah, but Adam… Adam had never been so horny in his whole fucking life. Noah looked fierce and so fucking sure of himself that it made Adam want to drag him out to the car and fuck him right then and there.

But there was no time for that. There was truthfully no time for any of it, including Noah perched in Gary's lap, head tilted, as if he was truly trying to gauge the man's fear.

"Noah likes to play with his food before he eats it," August said. "Excellent."

Noah stood but continued to stare down at the older man.

"I mean, it's only fair he's the one who gets to kill Gary," Avi said. "Right? That kill belongs to Noah."

Adam snapped his head around. "Noah's not killing anybody. Just because he's being inducted into the family doesn't mean he needs to be initiated with blood."

"Every one of us had to make our first kill," Archer said, as always sounding inconvenienced.

"Noah said it himself," Avi reminded. "He said this was a test. Dad is clearly using this as some sort of experiment. If Noah is part of this family, he's going to have to get his hands a little dirty."

"No—"

Noah cut him off. "I'll do it."

"You don't have to," Adam swore.

Noah looked at Gary, his gaze almost frigid. "I don't have to. I want to. But not until it's over. I want him to watch the others die first."

"Then it's settled," Archer said. "Get the man's phone and let's get this over with."

TWENTY-FOUR
NOAH

"What if they don't show?" Noah asked again for the hundredth time, chewing on his thumbnail as he watched Adam gaze out the window through a pair of binoculars.

They sat in an abandoned shack that had once been a bait and tackle shop, approximately five hundred yards away from an old wooden building that had once been a fish hatchery, whatever the hell that was. Adam had said the whole marina had shut down years ago and had sat abandoned for more than a decade. It was one of the forgotten properties in Thomas Mulvaney's vast portfolio.

"They'll show," Adam promised without looking up from his post. "Your idea was smart. Even my father thought so."

That wasn't entirely true. Thomas had said the plan was reckless and risky. But he'd also said he was going to sit back and let it play out. He was putting a lot of faith in Noah. Too much faith if he was being honest. Noah's bravado from the other day had vanished in a puff of smoke the moment they'd posted up in this dirty dilapidated shack that reeked of rotting fish, even though there were none to be found.

Still, the area was perfect for their purpose. The rotting wooden building would go up like a tinderbox once they were all inside, and—unlike Gary's cabin—was unlikely to start a forest fire. Thomas didn't strike Noah as much of a conservationist, so he imagined it had more to do with unwanted attention than saving wildlife and vegetation.

Noah shook his head, chewing harder at his nail until Adam had reached up and tugged his hand from his mouth without looking, dropping it to Adam's jean clad thigh.

"You're going to chew off your own hand like a bear in a trap. If you need a distraction, I have something you can play with," Adam said, clearly amused with himself.

"Oh, for fuck's sake," Archer muttered in Noah's ear.

"Yeah, coms are live. Try not to act like heathens," Atticus added.

It felt weird hearing other people in his ear, but there was something weirdly exciting about it, too. The adrenaline rushing through his veins made him jittery, his heart racing like he'd had too many energy drinks.

Adam chuckled. "Baby, relax. I can literally feel your nerves from over here."

"Here being six inches to your left?" Noah sniped, feeling suddenly sulky.

"We don't have time for marriage counseling today," Avi said, voice low. "How about we save the hurt feelings for when we're on the other side of this pile of bodies? No?"

Adam continued on like his brothers hadn't even spoken, looking only at Noah. "Relax. Everything is going exactly as planned."

"You know who says that? That one person in every movie right before it all goes to shit," Noah said, earning another amused smirk from Adam.

Adam was right, though. Gary had sent out the distress call, alerted his pervy friends that they had a verifiable threat to their operation and he was calling an emergency meeting to figure out how to rectify the situation as quickly and quietly as possible. He'd been impressively convincing. Noah assumed it was the hunting knife pressed to his balls and not a sudden attack of conscience.

He gnawed on his lip. "Seriously, though, there's twenty of them and only six of you."

"Seven," a strange voice corrected in Noah's ear.

"Seven?" Noah echoed.

Adam nodded. "Yeah, Aiden is here, too. He flew in for the kill. Say hi."

"Hi," Noah said before shaking his head. The mystery brother had made an appearance just for this? Was that supposed to make Noah more nervous or less?

Adam gave a wild cackle. "Look," he said, handing Noah the binoculars.

Noah put the lenses to his eyes, watching as a car slowly pulled up to the entrance. They sat for a good five minutes before they slowly exited the car, glancing around in a way that screamed the man was doing something shady. Hard to believe these guys were criminal masterminds.

When the wind caught the man's suit jacket, Noah caught sight of a gun holstered to his side. His heart dropped into his stomach. He should have considered they'd come armed. "He's got a gun," Noah said to nobody in particular.

"He'd be a fool not to," Atticus said. "We anticipated that."

Adam didn't seem troubled by this new information either, smiling in Noah's direction. "Told you they'd come. They have too much to lose."

"Yeah, but they could have just run," Noah countered.

Adam took the binoculars back. "Sure, they could have, but it's not easy to abandon a whole life. Especially not when you seemingly have the world at your fingertips. These men think they're untouchable, so they'll do whatever it takes to maintain that power. Most of them are probably going in there intent on killing the messenger. It's why they didn't think it odd for Gary to say he'd arrive last. They need to believe they can make this problem go away."

Noah watched the wind pick up Adam's dark strands, fanning them across his forehead, the sunlight making his pale blue eyes look almost white. "Shit. You look really hot right now," Noah murmured.

"Again, coms are hot. Keep it in your pants, boys," Archer muttered.

Why were people always saying that to them?

One of the brothers gave a frustrated grunt, but Noah couldn't tell who until they spoke. "This is stupid. We do so much better alone. We could have just killed all twenty separately in one night. You know?" Avi asked. "What do they call that?"

"A serial killer?" Noah asked, exasperated.

"No, serial killers have a pattern," Asa said, sounding like he was searching the farthest reaches of his brain. "A spree killer. We could have been like spree killers."

"That would have been, like, three kills each," Atticus chimed in.

"Two for one of us," August corrected.

"I hate math," Aiden muttered.

"And twenty separate crime scenes to clean up," Noah reminded them.

"I'm just saying, killing three guys in one night would have been cool," Avi pouted.

"But, instead, you get to kill twenty guys during the day, with your brothers, as a family," August said.

"Other families just have barbeques," Archer said, tone dripping with sarcasm.

That seemed to be his default setting. His unkempt hair and eye liner made him look like a pirate. A hot sarcastic, drunken pirate.

"Well, you're in luck. In about thirty minutes, it's going to smell a lot like barbeque," August assured them.

That killed the conversation for a short time. Noah grew restless as each man parked their vehicles and filed into the old building to wait for Gary, who was still stashed in the back of Atticus's trunk. Acid pooled in Noah's stomach, his heart hammering in his ears.

When the last man arrived, Archer came over the speaker once more. "All targets are on site."

Adam grinned at Noah. "It's go time."

Noah followed Adam from the bait shop to the

windowless fish hatchery. They all had jobs to do. Noah was the lookout. Archer barricaded one of the two points of entry, the wooden double doors at the back of the building. Asa and Avi took the cans of gasoline, thoroughly saturating the wood and the surrounding ground. Adam dismantled the water line at the dock to ensure no stragglers had access to anything that might help put out the fire. Atticus was at the car, making sure Gary was where they'd left him, and August stood at the closed front doors of the building, holding a metal device in his hands. It was an iron locking mechanism, like something out of Game of Thrones. Noah supposed it was only appropriate. They were about to have their very own Red Wedding.

Aiden didn't participate much. He stood beside Noah, arms crossed over his chest. He didn't look like any of his photos. The clean cut boy was long gone, replaced by a man, who looked like he spent his nights sleeping on park benches but was somehow still cute even with his hand floating over the Glock at his side.

They were all armed. Though it was unlikely anyone would make it out, the wood was old and somebody might be able to kick a piece free.

August was just about to chain the door when Asa pulled a generic butane lighter from his pocket. He flicked the starter, but it sparked and then went out. Once. Twice. Half a dozen times.

"Oh, no. Take your time," Aiden drolled. "It's not like people won't start to suspect something any minute now."

Asa looked at the others sheepishly. "Um, anybody have

any matches?"

"Jesus Christ. You have got to be kidding me," Atticus hissed.

"Fuck this," August muttered, freeing his phone from his pocket and pulling his com from his ear, replacing it with his earbuds.

"What's he doing?" Noah asked, his pulse skyrocketing, watching as the others pulled their weapons free. "What the fuck is happening here?"

Adam grabbed his face and kissed him thoroughly. "You stay here. You shoot anybody you see who isn't us. No hesitation."

"What the fuck is happening?" Noah asked again.

August pulled two knives free from God knows where, twirling them in his hand like a carnival performer before kicking the door open like a SWAT team, all attendees turning on them, faces slack. Adam could only watch as the others followed suit, giving Noah one last look before closing the door on him.

August's voice could be heard even through the wood panels. "Hello, gentlemen. I'm afraid your friend won't be attending your meeting."

That was when the screaming started.

TWENTY-FIVE
ADAM

By the time Adam pushed the doors back open, every muscle ached, his ears were ringing from the gunfire, and all seven of them were dripping in blood. Luckily, most of it wasn't theirs. As suspected, none of those men managed to put up much of a fight. They were too busy trying to make sense of the situation. The few that were armed had been shaking so badly they hadn't even had time to fire a shot. It was literally like shooting fish in a barrel. Or gutting fish in a barrel if you were August or the twins.

As soon as Noah saw them, he dropped the gun he had trained on the entrance and leapt into Adam's arms like it was the end of a rom-com. Adam laughed as Noah clung to him, arms and legs encircling his body.

"I didn't think you were ever coming out. I thought you were all dead," he said as Adam set him back on his feet, gaze snagging on August, who was bobbing his head to a beat only he heard, eyes closed like he was attending Sunday morning service and he'd caught the Holy Spirit.

"Well, maybe not August. But I thought the rest of you guys weren't coming back. I didn't know what to do. Do you have any idea how long you've been in there?"

Archer cocked a bloody brow. "Do you have any idea how much work it is to kill twenty men? I'd say we deserve a goddamn gold medal for our work today."

Noah frowned, but Adam didn't let him get caught up in Archer's perpetually bad mood. "We're fine. Everything's fine. But we do have to find a working lighter. The fire still has to happen—somehow—or our next family gathering will be at our murder trial."

Atticus sighed, looking down at his blood spattered hands. "When is Noah going to take care of the pedophile in my trunk? If he hasn't already died of heat stroke, that is. He needs to be in there when we torch the place. At the moment, all roads lead to Gary being the culprit. His phone. His associates. If nothing else, it will buy us some time."

Noah's tongue darted out over his lower lip. "Now. Let's do it now. Atticus is right. It needs to be here. I want him to see what happened to the others."

Asa and Avi looked like they wanted to high five each other. "We'll go retrieve him."

Noah didn't answer, so they just walked away in the direction of Atticus's car. Adam took his hand and led him around the side of the building where they could be alone. He cupped his face, blood smearing across Noah's fair cheeks. "I can do this for you. I don't give a fuck what the others say. You are already a part of this family. You don't have to kill Gary to prove that."

Noah met his gaze. "I want to do it. He's had this coming for years. I'm only sad that the other children he hurt won't get their turn at him. It's not right."

"Maybe it's enough just to know he's dead," Adam said, kissing Noah's forehead.

"It's not. Even if their victims see that they're dead, the world will never believe they were monsters. Not unless we show them."

"We knew that going in."

Tears sprang to Noah's eyes, but he blinked them away, seeming annoyed by the sudden display of emotion. "Yeah, but I don't want these fuckers dying heroes…or martyrs. The world needs to know what they've done. They need to see who they really were."

"Meaning what, exactly?" Adam asked, already knowing the answer.

"I want Calliope to turn over what we've found to the cops. She can send it anonymously. Through the internet. I want their victims to see that they're no longer in danger and to know they'll be believed when they come forward with their stories."

Adam mulled it over. Noah had a point. None of those men should die with their reputations intact. Besides, they hadn't gotten all of them, just the major players. There were so many others that participated or were, at least, complicit. They should all go down for it. Adam preferred they went down with a bullet to the head, but if Noah wanted them exposed to the world, so be it.

"Okay. If that's what you want, we'll do it."

"Your father won't like it."

Adam shrugged. "My father didn't like this plan either. But he respected your decision."

Noah chewed on his lip for a minute before saying, "Why is that? He doesn't even know me. I have no training, no experience. This almost blew up in our faces. Why would he just let me call the shots like that?"

That was a good question, but it was one Adam suspected he could answer. "You know, I always wondered what would happen to us if my father died. Atticus thinks he'd just take over as head of household, but that would be a lot like the inmates taking over the asylum, you know? As much as he tries to pretend he's the level-headed one, it's all an act. You put a weapon in his hand and he's just as lethal as the rest of us."

Noah frowned. "Okay?"

"And I think my father sees a lot of himself in you. I think he's seeing if you're…groomable."

"Groomable isn't a word," Noah said, irritated. "What do you mean?

"I mean, I think he wants you to take over his work someday."

If possible, Noah seemed to frown harder. "Like…take over as in deciding the fate of criminals? Who lives? Who dies? He wants me to be the Charlie to your angels?"

Adam snickered. "I don't think any of us qualify as angels."

"How can your father be so sure about me when we've only met a couple of times?" Noah asked, bewildered.

Adam laughed, wrapping his arms around him. "What choice did he have? What choice did any of them have? They knew I'd never let you go."

"That you'd tie me to the radiator if I tried to leave," Noah said, voice muffled against Adam's sweat and blood soaked shirt.

"I'd prefer the bed, I think," Adam said, kissing the top of Noah's head.

Atticus rounded the corner, looking annoyed at catching the two of them in an embrace. "Make out later, please. August found some matches in his trunk, so let's get this dude dead already. I'm expected to attend a dinner for one of Dad's charities tonight."

Adam rolled his eyes before looking at Noah. "You ready?"

Noah nodded, taking a deep breath and blowing it out. "Yeah. Let's do this."

TWENTY-SIX
NOAH

The scent of blood hit Noah first, filling his nostrils until it felt like he was choking on a million copper pennies. The carnage came next. His shoes slipped in the pools of blood as he did his best to navigate while his eyes adjusted to the dim light of the room. The fallen men were everywhere, still splayed however they'd landed, and in the center of them all was Gary…tied to that same folding chair, screaming and sweaty.

"Did you bring the folding chair?" Noah asked absently.

Avi nodded. "We thought it might help. You know, being your first kill and all, we didn't want him making a run for it."

Noah's brows raised, a warm feeling washing over him. "Thanks, that's…kind of sweet, actually."

The boys beamed at him.

Noah pulled his gun free and aimed it at Gary. "Take his gag off."

The boys looked at each other, then Adam.

"You heard him," Adam said.

They yanked the gag free, and Gary immediately started to babble. "Please, Noah. Please. Don't do this. You're a good boy. Not like us. Not like them." He looked at the seven men surrounding them. "They're monsters, but you…you were always a sweet boy. Your father loved you. I loved you."

Noah listened to it all, surprised at how little he cared about the man pleading for his life.

"I can do this," Adam said again.

"Give him a minute," Archer said, surprising Noah.

"Yeah, this wasn't easy for any of us and we don't even have the ability to feel bad about what we do," Aiden said.

Noah found himself getting kind of choked up. These men—these deviant, murderous psychopaths—were his family and they were being weirdly supportive. They thought that he was afraid to kill Gary or was having second thoughts.

"I don't want to kill him," Noah said. When Gary's shoulders sagged with relief, Noah tacked on, "Yet."

"Well, we don't have a lot of time."

Noah aimed at Gary's left knee cap and pulled the trigger, the man's screams washing over him. "That's for everything you fucking monsters did to me." He took aim at Gary's right kneecap, firing without hesitation. "That's for everything you did to the others." He pointed the gun between Gary's legs, a grim satisfaction filling him as Gary started to shake his head. But it was too late. Noah fired. "And that's just because."

"Not that I don't appreciate a good performance," August said, "but can you put the man out of his misery? His screams are annoying and we have to start cleaning up. We don't have all day."

Noah raised the gun. "Sure."

The bullet struck right between Gary's eyes, leaving only the tiniest of holes. Noah stared at it, ears ringing, watching a tiny line of blood trickle down the man's nose. Almost immediately, there was a flurry of activity. August snatched the gun from his hand and the boys untied Gary, dumping him among the others.

They didn't set the fire right away. Atticus forced them all to strip naked and dive in the water to scrub the blood off. Their clothes were collected in garbage bags with new clothing distributed to each of them. Weapons were collected in a metal box to be melted down later, and the bloody clothing would be burned off site where August could be certain it was gone.

Striking the match was the very last thing on their list. Noah stood back, watching as the small flame erupted, chasing the trail of gasoline around the building before catching the wood. The building was almost immediately engulfed in flames. Still, they all stood, watching, until they were certain nothing would keep the fire from doing its job, before going their separate ways.

They were far from the scene when Adam finally looked over at Noah. "You okay?"

Noah shook his head. "My ears are killing me. At the range, they give you ear muffs." He tugged on his earlobes as if that might help the problem.

"I meant are you okay with what you did? To Gary?"

Noah nodded once more. "Maybe I should feel guilty or, at least, have some kind of regrets. Maybe it will come later, but I honestly just feel…relieved. Like it's all finally over."

"It is," Adam assured him before adding, "Well, it will be once Calliope forwards the evidence to the appropriate law enforcement officials."

Noah yawned. "Can we go home? I want a shower and Thai food. And maybe ice cream."

Adam nodded. "Yeah. Sure."

They were just pulling into Adam's parking space when he said, "Did you mean it?"

Noah tried to think back to the million things he could have meant. "Mean what?"

Adam put the car in park and then turned in the seat to look at Noah. "The text message. Did you mean it?"

Noah could feel himself flushing. "Which part?" he hedged.

Adam grinned. "The part where you said you loved me?"

Noah's gaze dropped to his lap, his heart pounding. He clutched his hands together to stop them from shaking. How was that question more stressful than murder? "I don't know. Maybe?"

Adam chucked his finger under Noah's chin, forcing him to meet his gaze. "You maybe love me?"

Noah wanted to say it. He did. He wanted to say he loved Adam, but the words wouldn't come. So, he just nodded.

Adam's grin widened. "Well, I maybe love you, too."

Noah's chest tightened, his face twisting into a grimace.

"Don't say that. Especially if you don't mean it."

Adam frowned. "I do mean it. I mean, I think I do."

"You think you do?" Noah echoed.

Adam nodded earnestly. "Like, I don't know what love feels like, but I know that whatever I feel for you, I've never felt for another person—ever. So, who's to say that's not love?"

"I don't know," Noah said. "Maybe it is."

"So, maybe I love you."

Noah shook his head, a stupid grin forming on his face as he leaned across the console until they were nose to nose. "Then maybe I love you back."

EPILOGUE
Noah

"You know, when you said you would chain me to the bed if I ever tried to leave, I thought it was just possessive posturing," Noah said around a laugh, tugging at the metal links attached to the leather cuffs around his wrists and ankles, tethering him face down to the four corners of Adam's bed.

His laugh quickly became a moan as Adam's lips trailed from his hairline along his spine. He hissed as Adam's teeth sank into the fleshiest part of his ass, wondering if there would be teeth marks later. The thought made his dick throb, and he rubbed against the bedding below. He loved when there was evidence.

"Possessive?" Adam murmured. "That doesn't sound like me at all."

Before Noah could call him on his obvious lie, Adam's tongue teased along his balls, sucking at them before spreading him open to lave across his hole. Fuck, that felt so good.

Noah's breath hitched. "You know, I still have to leave, right? Your father is paying a fortune for me to go to this top secret ninja training place for wannabe mercenaries. I can't say no. It's part of his plan."

Thomas hadn't been lying about ensuring Noah received proper training. Over the last six months, he'd worked with personal trainers, a martial arts instructor, had clocked numerous hours at a shooting range, and had even completed a pseudo SWAT training course with a bunch of overly muscled meathead types, who just wanted to feel like 'real' cops.

"You'll make your plane," Adam promised, moving up to blanket himself over Noah, his hard cock snug against his entrance. "But you'll do it with my cum still inside you."

Adam's words had Noah working himself against the mattress, whining in frustration when he got no relief. "Adam…"

His name was a plea, but it fell on deaf ears. Noah was well aware that Adam hated whenever he left, whether it was for five hours or five days. Adam was wild whenever they were apart. His brothers found it amusing. Noah pretended to find it annoying but, deep down…he fucking loved it.

This was always his punishment. This frustratingly slow one-sided fuck that would go on until Adam decided it was over and that Noah had earned his orgasm.

"I love you like this," Adam said. "Naked. Helpless. Completely at my mercy."

A warm rush washed over Noah. Adam used the word

love a lot. So much that Noah was starting to believe it was true. Still, they didn't talk about it, poke at it, or examine it too closely. There was no reason to. Their relationship worked. It just did.

"You can't just tie me to the bed every time I do something you don't like," Noah chided, breath leaving in a rush as Adam sank into him in one thrust.

"Oh, we both know that's not true," Adam crooned against Noah's ear. "I can do whatever I want to you in here. Remember? That was your rule."

Noah's toes curled, every nerve ending sparking with pleasure as Adam lazily used him, fucking into him by rolling his hips, barely moving but, somehow, so deep inside.

Noah turned his head to the side, another breathy moan escaping before he said, "Okay, true. But I didn't mean you could drag me into a bedroom every time I did something you didn't like."

Adam bit down on the shell of his ear, hands sliding under Noah's chest to curl over his shoulders, holding him in place so he could go even deeper. "Then you should have been more specific. Too late to stop now."

Noah didn't want him to stop. In fact, he rather liked Adam's cave man problem solving skills, even if his solution was usually to drag Noah into the nearest empty space and fuck him senseless.

There was just something about being—how did Adam put it?—completely at his mercy. To know that hands that killed without an ounce of regret were the ones now holding him in a vise grip so he could fuck him harder. That a body crafted to make his kills more efficient was contracting over him, driving deep into him, wanting to leave as many marks as he could to show the world Noah was his.

The duality of their lives would never stop being strange to Noah. One minute, they were at a black-tie dinner, where people still whispered about the fire and the scandal that had erupted soon after. The next, Adam was packing his kill kit while Noah walked him through his target's dossier. Adam was right. Nothing ever blew back on them. Calliope kept on top of the case, listening to police chatter. The cops were still clueless as to who had murdered twenty pedophiles, but it was clear they thought the trash had taken itself out.

Being a Mulvaney made Adam Teflon. And Noah belonged to Adam. That knowledge was a heady thing. Being untouchable. It made Noah reckless. Fuck. It made him dangerous. Far more dangerous than Thomas's mercenary training ever would. Because Adam would do anything to protect Noah. Anything. He was like a vicious junkyard dog, and Noah held his leash.

Except in the bedroom. Never in there. In bed, Noah got to let it all go, let Adam make the decisions, let him do whatever he wanted. And, right then, he clearly just wanted to use Noah for his own pleasure. And he did. He rolled his hips, his movements getting faster, harder. His breathing harsh and panting against Noah's ears as he muttered, "Fuck, you feel so good."

Noah closed his eyes, enjoying the friction of the sheets against his dick and the fullness of Adam inside him, knowing he'd get his as soon as Adam finished. A few more thrusts and Adam's forehead dropped to Noah's shoulder, body twitching as he came with a harsh sound.

After a few minutes passed, Adam slipped free of Noah, freeing his ankles from the restraints. But only his ankles. He sucked in a breath as Adam tugged his hips into the air. "Open your legs for me."

Noah did what Adam asked, a low moan slipping from his lips as Adam's hand wrapped around Noah's aching erection. There was no teasing now. Adam jerked Noah with long, efficient strokes until sparks were flashing behind his lids. "Oh, fuck, I'm so close already. Don't stop. Please."

"You're way too coherent," Adam muttered, working three fingers back into his slick hole, finding that tiny bundle of nerves just inside and massaging over it.

Noah's blood was made of fire, his whole body covered in perspiration. "Oh, my God. Yes. Keep—oh, fuck—keep doing that. Please, Adam. Fuck. Yes. Yes."

And then he was coming hard, the kind of orgasm that made his vision go black and his soul temporarily leave his body. By the time he could put a coherent thought together, Adam had released him from the restraints and rolled him onto his back to hover over him on all fours.

"What are you doing?" Noah asked, amused.

Adam grinned. "Making sure I didn't fuck you into a coma. You looked a little…out of it."

Noah rolled his eyes. "You do this to me every time I leave. When I went to meet my mom, I could barely sit for three days. Do you know how awkward it was having the woman who gave birth to me ask why I was wincing every time I sat down?"

Adam chuckled. "If I recall, it was you who wanted to be spanked before you left. You told me to make it hurt. Your words, not mine."

"I cannot be held responsible for what I say when there is a sex toy vibrating against my prostate," Noah said, sounding huffy.

Meeting his birth mom had gone alright. It wasn't the teary, heartfelt reunion they often showed on the news. She didn't throw her arms around Noah and sob at the return of her long, lost son. And that was okay. He probably wouldn't have known what to do with that kind of attention anyway.

Noah was an adult, and she was a stranger with a new family and a new life. It wasn't awkward or unpleasant. Everybody had been gracious and welcoming. Noah had met his mother's new husband—a cattle rancher named Chad—and their three teenagers, Andreina, Marcella, and…Loretta. After Chad's dead mom.

They hadn't spoken of anything of substance, really, even though they both probably had a million questions for each other. But Noah wasn't sure he wanted to know the answers to his questions, wasn't sure he'd look at her the same way if he didn't like the answers. And he didn't want to ruin her life by telling her what he'd been through. She didn't deserve to live with that knowledge. None of it was her fault.

They'd parted at the airport with hugs and a promise to talk again soon. And they did. She would call him once a month or so to check in. Would hesitantly ask about Adam.

Would give him updates about Chad, the girls, the ranch, and it was nice. Easy. Someday, maybe she would even feel like his mom. But not yet.

Noah had gone into it with no false expectations. He already had a family. One that he didn't have to keep secrets from. Adam's family. His completely insane, fucked up family. They knew all his secrets. And he knew theirs.

"Hey, where'd you go?" Adam asked, tapping on his forehead.

Noah pulled himself from his thoughts. "Just thinking about your family."

Adam dropped down to his forearms until they were nose to nose. "I just fucked you into a blackout and you're thinking about my brothers… Some guys might find that insulting."

Noah rolled his eyes, giving Adam a playful shove until he toppled over onto his back. Noah rolled off the other side before Adam could find another excuse to drag him back to bed. "Good thing you're not 'some guy.'"

Adam hopped to his feet, coming around to where Noah stood, wrapping his arms around him. "I'm not?"

Noah scoffed. "You know you're not. Why do we have to play these games?"

Adam ignored him. "So, what am I?"

"The guy whose father is going to kill me if I don't get in the shower right fucking now," Noah said, looking at the clock on the wall.

"But I don't want you to go," Adam whined.

"Yes, both me and my ass are very aware of that."

Adam cupped said ass. "I'm not letting you shower until you say it."

"Say what?" Noah asked, blinking up at him with mock innocence.

"You know what." Adam gave him the big, sad puppy dog eyes. "Please?"

They were so contrived, yet they worked every fucking time. "Fine."

Noah flushed. It was such a stupid, embarrassingly sweet ritual they'd created. One that would make Noah cringe if he saw it in a book or movie. Hell, he would probably murder to keep it quiet because it was just too precious for two twenty-something-year-old killers. But Adam loved hearing it. And often. Noah didn't know exactly why. Still, he sighed. "I maybe love you."

A wide grin spread across Adam's face. "I maybe love you, too."

They were building a life together on that maybe. And it was a good one. More than Noah could ever have imagined.

DEAR READER,

Thank you so much for reading *Unhinged,* Book 1 in my Necessary Evils series. I hope you loved reading this book as much as I loved writing it. Look for August's book, *Psycho,* coming soon.

If you've read my books before, you have probably come to realize that I have an addiction to writing about the psyche and exactly how both nature and nurture often play a part in who a person becomes. I spent years working as an RN in a psychiatric hospital, most of those spent with children aged anywhere from five to eighteen. It took a big toll on me and my own mental health, which is why writing these characters has become my own form of therapy. While sociopathic bodyguards and megalomaniacal cult leaders are all works of fiction, my heroes and villains are all drawn from real people who I encountered in my time as a nurse.

The extreme child sexual abuse experienced by Noah might be fiction, but all we have to do is turn on a television or open a news app to know that it's still a very common occurrence. I tried not to go too deep down the rabbit hole of those experiences, not because I wanted to trivialize them but because this is a love story.

This is all a rather maudlin way of saying thank you for reading my books and loving my characters and allowing me to use these books as my own therapy sessions.

If you guys are really loving the books, please consider joining my Facebook reader group, **Onley's Oubliette**, and signing up for my newsletter on my website so you can stay up to date on freebies, release dates, teasers, and more. You can also always hit me up on my social media and find all my links here. You can find me literally everywhere, so say hi. I love talking to readers.

Finally, if you did love this book, (or even if you didn't. Eek!) it would be amazing if you could take a minute to review it. Reviews are like gold for authors.

Thank you again for reading.

ABOUT THE AUTHOR

ONLEY JAMES is the pen name of YA author, Martina McAtee, who lives in Central Florida with her children, her pitbull, her weiner dog, and an ever-growing collection of shady looking cats. She splits her time between writing YA LGBT paranormal romances and writing adult m/m romances.

When not at her desk, you can find her mainlining Starbucks refreshers, whining about how much she has to do, and avoiding the things she has to do by binge-watching unhealthy amounts of television in one sitting. She loves ghost stories, true crime documentaries, obsessively scrolling social media, and writing kinky, snarky books about men who fall in love with other men.

Find her online at:
WWW.ONLEYJAMES.COM

Printed in Great Britain
by Amazon